THE MINISTER'S WIFE

JOHN ANTHONY MILLER

For family – and all that's most important

ACKNOWLEDGEMENT

Special thanks to Donna Eastman at Parkeast Literary and the staff at Next Chapter.

ALSO BY JOHN ANTHONY MILLER

WWII Fiction

To Parts Unknown

In Satan's Shadow

All the King's Soldiers

When Darkness Comes

Historical Mysteries

Honour the Dead

Sinner, Saint or Serpent

The Widow's Walk

A Crime Through Time

The Drop

Cold War Thriller

For Those Who Dare

Medieval Fiction

Song of Gabrielle

1

EIGHTEEN MILES NORTHEAST OF PHILADELPHIA

September 18, 1777

A bigail St. Clair gazed at the Delaware River shimmering in the morning mist, the road to Philadelphia twisting beside it. After two years in New York, she was coming home. Her family was intensely loyal to the Crown, her father linked to London by both business and tradition, and they had left when the rebellion began, choosing not to remain in a city soon to serve as the colonial capital. She was wary of her return, knowing shadows from her past could easily find the present. Secrets, it seemed, were so very hard to keep.

"It won't be much longer," said her husband, Solomon St. Clair, as their carriage rattled down the road. The newly appointed minister to the Philadelphia Anglican Church, he was a bit portly, with brown, curly hair and round spectacles. Known for his intellect and an interest in philosophy, his passionate sermons merged the ancient world with the modern, contrasting good with evil.

Abigail stretched, leaning back in her seat. "It's been a tiring journey," she replied. Attractive, with blonde hair that framed her face and fell to her shoulders, her green eyes housed a curious twinkle that few ever failed to notice.

The road cut through a wooded slope that stretched to the river below, the water sometimes screened by shrubs and trees. It was quiet, an empty lane with no carriages, wagons, or riders, only the sound of the wagon wheels rolling down a rutted road competing with songs the birds were singing.

"A few miles more and you'll be back in the city you once called home," Solomon said.

Abigail was quiet, thinking of those she would see: friends, foes, and some who meant much more than she could ever admit. She wondered how much the city had changed since her departure now that it served as capital to a nation forming from seeds of rebellion.

"You'll soon see old friends," Solomon continued.

"Yes, I should think so. I'm anxious to visit my cousin, who now resides in my father's house. But I shall miss my sisters terribly—three of the closest friends a woman could ever want or need."

They sat quietly, each minute that passed bringing their journey closer to an end. Trees surrendered to fields, an occasional farmhouse dotting the terrain, split rail fences containing cattle who curiously watched the carriage and two wagons that trailed behind it. Solomon withdrew a Bible from his leather satchel and was soon immersed in the Scriptures.

They had traveled almost an hour when they came to a crossroad. At first it seemed deserted, two roads intersecting to wander in different directions. But as their wagons passed through, they heard galloping horses.

Abigail opened the window and leaned out.

"What is it?" Solomon asked.

"A band of soldiers."

He looked at her strangely. "Surely they won't bother us."

She watched a moment more and turned to face him. "I'm not so sure."

The carriage came to a halt, the horses neighing in protest, as six colonial soldiers blocked their path. Wearing tricorn hats with blue coats and white breeches, satchels hung from their shoulders, carrying powder and shot. They gathered behind a lanky man who appeared to be their leader, their rifles at the ready.

"Where are you going, friend?" the leader asked.

"To Philadelphia," said their driver. "We move the minister and his wife."

The rebel leader dismounted. The sound of his boots trampling grass along the side of the road proved he was coming closer. When the footsteps stopped, the door abruptly opened.

Abigail gasped and moved closer to Solomon.

The rebel leaned in. "Morning," he said, tipping his hat. "I'm Captain Howard of the colonial army."

"Is something wrong, Captain?" Solomon asked. "We near the end of our journey, and only hope to have it completed."

"What are your intentions?" Howard asked.

"Why would you care, good sir?" Abigail asked, acting braver than she felt.

"The city is home to the Continental Congress. I only ensure no threat is posed."

Solomon's eyes widened with disbelief. "Surely you don't fear us?" he asked. "I'm Solomon St. Clair, new minister of the Anglican Church. This is my wife, Abigail."

"We came from New York," Abigail added.

"And the wagons contain your belongings?"

"They do," Solomon said, indignant. "You may search them if you like."

The captain studied them a moment more, a rugged man with a two- or three-day growth of beard. "The British plot to take the city," he said simply.

"Do you honestly believe we pose a threat, Captain?" Abigail asked.

Howard hesitated. "It isn't the army we fear. But those they send to watch us."

Solomon had a confused look on his face. "I don't understand."

"I do," Abigail said tersely. "He thinks we're spies."

"Words I never spoke," Howard said, a slight smile breaking. "I only voiced the ways of war that the British tend to use."

Abigail knew the city of Philadelphia, and its inhabitants, even if she hadn't been there for two years. "Many residents are loyal to the Crown," she countered, trying not to be rude. "The British have no need for a minister and his wife for tasks that others already perform."

Howard showed a mild curiosity, as if surprised strength and beauty could coexist. He nodded with respect. "Perhaps true, ma'am."

"Can we then be on our way?" Solomon asked.

Howard hesitated. "Not just yet," he said warily. "I need to ensure you are who you claim, and not rehearsed pretenders."

Solomon sighed, ruffled. "If I removed a cassock and collar from my luggage, would they then tell the tale?"

Howard seemed amused. "A disguise any man could offer." He paused a moment, pensive. "Who is the minister you replace?"

"Mr. Benjamin Harper of the Anglican Church."

The captain seemed satisfied with his reply and backed out of the carriage. "Mr. Harper is a good man. I hope that you are, too."

"Attend my services," Solomon suggested. "Decide for yourself."

"Perhaps I shall," Howard replied. "You may go. Welcome to the city of Philadelphia."

"Good day, Captain," Abigail said.

Howard motioned to his men. "Clear the road."

The captain closed the door and vanished, his boots trampling the grass. A moment later the carriage moved forward, slowly at first and then a bit faster. Abigail looked out the window at the captain and his men astride their horses on the side of the road. As her gaze met his, he nodded and tipped his hat.

They traveled only fifteen minutes more before they came to the outskirts of Philadelphia. A town of fifteen thousand, the city was arranged in square blocks, numbered streets running north-south, parallel to the Delaware River, named streets running east-west. The dirt road soon became cobblestone; brick townhouses and wood frame dwellings nestled beside the road. Trees sprouted between curb and pavement, their sprawling limbs bathing the street in shade. The closer they came to the city center, the more activity they encountered—pedestrians passing, horses' hooves clicking on cobblestone, residents on their stoops, coming or going or enjoying the day. It was a familiar sight to Abigail. She had come home.

But she doubted it was the same city she had left. For it was here that her heart had been broken—a wound so severe it would never heal, the scar it left lasting all of eternity.

2

TWENTY MILES WEST OF PHILADELPHIA

I an Blaine, a cabinetmaker loyal to liberty and those who fought to obtain it, galloped down Old Lancaster Road, destined for Trudruffrin, where the British army was supposedly camped. A leather pouch slung over his shoulder contained sketches of cabinets and wardrobes along with personal provisions. If stopped by the British he would claim he traveled to solicit customers or purchase supplies for a business started by his grandfather and passed down through generations.

It wasn't a complete lie. He often sought sales in nearby towns. But he wasn't dashing down Lancaster Road to visit customers. He searched for the British. When he found them, he would bring any information gathered back to Philadelphia where an unprotected Congress anxiously waited. But he knew if he was caught and couldn't convince the enemy that he was simply selling his wares, he would hang by his neck until dead.

A tad above average height, he was a handsome man with brown hair tied in a ponytail that fell just short of his collar. Almost twenty miles from the city, his horse was bathed in sweat, his journey made in haste. When he reached the White

Horse Tavern, a two-story stucco building that sat on a cross-roads and did a brisk business for those traveling to and from the city, he saw carriages and horses parked before it, the patrons inside enjoying a meal. Just ahead, British pickets waited, ready to challenge any who continued down Old Lancaster Road.

The presence of sentries suggested an encampment a few hundred yards away. To avoid them, Ian took a fork in the road that led to the left, down a dirt road for a mile or more. He turned right at the next crossing and came to St. Peter's Church, the steeple sticking above the trees, the building dark and empty. He again turned right, toward the British, and led his horse off the road and into the trees, slowing to a walk. When he got close to Old Lancaster Road, he dismounted and teth-ered his steed to a branch, tucked away in dense foliage but still close to the road. A sprawling oak, once hit by lightning, its largest limb split and charred, would serve as a landmark when he returned.

He crept through the woods just south of the British. Step-ping softly through the foliage, he ducked behind a shrub when he saw British pickets along the forest fringe, barely fifty feet away. He then slipped behind a stout tree and peeked at the enemy encampment, a sea of white tents sprawled across a clearing, half-loaded wagons parked beside them. Orange flames from campfires licked the landscape, gray smoke spiraling upward and fading as it reached the clouds.

Tripods built from branches held boiling black kettles above the fires, and Ian could smell the aroma of simmering stew. The red coats and white breeches that the British wore contrasted sharply with the green landscape and made them easy targets if he was an army instead of a man. He stepped through the brush, tracking the number of tents, men, cannon, and wagons, assessing their strength and trying to determine if they would march on Philadelphia.

After observing the camp from several locations, he knew it wasn't permanent. The tents were close together, many men squeezed into clearings bordered by trees, relying on pickets to warn of an approaching enemy. Few supplies were stored near those who needed them, wagons loaded with crates or produce stolen from nearby farmers. Even the stacks of firewood were slight, suggesting the men should be ready to march as soon as the command was given. Philadelphia was their objective, where its citizens and Congress assumed the colonial army under General Washington would keep the enemy at bay—just as they had in the months preceding. But Ian had found an army with an unmolested path to the city. The Patriots, it seemed, had been outflanked.

He crept forward, hiding where the foliage was thickest, daring to come closer. The same scene was continually repeated: clusters of tents, soldiers gathered around campfires. stacks of rifles and firewood. A few farm animals—cows, goats, cackling chickens—provided food to fuel the army, kept in pens or tethered to trees. Ian sneaked along the edge of the camp, staying just beyond the guards, hiding in shadows cast by a setting sun. After moving west for a half mile, the British yielded to Hessians, German mercenaries hired by the Crown, their infantry, cavalry, and cannon staged and stored and ready for battle.

"There must be ten thousand men," he muttered, impressed by the size of the army.

He hadn't observed the entire camp, but he had seen enough. He had to warn Congress to evacuate before the British marched, before they were trapped, and the war lost. He went back the way he came, sneaking through shrubs, surveying the camp, coming closer when he dared, but watchful for the pickets perched at its perimeter.

As he wormed his way east, close to where he would fetch his horse, he made a mistake he knew could cost him his life.

He had come closer to camp than intended, crossing the picket line when he did so. He hid in a clump of maples, caught between the camp and its sentries, completely surrounded.

A crude cabin sat past the camp's edge. He suspected it housed an officer, probably high-ranking given the soldiers who stood guard around it. He studied the sky, the light quickly fading as dusk approached, and chose to remain until darkness arrived. He knelt behind shrubs, observing the cabin, smoke drifting from its chimney, two men stepping from the porch.

3

Oliver Hart was one of Philadelphia's wealthier citizens. Owner of a global shipping concern, he was tall and slender with black hair and haunting brown eyes. He sat astride a black stallion in the center of Old Lancaster Road, warily watching the sentries who protected the approach to the British camp.

"State your intentions," a redcoat demanded, as another pointed his rifle.

"I'm Oliver Hart from Philadelphia, come to meet with General Howe."

"What's the password?" the sentry asked. "You can't enter without it."

"Long live King George," Hart replied.

The sentry turned to his partner. "Take him to Colonel Duncan."

"But I'm supposed to see General Howe," Hart protested.

"We were told to take you to Duncan."

Hart was led into camp, white tents sprawling along both sides of the road, perched in clearings surrounded by trees.

Campfires burned, soldiers sprawling around them. Stacks of rifles, arranged in tripods, were staged and ready for use.

He ignored those who watched as the sentry led him forward. They came to a house near the camp's perimeter, small but functional, perched between groves of trees, a split rail fence rolling around it. Two soldiers flanked the door.

"Tell Colonel Duncan his visitor has arrived," the escort said.

Hart dismounted and tethered his horse to a hitching post. He stood there awkwardly, waiting for direction, a dozen soldiers watching him curiously.

A minute later, a man stepped from the cabin. In his forties, his uniform hugging a solid frame, he had the air of an aristocrat, or one who wished that he was. His hair was powdered, a ponytail in the back just above the collar, as was the fashion in both England and the colonies.

"Oliver Hart, of Philadelphia," Hart said.

The officer nodded. "Colonel Alexander Duncan."

Hart eyed the colonel warily. As a man whose business spanned the globe, he had the uncanny ability to assess people quickly. His instincts suggested that Duncan was dangerous. And Hart always trusted his instincts.

"Leave us," Duncan called to the soldiers guarding the cabin, his eyes still trained on Hart. He sat in a high-backed chair on the porch and motioned for Hart to do the same.

Hart sat beside him, glancing at the soldiers still clustered nearby.

"What are your intentions, Mr. Oliver Hart of Philadelphia?" Duncan asked.

Hart paused, collecting his thoughts. "I've been communicating with General Howe, through a courier, for the last two months. The general requested my presence."

"I speak for Howe," Duncan said curtly. "I may be a colonel, but I should be a general, as any man could attest."

Hart eyed Duncan cautiously, suspecting an ambition that ability didn't support. "I have two dozen ships, based in Philadelphia, which travel the world. I hope to ensure the city's residents are adequately supplied." He paused, wondering what might motivate Duncan. "An arrangement to benefit all involved."

"It will, I assure you," Duncan said. "Although I will direct any business conducted."

Hart hadn't expected an ultimatum. He only wanted access for his ships. "Yes, of course," he said. "Although I had envisioned more of a partnership."

Duncan eyed him cautiously. "It will be a partnership. But on my terms."

For the next fifteen minutes, Duncan dictated his expectations for conducting commerce once the British occupied Philadelphia. Hart listened, barely speaking, as his role became apparent. The plan was simple. Hart would do as he was told, nothing more.

"That concludes our discussion, Mr. Hart," Duncan then said abruptly. "I trust our agreement is satisfactory?"

Hart forced a smile, although he wasn't quite successful. He nodded and rose from his seat. "Thank you for your time, Colonel."

"We'll discuss the details after Philadelphia is occupied," Duncan said as they stepped from the porch.

Hart paused. "Can you tell me when that might occur?"

Duncan hesitated, wondering whether he could be trusted. "Soon, Mr. Hart, although it depends on the colonial army. Within the next two weeks, I'm sure."

Hart studied Duncan, a dangerous enemy, a more dangerous friend. "I only want to be prepared."

Duncan nodded, as if he really didn't care. "Philadelphia will be taken without a shot fired. I know that, but the residents do not."

"No, sir, they don't. None suspect the threat you pose. They have confidence in Washington's army."

"Then they're fools," Duncan muttered.

They walked to Hart's horse, ending their brief discussion, when a soldier raced past them. "Who goes there?" he shouted. Others followed with rifles drawn.

"What is going on?" Duncan demanded.

"Someone watches the camp, sir," the soldier said.

"Find him and bring him to me," Duncan ordered.

"He's in that thicket," another soldier said. "Circle around the far edge."

A half dozen men moved to the east, a few more to the west. They tread forward cautiously, surrounding the intruder.

"Come out," one of the soldiers called. "We'll shoot if you don't."

Hart watched as a man peeked from the shrubs. For a moment, their eyes locked. The man then turned and raced away.

"Ian Blaine," a surprised Hart stammered as the man fled.

"Who is Ian Blaine?" Duncan demanded.

4

I an gasped. He never expected to find Oliver Hart in the midst of an enemy camp. He turned and fled, darting between trees and shrubs, the redcoats racing after him.

"Stop!" a soldier yelled. "Stop or I'll shoot!"

Ian ran as fast as he could, swerving to make a difficult target. He eluded those that came from the camp and dove into foliage, buried in a thicket. Seconds later, the perimeter sentries ran toward him, passing only inches away. As soon as they were gone, he sprinted south, his gaze fixed on the damaged tree— the landmark used to find his horse.

A musket fired. The bullet came close, rustling through branches and ripping leaves. Ian barely paused, dashing for safety. He knew where he was going and the best way to get there. The enemy did not. They charged through shrubs, breaking branches, and snapping twigs, so close at times he heard their muttered curses.

Five minutes later, he reached his horse. A half dozen soldiers came toward him, spread through the foliage, stumbling through underbrush. He quietly mounted his horse and led him out of the woods. The road was deserted when he reached it, so he turned south toward St. Peter's Church, breaking into a gallop. Seconds later a redcoat emerged from the trees, knelt to steady his rifle, and took aim.

The rifle cracked. A puff of dirt pinged off the road. Ian leaned over his horse's neck. "Come on, boy," he urged, gaining ground.

Fifty feet farther, he looked back. Soldiers stood in the road, some loading rifles, ready to fire. Behind them, redcoats gathered horses, preparing to pursue. Ian raced toward the church as the British started firing. The bullets missed their mark, the shot more difficult the farther he traveled. Three horsemen quickly pursued, but Ian maintained his distance, even though his horse was spent from the ride to Trudruffrin.

A hundred feet farther, another glance showed they were gaining. If he stayed on the road, they would catch him. But he was familiar with the countryside, and they were not. With darkness approaching, his chance to escape was good. He just had to outsmart them.

He approached the intersection—the road that eventually led to the White Horse Tavern. Four horsemen were coming from the south, just beyond the church, opposite those who chased him. He couldn't see if they were British, travelers destined for Old Lancaster Road, or Patriots searching for signs of the enemy.

"Stop him!" a soldier called from behind. "He's a spy!"

Ian frowned. Those in front were British. They increased their pace and came towards him, pulling pistols from their holsters. He was trapped between pairs of pursuers, three men behind and four in front. He had to get off the road.

He veered to his left, scanning the landscape, searching for a path to escape. He galloped across a field of wheat and leapt over a split-rail fence, urging his horse forward. Groves of trees interrupted the fields. Once hidden within them, he could elude the enemy. The soldiers who came from the south swung off the road and fanned across the field, trying to intercept him.

The sharp report of a rifle ripped the air, followed by another. Leaves of a nearby maple shredded as bullets sped through them, whistling as they passed. Ian galloped forward, searching for a stream he knew cut through the woods. Once he found it, he could work his way back to the tavern.

More shots were fired. Ian felt the sweat on his horse's neck and knew it couldn't run much longer, not at the pace they maintained. The British fired again, a volley, but Ian made it to the trees as bullets pinged around him, embedding in trunks with sickening thuds.

He slowed as he entered the woods. Little light pierced the foliage, making it harder to see, but difficult for the enemy to find him. He crept forward, using shrubs as cover, guiding his horse to thicker brush.

A few minutes later he found the stream. It wasn't deep, barely a foot, and he forced his horse into the water. If he followed it, he would exit the woods in less than a mile, somewhere between the camp and the tavern. He just had to elude the enemy.

He hurried forward, wary of his horse's footing, trying to get as far away as he could. The redcoats reached the stream a moment later, the two groups combined, judging by the noise they made.

"Which way did he go?" a British soldier called.

Ian dismounted and led his horse through a thicket. They stood quietly, sheltered, as the soldiers came down the stream. Hiding behind shrubs, peering into approaching darkness, he caressed his horse's head, trying to keep him calm.

"He may have gone south," a second soldier said, as if they couldn't decide.

"We better find him," another replied. "Duncan wants him captured."

They came closer. Horses sloshed through water. Faint shadows showed as they moved through the stream, seven men on horseback. Ian stayed completely still, his heart racing, calming his horse so he made no noise, hoping the enemy would quietly pass or give up and turn around.

"We won't find him now," a soldier muttered. "Especially with darkness coming."

The enemy turned upstream, splashing through the water, talking amongst themselves. The noise grew fainter, and a few minutes later, Ian couldn't hear them at all. He waited a moment more and peeked from the foliage. No one was near, none of the soldiers lingered. He coaxed his horse forward, walking him for the next hundred yards.

The stream meandered through rolling terrain, twisting and turning but making it back to the road. After one last check for the enemy, Ian climbed on his horse and eased him downstream until they came to Old Lancaster Road. After ensuring no British were near, he left the woods and cautiously entered the road. He walked for fifty feet, not knowing how close any sentries might be, whether any watched him, prepared to fire. When no command came, and no shot followed, he picked up his pace. As soon as he came to the White Horse Tavern, he galloped toward Philadelphia.

He had to warn Congress.

5

Abigail and Solomon St. Clair had arrived at the rectory midafternoon. A modest two-story brick building with green windows and shutters, it sat on the corner of a narrow lane dominated by the Anglican Church, where Solomon would serve as pastor. The wagons that carried their personal belongings—clothes, books, linens, and collectables—had been quickly offloaded, books placed on shelves, fresh linens put on the beds, clothes stored in wardrobes and dressers. Much of the furniture remained in the rectory regardless of the pastor, property of the church. What little the St. Clairs had brought only served to compliment what was already there.

A cozy study next to the kitchen contained a desk, two leather chairs, and a tiny table. Solomon sat and rubbed his chin, intensely focused. Upcoming sermons were far from his mind. He had a delicate problem to solve.

Abigail eyed him closely, a chessboard on the table between them. With an intellect that surpassed her husband's, regardless of his brilliance, she usually beat him in chess, as well as many other pursuits. She now had him trapped, as she normally did, and he desperately sought to save his queen.

Sometimes a bit cocky, it seemed he thought he had a solution. But he didn't.

She hid a smile. "Take your time," she said. "Not that it will help you."

He chuckled. "I refuse to let you win three games in a row."

They were interrupted by a cry from the street, followed seconds later by two more, each louder. People rushed past the parsonage, their voices carrying but their words not clear. For a forgotten lane off Second St., the commotion wasn't expected. Solomon looked away from the board, his attention diverted, and listened to a neighing horse, more people shouting, and wagon wheels rattling on cobblestone.

"What is all the racket?" he asked. "It's louder than New York."

Abigail gazed at one of her knights. "I suspect it's an isolated incident."

"All while I'm trying to focus," he muttered.

She studied the board with a wry grin. Solomon was in serious trouble. Protecting his queen was the least of his worries.

He moved a bishop, intended as a sacrifice, a clever maneuver—or so he thought. He sighed and leaned back in the chair, as if the inevitable had been averted. He looked at Abigail, trying to portray confidence, but not entirely successful.

She paused for a moment, only to make him think she was challenged when she actually was not. She didn't want to offend him. But she ignored the bishop he had just repositioned and moved a rook halfway across the board. "Check," she said, trying not to sound triumphant.

"Humph," Solomon groaned, looking at the board with surprise. "I certainly didn't see that coming."

The noise from the street began again. Another wagon,

more shouting, horses galloping by. It sounded like a city in turmoil, but there seemed to be no reason.

He looked at Abigail curiously. "What is happening out there?" he asked as he glanced at his pocket watch. "It's past ten o'clock."

"I'll go and check," she said. "You had best focus on the game."

She went into the foyer and opened the front door. The lane in front of the rectory was deserted, but a man on horseback raced down Second St., less than a block away. A wagon followed, loaded with furniture, a headboard tied behind the driver with a table and chairs stacked against it. Wooden crates took the rest of the space, settled against the tailgate.

Across the street, residents of a brick townhouse loaded furniture into their wagon, and those a few doors down were climbing into their carriage. Yet the rest of the residences showed no activity at all, save the candles flickering in windows. Abigail studied her neighbors, scurrying in and out of their houses, some watching, others departing, and wondered why they were so afraid.

"What is it?" Solomon asked, appearing behind her.

"People seem to be panicking," she said, perplexed. "At least some of them. But I don't know why."

"Let's go out and see," he said, leading her onto the pavement.

They walked down the lane to Second St. and watched another wagon pass, loaded haphazardly, three children in the back.

"Why are you leaving?" Solomon called.

"Congress is fleeing," the man said. "Best get out while you can."

"Are the British coming?" Abigail asked.

"If Congress is leaving, the British can't be far away."

6

It was late evening when Ian reached the city. He hadn't expected the chaos, wagons and carriages racing down streets, riders galloping past them. Colonial soldiers guided those leaving, ensuring routes taken weren't captured by the enemy. He made his way to Chestnut St., where his home and shop were located, put his horse in the barn, and hurried through the cabinet shop and up to the second-floor residence.

"The city is in turmoil," he said to his father as he entered the parlor.

"Washington ordered Congress to evacuate," said Patrick Blaine. He was lean, like his son, but not as tall. Blue eyes showed an honest man who knew a good day's work, his gray hair short and close to the scalp. Born in Dublin, he never lost his Irish accent, even though he had lived most of his life in Philadelphia.

"The British are camped out past White Horse Tavern. But I can't say for how long."

"They're soon to be leaving, I suspect," Patrick said. He sat in a chair by the window, watching the commotion in the streets below. "Were you able to scout their army?"

"I was," Ian said. "It's large, at least ten thousand. But the redcoats chased me away before I learned more."

Patrick eyed his son, concern etched on his face. "Don't underestimate them, lad," he warned. "They're trying to win a war. Same as we are."

"I won't," Ian said, feeling uneasy. But he already had. That's how he almost got caught. He glanced back at the street. "Will only Loyalists remain?"

Patrick shrugged. "I doubt it," he said. "Many who oppose the Crown will stay but mind their business. I suspect they'll get along just fine."

"But most who support the rebellion are known," Ian said as he moved from the window. "And we're among them. Should we leave, too?"

"Where would I go? Philadelphia has everything I need. Although a Catholic church is missing, mind you. But maybe someday."

Ian hesitated. "But our loyalties are known, the same as some now leaving."

"Our loyalties are known to those we trust," Patrick said. "There's a difference."

Ian was confused. "How do you know who we can trust?"

"We're businessmen, smart enough to keep our mouths shut when we have to."

"But as soon as the British arrive, we'll see who has two faces."

"Friends are friends in peace or war," Patrick said.

Ian hoped his father was right. They spoke honestly to those they trusted and said little to those they didn't. But life was about to change, in minutes, if not hours. "I want to fight back."

"You already did. You scouted the British army. A lesser man would have failed."

"But we could do more," Ian said. "Especially after the British arrive. We've eyes and ears. We only have to use them."

Patrick's eyes widened. "Are you suggesting we spy?"

"I am," Ian said firmly. "A task not easily done, I know. But we only need a contact, someone to get our information to the colonial army."

Patrick hesitated, as if making a decision he couldn't undo. "I'll take care of that."

Ian was confused. "You've already started?"

Patrick turned away. "A network exists, ready for the day that it's needed."

"Who runs it?"

"A man we can trust," Patrick said. "Only a few know his true allegiance."

Ian paused, thinking of friends and acquaintances. "I know of no one capable of such a delicate operation."

"I'll share a name if it's never uttered."

"I can be trusted," Ian assured him, knowing some would soon risk their lives. "As you well know. I'll carry the name to my grave."

Patrick eyed his son cautiously. "Barnabas Stone, owner of City Tavern."

Ian's eyes widened. "Big mistake. He's loyal to the Crown. Everyone knows it."

Patrick chuckled. "Do they now?" he asked in his lilting Irish accent. "Then I'm supposing it must be true."

Ian considered a man he had known his entire life. "If anyone can do it," he said, "it's Barnabas. No one would ever suspect him."

"I'll tell him you've joined us. But it's a secret you're never to share."

"Understood," Ian said. "I realize lives depend on it. Who else will assist?"

"I don't want to know," Patrick said. "Neither should you."

Ian realized how dangerous the city was about to become. "To limit damage if anyone gets caught."

"Exactly," Patrick said. "We make cabinets, socialize with those we did before, but include the British and any Loyalists who stand by their side."

"They show themselves already," Ian said bitterly. "I saw a traitor at Trudruffrin, meeting with the British. A man you would never suspect."

"Who?" Patrick asked, eyes wide.

"Oliver Hart."

7

The City Tavern, a Philadelphia icon, sat on the corner of Second and Walnut, a brick building with white windows and shutters, built like many of the dwellings that lined the city streets. It was owned by Barnabas Stone, a man large in height and girth with a shock of black and gray hair, ably assisted by Dolly Clarke, barmaid and part owner. A widow with graying hair, she was the usual companion of Patrick Blaine for dinner or walks along the riverfront. But often for much more.

"You showed a lot of courage," Barnabas said after Ian described what he saw at Trudruffrin, including his escape. He sat at a table at the front of the tavern, huddled with Ian and Patrick. They were alone—it was just before 7 a.m.—and the tavern had not yet opened, its curtains fully closed.

"I knew Congress was vulnerable," Ian said. "A customer told me that British pickets were posted on Old Lancaster Road, so I went to take a look."

"I think it's time to include Ian in our plans," Patrick said. "We can use the help."

Barnabas lightly touched Ian's arm. "A valued and trusted asset, for sure."

Ian nodded in appreciation. "It didn't seem a permanent camp," he continued. "The British are ready to move."

"I suspect they'll arrive within the week," Barnabas muttered. "Especially since Washington warned Congress."

"It's a sizable force," Ian said. "About ten thousand British and Hessians. They'll soon control the city and most of the land around it."

"They'll control much more than territory," Barnabas said. "They'll restrict who enters and leaves the city, determine what newspapers can print, control what words can be spoken. It won't be long before we've no knowledge of what's happening in the world—or even in our own city. All will be filtered through the enemy's lens."

Patrick frowned. "And some in the city will assist them."

"Most of the Loyalists are already known," Barnabas said. "But we need to be wary of those that aren't."

"Trust no one," Patrick advised. "That's safest."

"Many hide their loyalties," Ian confirmed. "Like Hart."

Barnabas was quiet for a moment, assessing enemy and friend. "Hart seems a man that minds his own business. I wouldn't have guessed he sides with the British."

"There must be profit in it for him," Patrick muttered.

Ian was worried for his welfare. "Should I be wary of him? I'm afraid of the power he might possess."

"Are you sure he saw you at Trudruffrin?" Barnabas asked.

"He looked right at me," Ian replied. "But it was almost dark. I was hidden behind trees and shrubs. I suspect he's not really sure."

"Let's hope he's not," Barnabas said. "But we can't take that risk."

"Should Ian have an alibi for the redcoats?" Patrick asked.

Barnabas nodded. "I suspect the British will seek me out as

soon as they arrive. Given the Loyalist reputation I've worked so hard to foster."

"You'll tell them I wasn't at Trudruffrin?" Ian asked.

"I'll tell them you were in Jersey," Barnabas replied. "And you take frequent trips for business."

"Many do," Patrick said. "For business and trade. So few would discount it."

"But if the British question me, how do I prove it?" Ian asked.

Barnabas grinned. "You've nothing to worry about, lad. I know the ferryman. I'll make sure he vouches for you."

Ian sighed with relief. "You're much more than a friend. I don't know how to thank you."

"We all need to be much more than friends," Barnabas said. "The war will soon get harder. Not fought in a field, but with whispers and glances."

"Will the ferryman's word be enough?" Ian asked, fretting. "We don't know when they'll question me."

"Avoid them when they first arrive," Barnabas suggested. "Even if you have to stay off the streets for a few days. If the redcoats can't prove you were in Trudruffrin, you have nothing to worry about. I'll make sure they can't."

8

9/30/1777 FOUR DAYS AFTER THE BRITISH OCCUPATION

Fox and Demayne was a restaurant on the waterfront sheltered by oaks that veiled the sun. One of the city's better eateries, it was known for fine food and a generous view of the Delaware River, the Jersey shore in the distance. Dinner was served daily at 2 p.m., advertised by both newspaper and flyer, and the restaurant contained two spacious rooms overlooking the water that were used for gatherings and special events. But with the revolution underway, and those loyal to the King of England mixed among those that rebelled, any event was strained, the guests secretive, their beliefs unknown to neighbors and friends, sometimes even to their own family. Their lives depended on it.

A gala to celebrate the arrival of the new minister of the Anglican Church was hosted by General Howe shortly after the occupation began. It was attended by many: British officers, leading businessmen, tradesmen, shopkeepers, and even some from other denominations. An addition to the city as esteemed as Mr. Solomon St. Clair should be rejoiced by all, regardless of allegiance, political beliefs, or religious affiliation. And it was.

After all the guests had arrived and were seated, General

Howe stood at the main table, and faced the rest of the room, prepared to make introductions.

"Ladies and gentlemen, I am honored and privileged to welcome Solomon St. Clair, Pastor of the Anglican Church, to the city of Philadelphia. The minister arrived shortly before I did," he added, pausing while the audience laughed. "Originally from London, Mr. St. Clair spent the last eighteen months serving the congregation in New York City. Residents of Philadelphia are blessed to have such a renowned theologian, famous for both sermon and discourse, to lead the congregation. Joining the minister is his lovely wife of only a year, Abigail, a former resident of Philadelphia until the recent rebellion, when she moved to New York with her family. Join me in welcoming both to the community."

The room erupted in applause as Howe sat beside Solomon St. Clair, emphasizing the importance of the city's new minister, an act that didn't go unnoticed by those in the room. Abigail was also seated next to her husband, nodding to a few familiar faces, those she had known before her departure.

A few minutes after the introductions ended, Ian Blaine entered the restaurant, dressed in his finest blue coat and breeches, a darker blue vest with a white ruffled shirt. He eyed the room as he came in, looking surprised by the number of guests. He walked across the wooden floor, past the table hosting the guest of honor, and joined his father sitting alone at a cramped table in the far corner.

"You're late, lad," said Patrick Blaine. "You're in for quite a surprise."

A waiter interrupted them. "Would you care for more Madeira?" he asked, referring to a sweet wine often fortified with a touch of brandy. The port was popular among the more privileged in the city and, although still enjoyed by the lower classes, they tended to prefer beer.

"Please, if you will," Patrick said with his Irish brogue. "Don't be selfish with what you pour."

Ian watched his father with amusement while the waiter filled their glasses.

"Thank you, lad," Patrick said when he was done.

The waiter moved to adjoining tables, meeting the needs of other guests. All were handsomely dressed: coats and vests for the men, dresses that flowed to the floor for the women. The citizens, it seemed, enjoyed a party regardless of who might host it.

"I'm not too late, it seems," Ian said, eyeing the room. "Just in time for refreshments."

"But too late for introductions," Patrick said solemnly. "Which were quite good, I might add."

"I probably didn't miss much."

"Oh, but you did," Patrick said, eyes wide. "You missed the minister's wife."

"Who might she be?" Ian asked, scanning the room. Then he saw her, sitting at the table with the guest of honor.

Abigail St. Clair wore a flowing green dress, her blonde hair spilling to her shoulders, her green eyes studying those in the room just as Ian studied her. She sat beside a man her own age or slightly older, a bit portly, his curly brown hair tumbling almost to his shoulders. A pair of round spectacles were perched on his nose, and he was engaged in discussion with General Howe as if they had been prior acquaintances.

"I wasn't expecting her, either," Patrick said, watching his son.

"She looks just as she did the day she left," Ian muttered, mesmerized.

Patrick saw the pain in his eyes. "You're still in love with her, aren't you?"

"Who wouldn't be?" he asked. "Look at her. I should go speak to her."

"Wait," Patrick said, grabbing his arm.

"What's the matter?"

"You didn't hear the introductions," Patrick said softly.

Ian couldn't stop admiring her. "What did I miss?"

Patrick hesitated, not sure how to temper words that must be said. "She's the minister's wife," he said softly. "St. Clair is her name now."

Ian turned away. He took a long sip of his port, letting it bathe his throat on its way to his stomach. "I refuse to believe it."

"It's best that you do," Patrick said, seeing his son's pain. "Because it's true."

Ian was quiet, furtively glancing at the head table, watching her, loving her as much as he did the day she left. "I still don't know what happened," he whispered.

"You don't need to," Patrick said. "It's over, just as her father told you. She changed her mind and moved away. Best for you to greet tomorrow, like I keep telling you. Yesterday is gone."

"I can't accept that."

"You'd better learn to," Patrick said. "I talked to her before you came. Just briefly, given those around her. She hasn't changed. Still as special as she was when she was with you."

"Is she happy?" Ian asked, his heart heavy.

"Seems to be," Patrick said, knowing his words stung. "She's newly wed, barely a year. Back in the city with her husband, the minister. Although I don't know for how long."

"I must see her."

"No, you must leave her alone," Patrick advised. "Let her live her life. She could have shared yours, but she chose not to. Wish her well and move on."

"I don't understand what happened. It never made sense."

"It doesn't have to," Patrick said.

The waiter brought their soup, and they ate quietly. Ian couldn't help glancing at Abigail, even more beautiful than before. He saw her stand, an empty glass in hand, and wander to the window, looking at the river and the ships that sailed upon it.

"I can't resist," Ian said, rising from the table.

"Don't make a fool of yourself," Patrick hissed, reaching out to restrain his son.

9

Abigail looked from the window, wharfs adjacent to the restaurant on the right, a park on the left with benches that offered views of the river and the city beside it. Wooden ships were tied to pilings, their sails furled, while smaller cutters sliced the water, destined for parts unknown. Trees bordered the banks, the leaves still green as summer faded, and for a moment she considered what a beautiful portrait nature would paint when autumn bloomed and the foliage turned orange, yellow and red.

She turned when Ian approached, sorrow etched on his face. For a moment, it seemed like she had never left, but then the hurt returned, ripping her heart from her body. She forced a smile, memories reborn that were best kept dormant. "Hello, Ian," she said softly.

"Abigail, how are you?"

"I'm well," she said. "I was wondering when I would see you."

He smiled. "You're a lovely sight. New York has been good for you."

"It has. But it's nice to be back in Philadelphia."

He stood awkwardly for a moment, as if wondering what to say. "May I get you another glass of Madeira?"

"No, thank you. I'm fine," she said. She looked at him closely, comparing him to the image she hid in her heart. He seemed thinner, not as happy. "How have you been?"

"Lonely, I suppose."

"Don't," she said, the wound as fresh as the day it was delivered. "It was your choice, not mine."

He looked at her, confused. "What do you mean?"

"My departure," she said. "I didn't have to go. And you know it."

"But you did."

"I saw no reason to remain," she said tartly. "Not after my father said you had no intention of marrying me."

Ian stared at her, his lips moving but with no words spoken. He finally managed a reply. "What are you talking about?"

She hesitated, confused by his reaction. He seemed shocked by what she said. She started again, but with more detail. "My father told me he met with you to discuss our future. Is that not true?"

"No, it is true," he affirmed.

"And you told him you had no intention of marrying me."

His face paled. "I said no such thing," he insisted. "Your father did meet with me. But he told me *you* had no intention of marrying me."

She stared at him, eyes wide. "But that's not true," she assured him, lightly touching his arm. "I never said that. I wanted to marry you. I wanted to stay in Philadelphia. But after you refused me, I fled to New York in shame."

He closed his eyes for a moment, as if he carried a burden far heavier than it needed to be. "I would never refuse you," he whispered. "Not then, not now."

34

She was confused. She didn't know who to believe—Ian or her father. "But that's not what he told me."

"He lied," Ian said curtly.

"Ian," she scolded. "He wouldn't lie, and you know it. He had no reason to."

"I'm not so sure. He always thought you could do better. And it seems that you did."

"Stop it," she said crossly. "My father always liked you."

"Yes, he did. As a cabinetmaker. But not as his daughter's husband. I'm too far beneath you. You're from wealth. I'm an artisan."

"That's not true, and you know it." She was quiet for a moment, reliving the day that changed her life, in more ways than one. If what Ian said was true, she had been horribly betrayed. But why would her father do that?

"Maybe you should ask him," he suggested softly. "Because he changed more lives than yours."

She studied his face, so sincere, his haunted eyes filled with sorrow. "I'll write to him as soon as I return to the rectory," she promised. She knew something was drastically wrong. Her father would never hurt her. At least she didn't think he would.

"I never would have let you go," he whispered. "You know that. I loved you then and I love you now."

She smiled weakly, having wasted two years with a broken heart. "Not now," she said, glancing back at her husband.

He nodded, as if he understood. "The minister's wife," he said. "Congratulations. I'm sure your father is very proud."

She hesitated, knowing no explanation would suffice. "I had to live my life. And I thought you chose not to be part of it."

"Now you know that wasn't true," he said. "And it still isn't."

She turned away and they were both quiet, gazing at the river. "Are you married?"

He shook his head. "Why bother? No one could compare to you."

She smiled, nudging him lightly with her elbow. "You're a liar, Ian Blaine," she teased.

"No, it's true. I swear."

"I bet someone claimed you before I even got to New York," she said, trying to keep the conversation light, still reeling from what he had told her. "Who is it? One of my old friends?"

"No one," he insisted. "I swear."

She looked at him for a moment and realized he spoke the truth. "That's a shame," she said, but for some reason, she was secretly pleased. "But someone is waiting. You just have to find her."

"I thought I already had," he muttered.

She didn't reply, sensing his hurt, and steered the discussion in a different direction. "Are you still working with your father, building cabinets?"

"I am," he said. "Still on Chestnut."

"He's a good man. I miss his Irish brogue. I spoke with him briefly."

"Yes, he told me. I think he misses you as much as I do. How is your family?"

"They're well," she said. "My older sister Emma married Jacob Eastman, the banker. They're retuning to Philadelphia after Christmas. I'm very excited about it."

"And your sisters, Anne and Ruth?"

"Neither married, but they plan to return, also. As do my parents now that the British are here."

"Abigail, come here a moment," the man who had been sitting beside her called from across the room.

Ian turned to look. "Mr. Solomon St Clair, I presume?"

"You were always very perceptive," she said, laughing lightly.

"Does he know about us?"

She looked at him sternly. "No," she declared. "And I don't want him to. There's no need."

"Abigail," the minister called again, waving her toward the table.

"It seems he wants you close," Ian said, and then lowered his voice. "Although I can certainly understand why."

"Coming, darling," she called. She turned to Ian and smiled. "Take care of yourself, Ian."

10

I an walked back to his table, dazed by all that had gone wrong. He relived his discussion with Abigail's father, trying to determine why he had lost her. Could such a simple communication, either misunderstood or purposely misstated, destroy two lives? If intentional, it had served its purpose, leaving two lovers so heartbroken neither approached the other to verify fact from fiction.

"You're not looking well, lad," Patrick said as he eyed his son with concern.

Ian sat down and sipped his wine. "I exposed a web of deceit."

Patrick watched him closely, wondering what had happened. "It's too late to look back," he advised. "She's moved on and so should you."

"There's more than you or I had ever known."

Patrick wanted to console him. "I'm willing to hear it."

"She never said she didn't want to marry me, as her father stated," Ian said. "But he did tell her that I refused to marry her."

Patrick's eyes widened. "No one could be that spiteful, whether he wanted you to wed his daughter or not."

"Apparently he was," Ian said, fighting waves of despair.

"He must have done it to keep you apart. But why would he?"

Ian shrugged. "I guess he didn't think I was good enough."

"The scoundrel," Patrick uttered with distaste. "Who would do something so hurtful to his own daughter?"

"Apparently he would. But never admit it."

"He thought she would move to New York and never find out," Patrick said.

"She never would have if I hadn't told her."

Patrick paused, hoping his son's pain would ease. "Was she as surprised as you?"

"She seemed to be. A bit angry at first. She intends to write her father and demand an explanation."

Patrick gazed at the head table, the minister and his wife seated at the center. "But I'm thinking it's a wrong that can't be righted. At least now."

Ian looked at Abigail, her smile bright, her eyes twinkling. "No, it doesn't seem so. Her father probably arranged her marriage."

"To ensure you were forgotten," Patrick said softly.

Ian turned to face his father. "But I wasn't."

The main course was served, beef with peas and beans, a mug of malt beer and a chunk of bread. They were quiet while they ate, enjoying the meal. Fox and Demayne was the finest restaurant in the city, although several others were close, and the food was much better than what they might have had at home.

Ian kept glancing at the head table, ignoring the British uniforms, hoping to make eye contact with Abigail—although he wasn't sure why. But she seemed preoccupied, trying to eat while engaged in a conversation with her husband. Occasionally she met his gaze, but either turned away or smiled subtly.

"It is a nice welcoming for the new minister," Patrick said as he gazed around the room, trying to divert Ian's attention from Abigail. "Although I could do without the redcoats."

"It is," Ian agreed. "A hundred people at least. Even General Howe. The minister's friend, it seems."

"All the more reason to be wary."

"And I will be," Ian promised.

"The minister is supposedly a learned man," Patrick said. "Quite popular in London and New York."

Ian dipped his bread in the gravy and chewed thoughtfully. "That's something I don't understand," he said. "If the minister is so brilliant, and so respected in New York and London, why come to Philadelphia?"

Patrick nodded to two couples seated at the next table, one a former customer. "He wouldn't."

Ian was confused. "Then why is he here?"

"I'm sure there's much we don't know," Patrick said. "But I doubt he's here voluntarily, especially with Abigail's family in New York. He was either forced, he's indebted to someone powerful, like Howe, or it's some sordid secret yet to be revealed."

"Probably the latter."

"Exactly my point," Patrick said, and then sipped his port. "Whatever it is, they have a purpose in Philadelphia. Until we know what it is, we should be careful, even at Sunday service."

"I should avoid her," Ian mumbled. "Even though I don't want to."

"It doesn't matter what you want," Patrick said. "You need to do what's best—both for you and the cause. It's better to leave her alone."

Ian ate some of his beef, followed by a forkful of peas, and considered the options. "Maybe they're spies," he offered.

"I had the same thought," Patrick replied. "It's a perfect ploy. The minister, who all will trust, and Abigail, formerly from Philadelphia. She knows the city and its residents—who supported the rebellion and who sided with the king."

"She does know everyone's secrets," Ian agreed. "Including ours."

"All the more reason for us to seem neutral. We don't need trouble, even though it still may find us. We've no way to know what she'll do."

Ian again looked at the head table. "I don't think she'll do anything to harm us."

"Maybe not," Patrick said. "But I bet her husband will."

Ian turned to his father. Little escaped him. He was a good judge of character, blessed with common sense. "Then we must find out."

11

Once the celebration ended, Abigail and Solomon took their carriage back to the rectory. Solomon sat in the parlor, preparing for evening tea, while Abigail wandered into his study.

"I'll just be a minute," she called. "I want to compose a quick note for my father."

"Tell him we're settled in the city, and I was honored by our reception."

Abigail sat at the desk with paper and quill. It was a difficult note to write. She couldn't accuse her father of destroying her relationship with the man she loved. She would have to delicately request an explanation. She deserved the truth, and so did Ian.

When she finished, she added quick messages for her three sisters, put the letter on the table in the foyer for Anna, their housekeeper, to post, and went into the parlor to join Solomon. Tea had already been served, and he sat quietly, his cup to his lips.

"I was truly humbled," he said as she sat across from him.

She took her tea from the table. "They're good people who are honored to have you serve their city."

He sighed, casting her a guarded glance. "I would have preferred to remain in New York."

She frowned, the discussion distasteful. "A deed of your own doing."

He was about to speak but decided against it. Changing the subject seemed a safer course. "I felt no tension as I expected given the British occupation."

"I suspect the Patriots hide their allegiance. They have no choice."

"You know the people," he said. "How many support the rebellion?"

She thought of those attending, some she had known for years, others she had never met. "More than half, I'm sure," she said. "Philadelphia was the colonial capital only a few days ago."

The minister sipped his tea. "I'm sure they realize we're loyal to the Crown."

"I suspect they seek a pastor," she said, correcting him. "Politics is not their concern."

Solomon was quiet for a moment. "I think, once more, you may be right."

She considered the guests, their faces filtering through her mind, and then she fixed on Ian, and her emotions, dormant for so long, began to stir.

"Don't you agree?" Solomon asked, leaning toward her, interrupting her thoughts.

She hadn't been listening, but assumed he still dwelled on the reception. "It was a room filled with fascinating people," she said. "But the most brilliant minds were missing."

He was confused. "Who might they be?"

"The Continental Congress. You're far more suited to their

discussions, especially the philosophy—Rousseau, Locke, the Greeks."

"Yes, perhaps," he mumbled. "I have heard others praise them."

"Many thought they would change the world," she said softly, wondering if they ever would. They were good men, caught in a conflict gone wrong. Each day that passed brought them closer to British justice, closer to a hangman's noose.

"I suppose Philadelphia is different than you remember," Solomon continued, "if you're focused on a traitorous government."

She thought of Ian, a man she had loved above all else. His twinkling eyes were a bit dimmer, but he was just as handsome, his words just as soft. She had known she would see him when she came back to Philadelphia and, if she was willing to admit it, she realized he was the primary reason she had agreed to come.

"It couldn't have changed that much," Solomon said, sensing her hesitation. "Other than the absence of Congress."

"In some respects, it's the same," she said. "But in others, it's very different."

He paused, as if considering those he had met, and those he would never know. "We'll have to become acquainted with the congregation. Do you remember many?"

"Yes, I do," she said. "Like Patrick Blaine, the cabinetmaker. A few years ago, he donated funds to start one of the libraries."

"Who was the man so flattered by your attention?" he asked, peering at her through his glasses, his gaze suggesting more than a mild interest.

She paused, knowing he had no need to know. "The cabinetmaker's son."

"What was he talking about?"

She shrugged. "We only discussed dinner. The wine mainly."

"Nothing more?"

She slowly shook her head, trying to make a meeting between former lovers seem like an innocent encounter. "No, but he did tell me where his shop was located, should we need cabinetry."

He glanced around the rectory. "We have ample furniture, I would think."

"We've little storage," she replied. "I am in need of a wardrobe or chest."

He paused, considering the expense. "Chest is preferable."

"It's something I should explore," she said, wondering what her second meeting with Ian might bring.

"If the cost is reasonable," he said. He was quiet for a moment, still learning about those in his congregation. "Are the cabinetmakers loyal to the king?"

She hesitated, even though she knew the answer. "I suspect, like any businessmen, they sell their wares to whomever will purchase them."

He nodded, his thoughts elsewhere. "I only ask because General Howe will seek our assistance to identify friend from foe."

"Your place is at the pulpit," she said warily, "and mine is by your side."

"Yes, perhaps," Solomon muttered. "But Howe rewards his friends."

"And foes?" she asked, knowing where Ian's loyalties lay.

"Disaster lurks," he warned. "Yet none know it's coming."

12

The following afternoon, Abigail sat in the parlor reading a botany book, Solomon beside her poring through a philosophical dissertation. After she scanned the pages, studying some illustrations, she set it down and opened a book on ancient civilizations.

"I don't understand why you can't read one book at a time," Solomon said, gazing at her through his spectacles.

"I like to go back and forth. Read one for a while, and then switch to a second."

"It makes no sense at all," he mumbled, turning the page. "I find it annoying."

She looked at him curiously. "Why should you even care? I'm the one reading them."

They were interrupted by a knock on the front door. Anna Knight, an attractive widow in her late thirties who served as housekeeper, cooking and cleaning for the minister and his wife, emerged from the kitchen.

"I wonder who that could be," Solomon muttered.

"I'll see who it is, sir," Anna said as she went into the foyer.

Although sometimes nosy, she seemed loyal during their limited time in the city.

Abigail peeked over the top of her book. They didn't receive many visitors, and she was wary, especially since the British had just arrived in the city.

Anna opened the door, talked briefly, and stepped into the parlor. "A British colonel is here, sir."

Solomon arched his eyebrows. "Did he say what he wanted?"

"He wishes to speak to you," Anna replied. "Two of his orderlies are with him."

Abigail set her book on the couch. "We had best entertain them," she whispered.

Solomon cast her an anxious glance. "I suppose you're right. But who knows what they'll want?"

"I'll be on my best behavior," Abigail said, smiling—to lessen the tension if nothing else.

Solomon stood and prepared to greet his visitors. "Show them in, Anna."

A moment later, Anna led a British officer into the parlor. Two soldiers followed, but remained at the entrance, as if standing guard.

"The minister, Solomon St. Clair, and his wife Abigail," Anna announced.

The officer wore white breeches and black boots, his red coat adorned with gold fringe and buttons. He nodded respectfully. "I'm Colonel Alexander Duncan."

Abigail forced a smile, suspecting he was about to impose. Duncan seemed pompous, a handsome man with his powdered hair in a ponytail. She eyed him cautiously, sensing danger.

"What can we do for you, sir?" Solomon asked.

"As I'm sure you're aware, Mr. St. Clair, our arrival in the city has created housing shortages for the army, especially the officers."

Solomon hesitated. "I assumed most of your men would man defensive positions outside the city."

"Much of the army is camped along Germantown Road," Duncan replied. "But a contingent remains in the city, staged in public squares, with a few along the waterfront."

"What do you need from us, Colonel?" Abigail asked, guarded. She assumed he had an aristocratic lineage, similar to most of the officer corps, and suspected he was not yet powerful, but soon might be.

"I seek lodging in your home," he said sternly, but politely. "Not the best situation for either of us, I'm sure, but a necessity given the situation."

Abigail glanced at the minister. She had no desire to house a British officer, regardless of how polite or powerful he might be. But she also realized there was little chance of avoiding it.

"The rectory is quite small," Solomon said. "Two bedrooms upstairs that my wife and I occupy, the kitchen, parlor, a spare room and my study downstairs."

"I see," the colonel said, the smile disappearing.

"The room next to my study is available, however," Solomon said hastily after observing the colonel's reaction. "We only use it for storage."

"Hardly used to its full potential then, is it?" Duncan asked, the politeness returning.

"No, I suppose not," Solomon agreed. "If the room is suitable, we would be more than happy to accommodate."

"It should do nicely," Duncan said abruptly, without even seeing it.

"We're honored to have you as our guest," Solomon said.

Anna, who had been standing by the soldiers in the foyer, stepped into the parlor. "I can get it ready for you, sir. And make it quite comfortable, I'm sure."

"Thank you," Duncan said with a polite nod. "Mrs...."

"Anna, sir," she said. "Anna Knight. Housekeeper and cook. Although I don't live on the premises. I'm a few blocks away. Just me and my twelve-year-old son ever since I was widowed."

"Thank you, Mrs. Knight," Duncan said, a smile curling his lips. "I appreciate your efforts. And will continue to do so, I'm sure."

Abigail groaned inwardly, but kept a smile pasted on her face. She decided to make one last attempt to avert the situation. "There is one problem. We have no room for your orderlies."

"Not an issue at all," Duncan scoffed. "An outbuilding will be fine. They don't need much."

Abigail glanced at Solomon, but he only shrugged. "We have a barn where the horses and carriage are kept."

Duncan nodded. "That should do nicely."

Abigail glanced at the soldiers, their expressions passive, and back to Duncan. "Are you sure?" she asked. "Larger homes are available. Some have space for your men."

"That's quite all right, Mrs. St. Clair," Duncan said, with a slight bow. "The barn will suffice. Especially when considering the alternative—a blanket and bare ground."

"We also have vacant rooms in the church," Solomon offered, as if he might avoid losing a room in the rectory. "One on each side of the altar."

"Thank you, I'll consider it," Duncan said.

"With the minister's blessing, I'll get the room ready," Anna offered.

"Yes, of course," Solomon replied. "Do what you can to make the colonel comfortable."

"I will, sir," Anna said, casting Duncan a sly glance. "I'll make sure he gets what he needs."

Duncan turned to his orderlies. "Help Mrs. Knight prepare the room, and get my belongings and bring them in."

"Yes, sir," one of the soldiers said, looking at Anna for direction.

Abigail rose from the couch. "We have a cot you may use, although not the best accommodation."

Duncan nodded respectfully. "More than adequate, I'm sure."

"We'll make you as comfortable as possible," Solomon promised.

Abigail eyed the colonel warily, knowing her life was about to change, possibly forever.

"It does come with benefits, I assure you," Duncan said.

Solomon gave Abigail a guarded glance. "What might that be, good sir?"

"I will ensure you have ample food and firewood," Duncan replied.

Abigail was puzzled. Why would food and firewood be of such concern? "Thank you, Colonel. We appreciate your assistance."

"It may not seem like much now," Duncan said smugly. "But both will wane quickly in the weeks ahead."

13

I an woke to a loud bang on the front door. He listened. The knock repeated, and he jumped from bed to dress. A visitor near midnight meant nothing good, especially with the British controlling the city.

Patrick rushed into his room. "It's the redcoats!" he hissed. "Five or six of them out in the street."

"Open up, Ian Blaine," a soldier demanded.

"You've got to get out," Patrick urged. "Hurry! I'll stall them."

"We know you're in there," a second voice called.

"Give me a second to get some clothes on," Patrick yelled down to the first floor, their living quarters above the shop.

"You've got two minutes," the British shouted.

"Tell them I'm in Jersey," Ian said as he finished dressing. "Just as Barnabas said."

"I'll try to convince them," Patrick assured him. "But you better hide fast." He rushed into his bedroom and started to dress.

Ian buckled his shoes. He raced to his bedroom window, overlooking the back of the house. A lean-to for wood storage and a barn for their horses, carriage, and wagon sprawled across the property.

"Open the door before I break it down," a soldier yelled.

"I'm coming," Patrick insisted.

Ian cracked open the window. Two soldiers wandered into the yard, turning the corner of the carriage house. He eased the window down so he wouldn't be heard, left his bedroom, and hurried into the parlor.

Patrick was at the top of the steps. "Get out," he whispered. "They'll search the house."

"I saw soldiers out back," Ian said.

"Last chance, Blaine," the British hollered.

Patrick pointed upward. "Roof."

"Break it down," came the British command.

"I'm almost there," Patrick called as he hurried down the steps.

Ian opened the parlor window. He looked at the alley between the shop and neighboring house. There was nowhere to go, no tree to climb, no way down to the ground. He dashed across the second floor to the kitchen.

Patrick opened the front door. "What do you want?"

"Where's Ian Blaine?" a soldier demanded.

Ian crept into the kitchen. He gently lifted the window while he listened to the conversation below.

"He's in Jersey," he heard Patrick say. "Why, what's the meaning of all of this?"

"Who are you?"

"Patrick Blaine, his father."

"I'm Colonel Alexander Duncan of His Majesty's government. We have reason to believe your son has been aiding the enemy."

Patrick laughed. "That's ridiculous," he said. "He's not even here."

"He was observed spying on a British camp two weeks ago."

"That doesn't sound like Ian. Where did this supposedly happen?"

"At Trudruffrin."

"It wasn't him," Patrick insisted. "I think he was in Jersey then, too. He travels back and forth."

Ian listened to his father's explanation, but the British offered no reply. The silence was eerie, a warning that something was coming—he just didn't know what. He guessed that Duncan studied his father suspiciously, doubting every word he said.

"Search the house!" Duncan ordered, his voice booming.

"I'm telling you, he isn't here," Patrick protested.

Ian climbed out of the window. He stepped onto a corbelled chimney and reached back to lower the sash. Crawling up the angled brick, he climbed onto the roof, grabbing the chimney so he didn't slip on the slate. He crouched, peeking from behind the brick, the back of the house on one side, Chestnut St. on the other. He could see the house across the street, a bakery on the bottom floor, the residence above it. The windows were dark, not a candle lit.

The British barged in, rattling through different rooms. They searched the first-floor workshop and lumbered up the steps to the residence. Wardrobe doors opened and slammed closed, furniture slid across wood floors, as they checked every nook where a man could hide. Ian knew Patrick followed them from room to room, insisting his son was in Jersey, but not quite able to convince them.

"Did you see anything?" someone called from the back door.

"No one left the house," came the reply from a soldier near the carriage house.

"Search the stable and lean-to."

Ian's legs started to cramp, but he stayed still, knowing the chimney hid him. A cloud passed over the moon and darkness shrouded the city, but it lasted only a minute.

"You're wasting your time," Ian heard Patrick say. He was standing in the kitchen, directly below. "I don't know how many times I have to tell you."

"When was he in Philadelphia last?" Duncan probed.

"A couple days ago," Patrick said. "He went to the minister's reception and went on the ferry when it ended."

"It seems strange he left after the celebration," Duncan sneered. "Why not wait?"

"He had no reason to," Patrick explained. "He makes frequent trips, sometimes several a week,"

"When does he return?" Duncan asked.

"Tomorrow morning," Patrick said. "You can speak to him then if you like."

Ian dared not move. He could imagine the colonel staring at his father, his patience ebbing.

"When was the last trip he took?" Duncan asked.

Ian cringed, hoping his father provided the right date.

"He went last week, left Thursday morning," Patrick said. "On the eighteenth."

"And when did he return?"

"Monday." Patrick replied. "And he left again a few days ago."

"How does he get to Jersey?"

"On the Arch St. ferry," Patrick said.

It was quiet, an unexpected silence lasting almost a minute. Patrick tried to plant doubt in Duncan's mind, and it seemed he was succeeding.

A different voice spoke, one of the soldiers. "We searched everywhere, sir. No one is in the house."

"There's a heavy penalty for those not truthful," Duncan warned.

"I'm telling the truth," Patrick insisted. "Why would I not?"

"Why does he go to Jersey?" Duncan demanded.

"To sell goods and get supplies," Patrick said. "Many businesses do."

A moment passed before Duncan spoke. "Let's be on our way," he directed his men. "It seems Mr. Blaine is telling the truth."

Ian's legs ached, his torn fingers gripping the brick. He waited a few minutes and peeked around the chimney. The British colonel and two soldiers walked to the back of the property. They stood near the lean-to, just in front of the carriage house.

"Did you find anything?" Duncan called.

Two soldiers appeared, one from behind the lean-to, the second from the barn.

"Nothing here, sir," the first said.

"I didn't find anything, either, sir," echoed the second.

"Then let's be on our way," Duncan said. "We'll return tomorrow."

14

Ian watched as the British left, exiting through the alley to Chestnut St. A carriage waited, the driver perched upon the bench seat. Duncan went to it, opened the door, and turned to his men.

"Go back to your stations," he said. "We've nothing more to do here."

Ian peeked from behind the chimney as Duncan climbed in his carriage and the driver urged the horses forward. The soldiers remained in front of the shop a moment more and then walked away, their figures melting in the darkness. Once Ian was sure they were gone, he crawled down the angled chimney, opened the kitchen window, and eased inside. As he entered the parlor, he saw his father peering outside.

"They're gone," Ian said quietly.

Patrick turned, startled. "Where were you?"

"I climbed out the kitchen window and onto the roof."

"It's good that you did," Patrick said. "They searched every inch of the house."

"The buildings out back, too."

"There's no doubt now. Hart saw you and told the British."

"So it seems," Ian said, not sure what to do next.

"They won't stop until they find you, no matter when it is."

"Barnabas said he could create an alibi, use friends as fake witnesses."

Patrick paused. "I'll talk to him in the morning. We'll need to plot everything carefully. We can't underestimate them."

"What do you think of this colonel?"

"Duncan?" Patrick asked and shrugged. "He's like all the rest. Probably bought his position. I doubt if he earned it."

"I think we best treat him with care," Ian advised. "He could be hard to fool."

"I told him you were in Jersey. Anything to keep him from dragging you away in the middle of the night."

"It gives us time to prepare. Although I'm not sure what we should do."

Patrick considered their options. "You had best disappear for the night, should they return. Just be careful in case they posted guards. Come back tomorrow, as if you're returning from Jersey."

"I'll find someplace to hide and see you in the morning."

"Make sure you time your return with the ferry," Patrick warned. "They're sure to be watching."

"I'll be careful," Ian promised, as he started toward the stairs.

"See that you are," Patrick said, worried for his son's welfare. "I'll get to Barnabas first thing. He can create an alibi and provide witnesses to support it."

Ian hurried down the steps. He paused at the back door, peeked out to ensure no one hid in the shadows, eased it open, and stepped outside. He moved along the back of the house, avoided the path the soldiers had taken, and crossed through a neighboring property, preparing to exit onto Third St. There weren't many places to hide once he was on the street, not with British patrols. He intended to stay in a house of worship, at least for the night. But just as he was about to turn down the street, he heard voices, distant but discernable.

"Is that a man in the shadows?" someone asked.

Ian ducked behind a fence and dropped to the ground, lying still. He peeked down Third and saw a British soldier posted on the far corner, watching the street. Four more were farther away. They started toward him.

Ian crawled along the fence. He stayed in the shadows, scurrying to a nearby building. He suspected the British had guards on both Third and Chestnut, maybe Walnut, too. Chestnut was close, but brighter, street lamps lit with candles. He slid along the building, through his neighbor's property and back to his own. He waited but heard no one approach. After a few minutes of silence, he rose and raced across his yard, ducking behind his neighbor's carriage house. He peeked around the corner. Two soldiers were coming toward him, rifles drawn, peering into the darkness.

"I saw someone race across the yard," the first soldier said.

"Maybe it's Blaine, the man we're looking for," his comrade replied.

Ian crawled alongside the carriage house. He moved quickly, staying close to the building, getting as far away from the soldiers as he could. When he reached the edge, he turned the corner, leaned against the building, and looked out.

The soldiers weren't far, fifty feet at most. They rooted through wood piles in his lean-to, just as they had done while he was hiding on the roof.

"I don't see anyone," a soldier said. "Are you sure it wasn't an animal—a dog or a cat?"

"I don't think so. It seemed like a person. But I suppose it could have been shadows."

"We'll look for a few more minutes," the other said as they came onto the neighbor's property.

Ian scurried fifty feet to an alley that led to Walnut St. He hid behind another carriage house and waited several seconds, barely breathing. He poked his head around the corner. The soldiers approached on the opposite side, searching, and he pulled back so they couldn't see him.

He waited, eyeing the different buildings. Boots crunched the grass, footsteps coming closer. He couldn't stay where he was. In seconds they would see him. He had to take a chance, risk being seen or heard. He raced another hundred feet, stepping as gently as he could to make no noise, and came out on Walnut St. After ensuring no one lurked about, he edged toward Third, waiting on the corner. He paused, his back against the wall of a quilt store. A few seconds later he peeked down the road. The soldiers stepped out of an alley onto Walnut, not far away.

He didn't move. He could hear their boots thumping the pavement as they walked towards him. They no longer hid their presence, talking loudly, their search abandoned. If they had seen him, they would have raced after him. But they didn't.

Ian knew two more soldiers were nearby, but he didn't know where. Since he couldn't see them, he didn't know what direction to take. He could easily escape from those that chased him, and stumble into those that didn't. But if he stayed where he was, they would find him.

A carriage came down Third, heading north. Ian waited in the shadows until it approached. Once he saw it carried no passengers, he ran alongside, ensuring the driver couldn't see him. He lightly stepped onto the back of the carriage, a ledge used to store luggage, his body flat against the frame.

The horses' hooves clicked on the cobblestone, the metal rim of the wagon wheels kicking a mild blue spark from the friction on the road. The carriage moved quickly, the streets abandoned, no one about in the wee hours of the morning. The driver turned onto Market, headed toward the river, but then swung left onto Second St.

A soldier patrolled the street, ensuring the curfew was kept, the citizens contained. Another carriage passed, a man on horseback, but no pedestrians. When they reached a dark area of the street, hidden under the protective canopy of arching oaks, Ian stepped softly off the back of the carriage.

The soldiers who pursued him were blocks away. Except for an occasional sentry, the streets were deserted. Ian studied the Anglican Church just down the road. He glanced up and down the street, gazed at the dark windows in the brick townhouses to ensure no one watched, and stole along the edge of the pavement.

The back of the church faced Second St., the entrance on a narrow lane. Ian crept among shrubs on the side of the church until he reached the alley that the entrance faced. He studied the buildings across the street, ensuring he wasn't being watched, and sneaked around the corner of the church. The rectory sat diagonally across the street, a brick building dwarfed by the church and its steeple. He looked up and down the lane and hurried to the front door. He stepped in and eased the door closed behind him.

The church was dark, a single candle in a brass holder burning in the center of the altar. Ian tiptoed toward it and looked at two arched doors, rooms on each side. He chose the right, walked to the door, and gently opened it.

It was cramped and dark, with a desk likely used by the minister, a chest and bureau. A large wardrobe stood against the wall adjacent to the altar, a clothes rack in front of it, two coats hanging from hooks. He moved the coat rack into the room, stepped behind it and leaned against the wall. He stood for a moment, making sure he hadn't been followed, slumped to the floor, and closed his eyes.

15

Barnabas Stone lived alone on Second St. in a brick rowhome a few doors down from the City Tavern. He had managed to avoid lodging any British troops, although he wasn't sure how. He had offered, telling his British officer friends that he would be happy to accommodate. But most, it seemed, preferred homes with servants to ensure their needs were met.

He was in the parlor just before 7 a.m., preparing to leave for the City Tavern, when he heard a light tap on the back door. Accessed via an alley, the rear entrance was rarely used—not even by him. Something was amiss, he just wasn't sure what it was. He entered the kitchen, saw a man's frame through the window, hurried to the door and opened it.

"Barnabas, I need your help," Patrick blurted as he scanned the alley, ensuring no one watched.

"Come in," Barnabas offered, noting the frenzied expression on his friend's face. "Hurry. Before someone sees you and wonders what you're doing out there."

Patrick crossed the threshold and hesitated. "Are you alone?"

"Yes," Barnabas replied. "No redcoats here yet. But I don't know how long that will last."

"They came for Ian last night," Patrick said. "Around midnight."

"Sit down," Barnabas said, motioning to the kitchen table. "Can I get you anything?"

Patrick shook his head. "It was a colonel named Duncan, and four or five of his men."

"Where did they take him?"

"They didn't find him," Patrick said. "But they searched the whole house looking for him. He climbed out a window and hid on the roof."

"A smart lad," Barnabas said. "I'm impressed. Where is he now?"

Patrick shrugged. "Hiding somewhere. I told Duncan he was in Jersey, returning today."

Barnabas withdrew a pocket watch from his shirt and glanced at the time. "I'd best get down to the ferry. I'll make sure the ferryman vouches for him."

"I said he was in Jersey last Thursday, too," Patrick continued. "On the eighteenth. That's when Duncan claimed he saw him at Trudruffrin."

Barnabas was quiet, plotting Ian's alibi. "I'll need more than just the ferryman," he muttered. "If I'm to convince them."

Patrick calmed, watching Barnabas deep in thought, meticulously planning. "Other witnesses?"

Barnabas nodded. "That's easy enough. I'll talk to some who frequent the ferry, shipping product to Jersey."

Patrick sighed with relief. "Barnabas, I don't know how to thank you."

"No need," Barnabas replied. "This is just the beginning. We can't have the redcoats suspicious of Ian."

"It's Hart," Patrick declared. "The traitor."

"We'll deal with Hart," Barnabas promised. "But only when the time is right."

"I'm sure the redcoats are watching my house, waiting for Ian. I told him to time his return with the ferry's arrival."

"I'll take care of them," Barnabas said. "Some of the British breakfast at the tavern. They love Dolly's scrapple. And her hasty pudding, too."

Patrick was confused. "Does Duncan go?"

Barnabas shook his head. "No, I've never met him. But I think I'll start at the tavern, spread word among the redcoats that Duncan made a mistake."

"Do you think it will get back to him?"

Barnabas smiled. "I guarantee it will. Within the hour."

Patrick looked at his friend curiously. "How will you ever do that?"

"I'll say Duncan made a fool of himself, mistaking an upstanding citizen for a colonial spy. I'm sure someone will tell him. They'll do it quickly."

"Anything you can do to save Ian is greatly appreciated."

Barnabas stood. "I'd best be going," he said. "I've a lot to do before the ferry arrives."

"Should I leave through the alley?"

Barnabas nodded. "Better not to be seen with me. At least not now."

"Do you think this will work?"

Barnabas laughed. "Of course," he said. "I'll make sure it does."

16

Breakfast at the rectory was served around 8 a.m. Abigail found it awkward, sharing the table with a British officer. But although the arrangement was tense at times, Colonel Duncan was always polite, even if sometimes pompous.

"I'm told that church officials in New York sent you to Philadelphia," Duncan said as he ate his porridge.

Solomon hesitated, eyeing the colonel cautiously. "Yes, they did," he replied. "It was quite unexpected, but I must follow the church's direction."

"And since I had been raised it Philadelphia, we thought it not much of a burden," Abigail added, wondering where the conversation would lead.

"Your presence wasn't requested by powerful friends, was it?" Duncan asked before taking more porridge from the bowl. "General Howe, perhaps? I saw that he sat beside you at your reception."

Solomon chuckled. "No, I think not, although I do know General Howe very well. I simply serve God. He guides me to do what is right."

Duncan looked at him curiously. "I don't understand," he

said, prying. "Did Howe ask church officials to send you to Philadelphia? Or was there a different reason?"

Abigail glanced at Solomon, trying to get his attention. Duncan didn't need to know why they came to Philadelphia.

The minister paused, collecting his thoughts. "Church leaders suggested an assignment in Philadelphia. But I suspect they were prodded by General Howe."

Abigail sighed with relief. Secrets were meant to be kept. Regardless of who wanted them revealed. Solomon had secrets. But then, so did she.

"I would think you could go wherever you wanted," Duncan pressed. "Especially given your reputation. Your sermons are legendary, even to those not versed in theological dissertation."

"Thank you, Colonel," Solomon said humbly. "I'm honored."

Abigail eyed Duncan warily, wondering why he was so complimentary. Although he appeared to have no motive, she suspected he did. "Philadelphia offered an opportunity that might not be available elsewhere."

"Because it was the colonial capital?" Duncan asked warily. "Is that why Howe wanted you here?"

"Hardly," Solomon said with a light laugh. "Congress evacuated the day we arrived. We had no exposure to them, or their followers."

"You're not one of the general's spies, are you?" Duncan asked, a twinkle in his eyes.

Solomon laughed. "I'm a minister, Colonel. Nothing more."

"We did hesitate to leave New York," Abigail said. "My family is there and I'm quite close to my sisters."

Duncan ate some porridge. "It'll be interesting to observe the congregation," he said. "Some still support the rebellion, as I'm sure you're aware. How will you approach them—with hammer or honey?"

The minister seemed surprised. "I think a benevolent

approach would be best. I only try to do what's right, to serve the Lord. That's the message I shall bring."

Duncan sat back in the chair and eyed him cautiously. "At least initially."

Abigail wondered what he meant. She knew Duncan was dangerous. Even though he was polite, charming when he wanted to be, his steel eyes could cast a cold gaze when his wishes weren't honored. She suspected a fiery temper brewed within the confines of a calm exterior.

They finished their meal and, as Anna cleared away the dishes, Duncan reminded them of a prior conversation. "You mentioned rooms in the church where some of my men might be housed."

"Yes, there's a room on each side of the altar," Solomon said reluctantly, as if he hoped the colonel might have forgotten. "Although one is used as my office."

"But you have an office here in the rectory," Duncan said politely.

Abigail realized Duncan was cunning. Solomon lived in a different world—one of philosophical discourse and theological discussions—and he was about to be outsmarted.

"I use my study for my writings," Solomon said. "Sermons and articles for publication."

Duncan looked confused. "Why would you need another office at the church?"

Abigail knew what Duncan was doing, but she suspected Solomon did not. The colonel might look confused, or appear to, but he was spinning a web in which to catch his prey.

"My church office is for official business," Solomon explained. "It's where I pay bills, render services, coordinate charity efforts."

Duncan paused, reflective, and after a moment, acted as if he had an idea. "I would think the functions could be combined," he said with arched eyebrows.

"But my books and personal belongings are here," Solomon continued. "I may not have room for church documents."

Abigail studied Duncan's expression. The trap had been sprung. It showed in his eyes.

"I see no need for two offices," Duncan said firmly. "You can surrender the office in the rectory, and house another officer, or conduct church business from the rectory, and offer that space to my men."

Solomon realized he was in no position to argue. He would seem selfish if he did. "Yes, I suppose," he said softly. "It's something I hadn't considered."

"Don't you agree?" Duncan asked.

"Of course, we do," Abigail said, intervening. She had no desire to lodge another British officer. If Solomon couldn't avert it, she would. "Since the space in the church is larger, it can better accommodate your men."

"Splendid," Duncan said. "I knew a solution existed."

Abigail couldn't let Solomon interact with the colonel. He was mismatched. "I can show you the rooms at the church," she offered hastily, "while Solomon works on his sermon."

Duncan rose from the table. "Let's go now," he suggested. "Before I review my troops."

The rectory was across the street and slightly askew from the church, both brick buildings with slate roofs. Abigail led Duncan to the church, and they walked inside. The altar sat at the rear, three large arched windows behind it, the sun's rays streaming in and spilling across the pews. On each side of the altar, uniform in design, were two closed arched doors.

"Solomon's office is to the right," Abigail said. "It's used for storage—cloaks and clothes he wears for service—besides his desk and some furniture."

"And the room to the left?" Duncan asked.

"All storage," she replied. "Items to support different church events."

"Both rooms have adequate space for my men?"

"Yes, of course," she said. "I just have some rearranging to do first."

"Not too much of an imposition, I assume?" Duncan asked.

"No, not at all." She led him to the room on the right, wondering why he was so polite. She sensed that's when he was most dangerous. She opened the door and stepped inside, the minister's desk centered in the room.

Duncan stood at the threshold, scanning the space. "This is more than adequate," he said. "The men are soldiers. I don't want to spoil them."

Abigail walked into the room and examined the contents. "I can move everything to provide more space."

As she approached the minister's desk, she looked to her left. Beside the wardrobe, leaning against the wall with a coat rack in front of him, stood Ian Blaine.

17

Abigail gasped, eyes wide.

"Is something wrong?" Duncan asked from the doorway.

She turned, smiling weakly. "No, of course not. Just more cluttered than I realized."

"Easily addressed, I'm sure," Duncan said. He gazed out a window that overlooked a cemetery.

Abigail stared at Ian, eyebrows arched.

His gaze met hers, pleading for help.

She moved away, bumping into the coat rack, and knocking a garment to the floor.

"Do you need help, Mrs. St. Clair?" Duncan asked, taking a step toward her.

"No, Colonel, I'm fine," she said, using his title so Ian knew who was there. She picked up the coat and rehung it, arranging it so it hid more of Ian. She didn't know why he was there, but she suspected the British were behind it.

Duncan came closer. "Is the second room similar to this one?"

She moved in front of him. "We can go and see it," she said, easing toward the door.

He ignored her, studying furniture. "This is a large room, bigger than I assumed."

Her heart raced. "Yes, it is," she said, glancing at Ian. He was as frightened as she was.

Duncan took another step forward. "My officers should be quite comfortable here." He moved around her and approached the wardrobe, Ian hiding just to the side of it. "Interesting furniture, too."

She stepped back, close to the coat rack. "The second room could house your orderlies."

Duncan nodded, admiring the wardrobe. "I find these carvings interesting," he said. He ran his finger over a vine carved in the wood. "I'm afraid I don't have the patience for it."

"Me, either," she said nervously. She could see Ian, Duncan couldn't.

"Most definitely the work of a craftsman."

"The other room is filled with tables and chairs used for church functions," she said, coaxing Duncan to leave. "But we can move them, if needed."

Duncan turned toward the door. "Since we do have extra space, we should use it."

She stepped between Duncan and the wardrobe and pointed to a bureau along the opposite wall—anything to divert his attention. "I would think that, after moving some of the furniture, this room could house several men."

"Yes, four or five at least," Duncan agreed. He turned back toward the wardrobe. "Although I might use this in my room at the rectory."

She stepped to the side, closer to Ian, offering partial protection. She opened the wardrobe, using the door to block Duncan's view. "Some of the minister's clothes for the mass," she said, pretending to study what was stored within. "I can bring all of this to the rectory."

"Please do," Duncan said. "I need to store my clothes, and this shall work perfectly." He continued to admire it. "It's quite handsome. Befitting a colonel in His Majesty's service, don't you agree?"

"Yes, of course," she said with a nervous laugh.

Duncan moved toward the door. "I could fit a dozen men in here, if needed. But my officers shall use it for now."

"Whatever you determine," Abigail said, her breath coming in short gasps.

"Thank you, Mrs. St. Clair," the colonel said. He left abruptly, his boots echoing on the floor, growing dimmer as he walked down the aisle.

Abigail looked behind the coat rack. "What are you doing here?"

Before Ian could reply, Duncan's footsteps stopped and grew louder. "Mrs. St. Clair," he called.

She kept her gaze on Ian. "What is it, Colonel?"

The footsteps came closer. He crossed the threshold and stepped into the room.

Abigail moved toward him, ensuring he advanced no farther. "Is there something else you need?"

"I'll send soldiers to assist you," he said. "They can move the furniture."

Abigail stood in front of him, determined to block his path. "That's so kind of you, Colonel," she said. "I appreciate it."

He looked at her curiously. "Are you sure nothing is wrong? You're behaving quite strangely."

"No, nothing amiss," she said, forcing a smile. "I only want to sort through a few things before your men move in and I'm anxious to get started."

"I'll leave you to your tasks, madam," Duncan said with a

slight bow. "My men are grateful for the accommodations and will make do with whatever you provide."

Duncan left the room, his footsteps echoing through the empty church. A moment later the front door opened. He exited and closed it behind him.

Abigail stepped past the coat rack and leaned close to Ian. "We only have a few minutes," she said frantically. "Why are you hiding?"

18

"What time is it?" Ian asked.

Abigail looked at him strangely. "What does that have to do with anything?"

"Duncan thinks I'm in Jersey, returning on the morning ferry."

"Is that why you're hiding here?"

Ian nodded. "He came looking for me last night, but I slipped out of the house and came here. My father told him I was returning today."

"The ferry doesn't arrive for another thirty minutes," she said, a confused look on her face. "But why would he care?"

Ian sighed. He had no choice but to trust her. But he was sure he could. They had loved each other once. Maybe they still did.

"You better tell me everything," she said firmly. "Especially if you want me to help."

He stood at a crossroads—a moment to define the rest of his life. He could lie, knowing whatever he said could be proven untrue, or he could trust the only person he ever loved

—and hope she wouldn't betray him, regardless of which side she favored.

"You haven't much time," she said, pressing. "Duncan's men are on their way."

"I'm going to trust you."

"You have no choice," she said. "I know you're in serious trouble."

"But I'm trusting you with my life."

She rolled her eyes. "A life I almost shared. Stop wasting time. Or Duncan will find you."

He realized nothing had changed, even if their lives had taken different paths. "Oliver Hart told Duncan he saw me scouting the British army outside of the city two weeks ago."

"Were you?"

He nodded. "Duncan came to arrest me last night," he said, his gaze fixed on hers, hoping she would understand.

"And your father said you weren't scouting the British," she said, completing the explanation. "It was someone else."

"Yes, he claimed I was in Jersey. Both then and now."

She studied him closely, her expression unchanged. "Duncan is quartered at the rectory. I had breakfast with him this morning. He never mentioned you."

"I think my father convinced him," Ian said. "But I'm sure my house is being watched. I have to return sometime after the morning ferry arrives. Or they'll know we lied."

"Ian, how do you manage to get yourself into such messes?" she asked, remembering a few while they dated. "This is serious. We're at war. I saw men hang for spying in New York."

He was quiet for a moment, watching her. "I made a terrible mistake," he said softly. "Your loyalties lie with the Crown."

"Why would you ever assume otherwise?" she asked. "That's why my family left for New York. As you're well aware, because I wanted desperately to remain here."

He smiled faintly. "It can still be remedied."

"Don't," she said, closing her eyes as if she didn't want to see what the future might hold. "Not now. It's hard enough. For both of us."

"You're right," he admitted. "It is. It never should have happened."

"But it did."

"Did you write your father to ask why he kept us apart?"

"Ian, don't," she said.

"Did you?"

She sighed, her lips firm. "Yes, I did."

"I thought you would."

"Now, stop it," she insisted. "We have to get you out of here."

"I can't show my face until after the ferry arrives."

"But the timing isn't right," she said. "Soldiers are everywhere."

"I have nowhere else to go."

"You can't stay here," she said, glancing around the room. "We have to think of something."

"Can't you hide me?"

"I don't know where. Unless you have a suggestion."

"You were always the smart one," he teased. "I'll defer to you."

She smacked him lightly on the arm. "Will you be serious?"

"Maybe I can hide in the wardrobe?"

"No, Duncan is taking it."

"Can I hide in the rectory?"

The church door opened, squeaking on brass hinges, followed by footsteps. Abigail peeked from the doorway.

"It's Duncan!"

19

Several blocks south of the rectory, Oliver Hart sat in the office of his palatial home. An early riser, he had already spent a few hours reviewing papers and reports, when there was a knock on the jamb of his opened door.

"Miss Malone is here, as you requested," said Jean Stark, his housekeeper. An older woman who had been in his employ for many years, she was a bit stout with a cherubic face, gray hair pinned close to her head, good-humored, and loyal.

"Is breakfast ready?" Hart asked.

"Just about," Jean said, wiping her hands on her white apron,

"What time is it?" Hart asked,

"After eight," she said. "You've probably been working for hours already. Just can't stay away, can you?"

He stood and stretched. "It's my passion," he said. No one knew him as well as Jean Stark. No one ever would. Housekeeper, cook, dear friend, surrogate mother—she played whatever role was needed.

"Miss Malone looks wonderful this morning," Jean said as they left the study. "Make sure you compliment her."

Hart smiled as they walked down a broad hallway accented with molded arches painted white. He turned into the dining room, ivory panels on the lower half of the wall, rich burgundy wallpaper on the top, with broad crown molding tying it together.

Mrs. Stark paused, about to turn left, to the kitchen. "Go on," she whispered. "Do as I tell you."

Missy Malone stood in the dining room, beside the mahogany table, gazing out a twelve-paned window. Hart's frequent companion, at least when he allowed himself time for anything other than his work, she had black curls that spilled to her shoulders and blue eyes that twinkled with mischief. Not born to wealth, her family owned a business on Spruce St. that built carriages. The aristocrats of the city always seemed surprised when she accompanied the wealthy Hart anywhere, much to the amusement of both.

"You look absolutely radiant this morning," Hart said as he walked in.

Missy's eyes widened. "Oliver, you are so kind," she said, beaming. "What a thoughtful thing to say. And so unlike you."

He winked at Mrs. Stark as she went toward the kitchen.

"What got in to you today?" Missy asked.

"I have my moments," he said as he walked toward her.

She hugged him tightly. "I'm looking forward to breakfast. It gives us some time together before you start your day."

"We'll both enjoy it, I'm sure." He led her to the table and seated her.

Mrs. Stark arrived a moment later with two glasses of cider. "Breakfast will be served in a few minutes. I prepared hasty pudding and scrapple. I'll bring in some tea."

"That sounds absolutely delicious, Mrs. Stark," Oliver said.

"I hope you enjoy it," she said as she bustled out of the room.

As soon as the housekeeper left, Missy leaned closer to

Oliver and touched his arm. "Whatever possessed you to march into the city with the British on the first day of the occupation? Some are still talking about it—you'd be surprised by what they're saying. I told them all you've gone daft."

He smiled. Missy could be blunt at times. "I didn't have much choice. Not if I want to work with the British. I don't want to know what people are saying because I can't do anything about it. At least not now."

"You've alienated anyone with rebel sympathies—half the city or more. Although you put smiles on your rich friends' faces. I've never seen James Darwin, the banker, look happier."

"I suspect there are many more like him," Hart said. "Those who support the Crown, always have, and always will."

They were interrupted by sounds from an adjacent room, another wing of the mansion—murmured voices, people walking, doors opening and closing, boot heels on wooden floors. The noise lasted a few more minutes and faded.

Missy looked at Hart, perplexed. "What is all that racket?"

"British officers," he said. "Four are lodged here."

She looked at him with surprise. "Do they have the whole first floor?"

"Yes, just about," he said. "The game room and second parlor at the end of the hall."

"How about the second floor?"

"No, not yet," he said. "They seem to prefer the side entrance, so they can come and go as they please."

"It must be torture for you. Someone who hates people."

He laughed. "I don't hate people; I just prefer to avoid them."

She rolled her eyes. "If I didn't bring cheer to your life, you'd live in absolute solitude."

"And I wouldn't complain," he teased, eyeing her playfully.

Mrs. Stark walked in with a breakfast tray. She set the hasty pudding and scrapple in the center of the table and put healthy portions on each of their plates.

"Mrs. Stark, this smells absolutely delicious," Missy said.

"Thank you, I hope you enjoy it," Mrs. Stark said. She leaned towards Missy. "It's nice to cook for someone who appreciates it."

"I appreciate you, Mrs. Stark," Hart said. "I'm just not as vocal about it."

Missy lowered her voice. "You're not cooking for the brood next door, are you?" she asked, motioning to the wall and the soldiers on the other side of it.

Mrs. Stark smiled. "No, at least not yet."

Missy wagged a finger at Hart. "Don't you let her," she said. "The poor woman works hard enough looking after you."

"I'll get your tea," Mrs. Stark said, smiling as she left the room.

"I don't know if it's possible to decline a request from the British," Hart said as he sampled his breakfast. "If they ask for meals, I shall have to provide them."

"I don't think it's acceptable to work that poor woman to death. If the soldiers want Mrs. Stark to look after them, tell them to ask me. I'll give them an answer they won't soon forget."

Hart smiled. "Yes, I'm sure you will."

She sipped her cider. "Why are you forced to accommodate the British officers?"

"I'm not," he said. He put down his fork and met her gaze. "I invited them."

She looked at him curiously, eyes wide.

20

"I'm sorry, Mrs. St. Clair," Duncan said as he crossed the threshold. "I had something to ask you."

"What is it, Colonel?" She stood in front of the coat rack, shielding Ian. Just as she had a few moments earlier.

"When does the ferry arrive from Jersey?"

She removed a pocket watch from her skirt and looked at the face. "In about thirty minutes," she said. "Why is something amiss?"

He frowned. "Do you know a man named Ian Blaine?"

She pretended to mull over prior acquaintances. "Yes, I do," she said. "But not well. The cabinetmaker's son?"

"Yes, him," Duncan said. "I suspect he'll be arriving on the ferry. I'm taking a few of my men to make sure he does."

Abigail's heart was racing. "Has he done something wrong?"

Duncan paused. "I'm not really sure. He was seen spying on the British camp two weeks ago—or someone who resembles him."

She appeared confused. "What does that have to do with the ferry?"

"I tried to arrest him last night," he explained. "But his father claimed he was in Jersey, returning today."

"And if he is, he's believed innocent?" she asked, acting as if she tried to understand.

Duncan hesitated. "I'm still not sure. If I had found him last night, I would have hanged him. To set an example if nothing else."

She gasped. "But what if he committed no crime?"

He shrugged, as if it really didn't matter. "Last night I was convinced he did. But now I'm not so sure."

"Why would today be different than yesterday?"

He studied her for a moment, as if wondering whether to trust her. "Do you know a man named Barnabas Stone?"

"Yes, of course," she said. "The owner of City Tavern. Everyone in Philadelphia knows Barnabas Stone."

"Mr. Stone gives the British valuable information about the colonials."

Her eyes widened. "I didn't know that."

"Not many do, so don't repeat it."

"I won't," she replied. "I promise."

"An hour ago, Mr. Stone told one of my captains that Blaine was in Jersey, just as his father had said, that he frequently travels back and forth."

"Was he in Jersey when he supposedly spied on your camp?" she asked, hoping to persuade Duncan of Ian's innocence.

"Apparently," he muttered. "At least according to Stone— and Blaine's father."

"Maybe it was someone else," she said, trying to plant doubt.

"Yes, perhaps," he reluctantly agreed. "Although I'm still not convinced. Why would he keep going back and forth across the river? I'm not sure I believe it."

"It's actually quite common," she said. "Shopkeepers do a brisk business in Jersey. Frequent trips are a necessity."

Duncan was quiet for a moment. "If Blaine is on the ferry, I'll leave him alone. At least for now. But I intend to find out more about him. Maybe I'll even have him watched."

"I can ask old friends if they've seen suspicious activity," she said, hoping she could somehow refute Ian's guilt.

He looked at her curiously, considering her offer. "No, not just yet," he said slowly. "But it is an interesting proposition."

She regretted having said it. "Not that any of my former friends would know what Ian Blaine does or doesn't do," she added with a nervous laugh.

"Yes," he muttered, his gaze fixed on her, his thoughts wandering. "We'll discuss it further. But it will have to be our secret. The minister can't know. Or anyone else for that matter."

"I don't keep any secrets from the minister," she lied.

"Except for this one," he said sternly.

She hesitated, startled by his harshness. "Yes, of course," she said softly. She was caught in a trap of her own making. She had only wanted to prove Ian's innocence—not betray former friends. "I'm happy to assist if I can, but I don't think there's much I can do."

"I have a few trusted sources," he said. "Like Barnabas Stone. For now, I'll consult them. But that could change at a moment's notice. I think you can help if the situation warrants."

She didn't like his tone, or the suggestion that they work together. She had to convince him that she had little, if anything, to offer. But for now, her focus was Ian. "As I recall, and I really didn't know him that well, but Ian Blaine was a hard worker, devoted to the family business. He doesn't seem the type to risk everything to get involved in the conflict."

Duncan eyed her closely, assessing what she said. "No, perhaps not," he said slowly, seeming to agree. "But I'll still summon some men and wait for him at the terminal."

"I suspect you'll find him on the ferry," she said. "If his reputation rings true."

Duncan started to leave but stopped, turning to face her. "Should you see him in the meantime, summon me immediately," he advised. "He could be extremely dangerous. I would hate to have anything happen to you."

Abigail stared at the colonel, eyes wide, feigning fear. "Of course, Colonel. I'll contact you without hesitation."

Duncan left, walking down the church aisle, his boot heels pounding the hardwood floor, the sound gradually growing dimmer. After he was gone, Abigail rushed back to the wardrobe, opened the door, and removed a leather satchel and some articles of clothing.

Ian stepped out from hiding. "What are you doing?"

"Hurry," she said. "Put these on."

"What is it?"

"The minister's clothes," she said. "You heard Duncan. You must get to the terminal and somehow appear as if you're getting off the ferry. Use this disguise. When you don't need it, put everything in the satchel."

Ian took the clothes, a black hat with a large brim, which would hide his face nicely, a minister's collar, and a cassock, the black jacket typical of a minister's attire. He dressed quickly. The cassock was long, coming past mid-thigh, only a short portion of his brown breeches showing, his white stockings rising to just below his knees. He wrapped the collar around his neck and fastened the cassock to the top button. Some of his shirt showed, but not much. It wasn't perfect, but he didn't think anyone would notice.

Once he finished, Abigail opened the window. "Climb out and make your way to Arch St."

"Why the window?"

"It faces the cemetery," she said. "Hide behind the trees and shrubs. Duncan could be waiting out front or even on Second St., so be careful."

He started to climb out the window, stopped and turned to Abigail. He grabbed her hand and squeezed it tightly.

"Thank you," he whispered, and hurried on his way.

21

Ian scrambled through the window and dropped to the ground, hiding behind an overgrown shrub. He scanned the cemetery and the lane beside it. No one was watching. Tombstones and crosses poked from the soil, scattered across the grounds, hidden among bushes and trees that sheltered the graves in shade.

He hurried across the cemetery, staying where shrubs were thickest. It stretched a hundred feet north, the church entrance to his left, where Duncan and his men might be waiting; Second St. was to his right. When he reached the short brick wall that defined the graveyard, he climbed over it and stepped into the alley. He paused, brushed himself off, and started toward Second St.

As he strolled to the corner, he acted as casual as he could. His minister's clothes weren't perfect, but he hoped no one would notice. He reached Second St. and turned north, resisting the urge to glance behind him, fearful Duncan or his men were gathered by the church. He went briskly down Second to Arch, passing two soldiers speaking German. They nodded politely, offering the respect a minister deserved.

When he reached Arch, he turned toward the river. It was much busier than Second and, as he passed pedestrians and redcoats, he played his minister's role with as much dignity as he could muster. His heart raced as three soldiers came toward him, but they only nodded respectfully as he passed.

"Good morning, minister," one of them said, in English.

Ian softly mouthed a reply and tipped his hat. He passed others, residents on their way to shops or to catch the ferry, but none looked at him strangely. The disguise was better that he thought. No one noticed his clothes were slightly mismatched or, if they did, they didn't think much of it.

He kept walking, nodding to those he passed, behaving as he assumed a minister would. After a few minutes, and traveling only a block, he realized he was safe—he wouldn't attract any attention. Now he only had to get the timing right—somehow get on the ferry, remove his disguise, and disembark —all before Duncan saw him.

When he reached the terminal, the wharf was cluttered. Crates and packages were stacked along the side, waiting to be loaded or removed. People milled about, in line to catch the ferry or greeting those about to arrive. A few animals—three goats tethered to a railing, and five crates of chickens—were set beside their owners, waiting for the ferry. Ian paused at the entrance, didn't see Duncan, and hurried down the wharf, passing a wagon loaded with bushels of corn. Two soldiers stood at the entrance, but they merely glanced as he passed.

"Good morning, minister," one said.

Ian tipped his hat, hurrying to the end of the dock. He saw the ferryman standing beside long wooden crates, a large hulking man beside him. Ian approached tentatively.

"Is that you, Ian?" Barnabas Stone asked as he stepped away from the ferryman.

A line had formed to board the ferry, and Ian ensured he

couldn't be heard. He leaned close to Barnabas. "The British came for me last night, but I escaped."

"I know," Barnabas replied. "I met with your father this morning and he told me what happened. I invented a story for the British, said you were in Jersey and Duncan was a fool for thinking otherwise."

Ian chuckled. "I'm sure they appreciated that."

"A bit dramatic, I admit. But I wanted to make sure word got back to Duncan quickly. I came here to make sure the ferryman vouches for you." He looked away, studying the wharf. "Why the disguise?"

"I was hiding in the church and Duncan came in. I overheard him say that he's coming here to make sure I'm on the ferry."

Barnabas glanced at those around him and then out to the river. "The ferry is coming in now. It'll just be a minute or so."

"I have to get on the ferry, remove the disguise, and get off the ferry, making it look like I just arrived. All without Duncan seeing me."

Barnabas studied the incoming boat and those waiting to board. "Stay here," he said to Ian.

The ferryman stood at the edge of the pier. Barnabas walked over, leaned close, and spoke in hushed whispers. They both turned to look at crates on the dock, scanned the boat that was close to arriving, and studied the people—some onboard that would disembark, others on the pier waiting to get on. They talked for a few minutes and Barnabas returned.

"What did the ferryman say?" Ian asked. "Can he help me?"

"Yes," Barnabas muttered, glancing at those nearby. "Move up to the front. The ferryman will let you on board just before the others get off. Hide behind the crates stacked at the rear of the boat. When people start to disembark, remove your disguise, and leave with them."

"I have to make sure no one notices," Ian said as the boat drifted up to the pier.

Barnabas nudged his arm. "That's the least of your problems," he said, pointing to the terminal entrance. "Here comes Duncan."

22

Ian ducked behind Barnabas as the British approached. "Duncan will see me," he hissed as the colonel entered the terminal, coming closer.

"We'll block you," Barnabas said. He stood beside the ferryman; Ian crouched in front of them.

The boat bumped the pier and the oarsmen tossed lanyards to the ferryman's assistant. He tied off the bow and then the stern. Passengers massed at the boat's exit. As soon as the planks were positioned, they would disembark.

"Make way for the pastor," the ferryman called as the ramp was laid in place. "He needs to get on board before you get off."

No one questioned the strange request. The sea of people parted, and Ian hurried onboard, easing through the crowd. Once on deck, he went behind wooden crates stacked six feet high, waiting to be offloaded. After ensuring no one watched, he removed his hat and collar, tossing them into the satchel. As the passengers filtered from the ferry, he took off his coat, folded it, and shoved it in the pouch. The redcoats were coming up the wharf, close to those who had just disembarked. Stepping out from behind the crates, Ian got at the end of the line.

The passengers slowly moved forward until only Ian remained. He stepped off the ferry and onto the ramp, nodding discreetly to Barnabas and the ferryman.

"Careful lad," Barnabas whispered.

Sixty feet down the pier, the line halted, a string of people waiting to move on: families, businessmen, travelers, and traders. Ian stepped to the side and looked ahead. Duncan blocked their progress, standing at the head of the line, questioning each passenger before letting them pass. Ian stayed at the end, ensuring everyone else went before him. He didn't want Duncan asking passengers if they had seen him onboard.

Duncan was flanked by two soldiers in white breeches and red coats. As Ian approached them, he stayed behind a family, husband and wife with two small boys. The British waved them past, not even asking a question. Ian stepped forward and a soldier held out his hand.

"Are you Ian Blaine?" Duncan asked.

Ian looked at him with a vague expression, as if he had never seen the colonel before. "Yes, I am, sir," he replied politely. "Is something wrong?"

Duncan hesitated. He studied Ian closely, trying to remember the fleeting image he had seen at the British camp. "You're returning from Jersey?"

"Yes, after a brief trip," Ian said, his gaze shifting from Duncan to the soldiers.

"How long were you there?" Duncan asked as signs of doubt crept across his face.

"A few days," Ian replied. "I left after the minister's reception."

Duncan eyed the crowd forming, waiting to take the ferry. Men unloaded crates from the boat that had just arrived and stacked them on wagons arranged in a row. "How often do you go to Jersey?" he asked, his voice softer, his tone hiding a twinge of defeat.

Ian shrugged. "I've gone several times during the last few weeks."

"For what purpose?" Duncan probed.

"My father and I own a cabinet shop," Ian explained. "I collect payments, procure material, and sell our wares." He paused and pointed to those around them. "Many other businesses do the same."

"I see," Duncan muttered. He fixed his gaze on Ian's face, his frame, his clothing, looking for any sign that he found the man familiar.

"Can you tell me what's wrong?" Ian asked, trying to stay calm.

Duncan eyed him warily. "What's in the satchel?"

23

Ian froze. If the British checked his pouch, they would find the minister's clothes. He shrugged, trying to seem nonchalant, even though his heart was racing. "Dirty clothes," he said. "A few receipts."

Duncan trained his gaze on Ian. "Search the satchel," he ordered the soldier next to him.

"I beg your pardon," Ian said, outraged. "They're my personal effects."

Duncan turned to the soldier. "Do it."

The soldier stepped forward and wrestled the satchel from Ian's shoulder.

Ian didn't resist. "This is uncalled for," he declared, trying to hide his fright.

The soldier opened the satchel. He reached his hand in, felt the garments, and peeked inside. But he didn't remove anything. "A coat and hat," he said, handing the satchel back to Ian.

Ian acted indignant, staring at Duncan as if he were a tyrant, and slung the satchel back over his shoulder.

Duncan glared at him a moment more and stepped aside. "You're free to go."

"Thank you, sir," Ian said, fighting to keep his voice from trembling.

Ian walked down the pier, trying not to rush or seem afraid. He resisted the urge to look back at Duncan, or at Barnabas, to see if he'd observed what happened. He didn't want to seem guilty. He had been fortunate. It could have been much worse. He never should have kept the satchel. He should have handed it off to Barnabas or hid it on the ferry.

He hurried down Front to Chestnut, turned and made his way to the cabinet shop. He went inside, found his father, and related what happened—how he hid in the church and Abigail saved him from Duncan, and how Barnabas helped him at the ferry.

Patrick was upset. "You need to be careful, lad," he warned. "The redcoats are smart. And they're devious."

"I'm fortunate Barnabas was at the ferry. I would have been caught if he wasn't."

"He's a good man," Patrick said. "You never would have got through all of this without him. Let's pray that it's over."

"If nothing else, we learned Duncan is dangerous," Ian said. "And Hart is a traitor."

"The British put Hart in charge of the port—import and exports."

Ian frowned. "A just reward for his betrayal, I'm sure. Although there's not much he can do. The Patriots control the river."

"It makes me wonder how long they will," Patrick said. "I'm sure the British have something planned."

"Do you think they'll attack the river forts?"

"Most likely. We need to find out when. But we have to be cautious."

"Abigail saved me," Ian said quietly. "I never would have escaped without her."

"Yes, she did. Just be grateful it was her. If it was anyone else, you'd be in jail right now."

Ian thought about squeezing Abigail's hand before he left the church, the look they shared. He hadn't realized how much he missed her.

"You're still not over her, are you?" Patrick asked, eyeing his son. "Even though she married another man."

Ian didn't want to discuss it. "Duncan is lodged at the rectory," he said, evading the question. "His officers and orderlies commandeered rooms in the church, beside the altar."

Patrick eyed his son, as if seeing something he wished he hadn't. "You have to avoid her, lad. She helped you today, but don't expect it again. She's loyal to the Crown. Don't ever forget that."

24

J ean Stark, Oliver Hart's housekeeper, stepped into his
study just after 8 p.m. Hart sat behind a walnut desk
centered in the room, cabinets and bookshelves along the
walls. A painting hung behind him, cluttered docks and ships
with sails, framed by two twelve-paned windows that overlooked a garden showing signs of autumn.

"Colonel Duncan is here," she said, coming close to the
desk.

"What does he want?" Hart asked quietly, peering into the
hall.

"He wouldn't say. But he claims it's important."

Hart frowned. "He claims everything is important."

She leaned across the desk. "I'm sorry, sir, but I just don't
like the man. He's polite—never said anything to offend—but
there's just something about him."

Hart was quiet, his lips taut. "Yes, there is," he agreed. He
hesitated, not interested in entertaining, but relented. "I
suppose you should show him in."

She left the room and returned a moment later. "Colonel
Duncan to see you, sir."

"Thank you, Mrs. Stark," Hart said as he stood to greet Duncan.

"Would you like anything, Colonel?" she asked.

"No, thank you," Duncan replied. "I won't be long. I just have some business to discuss with Mr. Hart."

Jean Stark left the room, closing the door behind her.

"Sit, Colonel," Hart offered with an outstretched hand.

Duncan approached a pleated chair in front of the desk but stood just behind it. "How are you adapting to your new role as Commissioner of Ports?"

Hart was confused. "It's a title more than a role, is it not?"

"It's whatever you want it to be."

"The colonial forts prevent a thriving port and pose a threat to the city greater than Washington's army. I'm not convinced a political appointment can solve that."

Duncan didn't reply. He walked across the room to a sideboard by the wall, a bottle of whiskey and glasses sitting upon it. He filled a glass halfway and turned to Hart. "Will you join me?"

"A special occasion?"

Duncan chuckled. "If you want it to be."

Hart nodded, confused by Duncan's visit. Unless it was only a quick stop for free whiskey.

The colonel poured another glass, came back to the desk, and sat in front of it. He handed Hart his drink and raised his in toast. "To a prosperous partnership."

Hart raised his glass and took a swig. "It's difficult to have a prosperous partnership with no outlet to the sea. I see many idle ships and empty wharfs that should be lined with cargo."

"A problem soon to be solved, I assure you."

Hart hesitated, reluctant to challenge the colonel. "Many of my competitors will fail if a path to the ocean isn't soon restored."

"Not my concern," Duncan said smugly. "Nor does it matter. British traders will take their place."

Hart didn't reply, seeing through the eyes of the victor. A loss on the battlefield was magnified many times over, impacting much more than the soldier.

"Can't you increase the river trade until we capture the forts?" Duncan asked.

"Yes, I can," Hart said. "But little produce or product can be found locally. Certainly not enough to sustain a city and an army of occupation."

Duncan hesitated. "I'm aware of the issue, but I'm not in a position to solve it. At least not yet. But be patient. A solution is on the way."

"I am patient," Hart replied. "But how patient will the residents be when they have no food to eat?"

"The forts will fall, I promise you."

"They'd better. Or we'll have a catastrophe to address."

Duncan took another sip of whiskey, studying Hart. "My family lost a fortune when the war began, goods shipped to the colonies that were confiscated. I intend to correct that."

Hart eyed the man before him, a hint of his motivation now exposed. He sought revenge and he made it quite clear, as he had in Trudruffrin, that he planned to recover any losses incurred. He was an ambitious man, seemed competent, but battled an inner hostility, as if he'd somehow been wronged and had to right it, perhaps his inability to obtain the rank of general.

"Do you have a method to track goods shipped, as we discussed?" Duncan asked.

"Yes, of course. Per our agreement. But not much moves without a route to the sea."

Duncan hesitated, his thoughts returning to the forts. "Can't you develop additional methods to obtain supplies? At least on a temporary basis. I have an army to feed."

"And a city soon to starve. Few alternatives exist. The river must be opened."

Duncan raised his glass and drained its contents. He put the glass on the desk and stood. "The British control the newspapers," he said. "Just to remind you."

Hart didn't know what he inferred. "Which suggests what?"

"I expect you to offer solutions for the shortages until the forts are taken."

"There are limited options," Hart said tersely. "And little chance for success."

"I have full confidence in you," Duncan said as he turned to leave. "That's exactly what the press will print. I'm about to announce that our newly appointed Commissioner of Ports is solely responsible to solve any and all potential shortages, from food to firewood."

"And if I can't?"

Duncan opened the door to leave. "Then I suspect a mob of angry citizens will descend upon your home. They'll hang you before I do."

25

Ian came down the stairs from the residence and entered the cabinet shop, dressed in brown breeches and a white shirt with a brown vest. He had the minister's jacket, collar and hat neatly tucked in the leather satchel.

"I'll be back," he called to his father, who was making a dresser in the back of the shop.

"We've work to do," Patrick protested as Ian closed the door. "Don't be forgetting what puts food on our table."

Ian walked down Chestnut to Second, the leaves on the majestic trees starting to change, traces of orange and yellow and red replacing the green. When he turned down the cobblestone lane that led to the rectory, he approached a woman holding a basket, a sleeping baby inside wrapped in blankets.

"Good morning," he said, peeking in the basket. "What a beautiful baby."

"Thank you," the proud mother said. "He's finally sleeping. It takes a walk to do it, though." She smiled and leaned toward him, as if confiding a secret. "Sometimes I feel like the crying will never end."

Ian laughed and went on his way. His smile faded seconds

later, replaced by sadness. It was part of his past he fought to keep dormant, but sometimes it was reborn, often with only the slightest persuasion. He barely remembered his mother. She died in childbirth, as did the baby, when he was only a toddler. From that day forward, it had only been his father and him. And his father's main priority was properly raising his son. Patrick was strict at times but provided enough love to play the part of both parents. But still, Ian never lacked female influences during his formative years. His father, with his Irish brogue and quick wit, the eyes that always smiled, was very popular with the ladies, and it seemed an endless stream had assisted him while Ian was growing up. Patrick's latest love interest, Dolly Clarke, an attractive widow with two teenage boys, owned a partial interest in City Tavern with Barnabas Stone.

When he reached the rectory, he knocked on the door and waited only a minute before Anna Knight answered.

"May I see Mrs. St. Clair?" he asked.

"In regard to what, sir?"

"A charity donation."

"Certainly, sir," she said. "Please step into the parlor. May I ask who's calling?"

"Ian Blaine."

Anna left and Abigail appeared a moment later, hiding a smile, her green eyes twinkling. "Mr. Blaine, how nice to see you. How are you?"

"I'm well," he said. He waited for Anna Knight to leave and then continued, talking softer. "I have something that may belong to you." He handed her the minister's clothing.

She looked back, ensuring Anna had disappeared and studied the clothes as if she didn't recognize them. "How did these come into your possession?" she asked in jest.

"A friend provided them."

"It must have been a very good friend," she said, her gaze

trained on his. "I trust you made it to the ferry, and all went as planned?"

He leaned closer, in the event Anna was nearby, and whispered. "It did. I can't thank you enough."

She smiled weakly, almost as if the failed past invaded the present. "You would have done the same for me."

"I would," he said. "And more. If I had another chance."

She looked cautiously to the hallway. "Has the danger passed?"

"For now," he said. "But I have to be wary of Duncan. If you could warn me, should he say anything relating to me, I would greatly appreciate it." He leaned closer. "Or tell me anything he might say regarding the conflict."

"Ian," she said, as if not wanting to get involved. "This will all end horribly. Please reconsider."

He hesitated, his gaze again fixed on hers. "When you really want something, it's worth fighting for. Even if you lose it. You can always get it back."

"Not always," she said softly, imploring him to understand. She realized his words had two meanings, referring to both them and the conflict.

"Will you help me?"

"I can't. You know that."

"Even if my life is in danger?"

She hesitated, almost as if yesterday was more than a forgotten memory. "My family's loyalties lie with the Crown. So do Solomon's."

"Where do your loyalties lie?" he asked. "Because before you left for New York, they were more closely aligned with mine."

"It was a time when I rebelled against my father," she explained, and then paused. "Although given what we now know, I had good reason."

"Have you received his reply?"

She shook her head. "No, not yet."

"We can always turn the clock back," he said. "Start where we were before you left."

"Ian, please. I'm married to another man. We're different people. Two years have passed."

"I think we're very much the same," he said. "You only need to admit it."

Anna Knight abruptly rounded the corner, emerging from the foyer. "Can I get you anything, Mr. Blaine?"

"No, thank you," Ian said, nodding to the maid. He was sure she overheard some of their conversation, but he didn't know how much. "I was just about to leave."

They walked to the door as Anna retreated to the kitchen.

"Until we meet again, Mrs. St. Clair," he said loudly, for the maid's benefit.

"Good day, Mr. Blaine."

"You saved me," he whispered. "I'll never forget it. I was trapped by ten thousand enemy soldiers, about to be hanged. If it wasn't for you, I would have been."

She gazed in his eyes for a moment and then looked away, ensuring Anna wasn't nearby. She leaned close. "Fifteen thousand," she said and quickly closed the door.

26

Abigail stood at the closed door for a moment, gathering her thoughts. She wasn't sure why she gave Ian the strength of the British army. Duncan had mentioned their numbers during dinner discussions, comparing British forces to Philadelphia residents. Even though she had made a mental note when she heard the figure, she never had any intention of sharing it with Ian, who clearly spied for the Patriots. It was something she blurted out. And she wasn't sure why.

It was hard for her not to love him, even after the way their relationship ended, designed to inflict the greatest hurt in both their hearts. Although she had yet to receive her father's reply, only a few short conversations with Ian led her to believe he was telling the truth and her father wasn't—even though she couldn't believe he would ever do anything to hurt her.

She went back into the parlor and sat in the chair, opening a translation of the *Iliad* by William Cowper. Although her eyes scanned the blank verse on the page, and she made every attempt to admire the iambic pentameter that formed the phrases, she couldn't concentrate. She began to wonder, for the first time since her arrival, if coming to Philadelphia had been wise. Although she had always known she would see Ian, a former lover she thought she had learned to forget during her two-year stay in New York, she quickly discovered she had been unsuccessful. Much of what she felt could probably be attributed to learning the truth—or at least the truth as Ian remembered it.

Without much forethought, she had created a dangerous precipice upon which she now walked, carefully balanced between two separate worlds. She had caught Ian hiding in the church, terrified he was about to be found by the British. If she no longer loved him and was the staunch Loyalist her family had taught her to be, she would have turned him in to Duncan. It would have been very easy to do. Ian would have hung as a spy. But she realized, failed relationship or not, she could never be responsible for anyone's death—especially his. She had loved him once, and she was beginning to suspect that she still did. It would have been best to avoid him or keep their interactions formal and polite. But she hadn't done that. Instead, she revealed confidential military information. So not only had her feelings for Ian lingered unaltered, but her loyalty to the Crown was now suspect, hardly as strong as she would have expected —or her family would have led her to believe. But many factors, it seemed, now influenced her—some beyond her control.

"Should I bring that donation over to the poorhouse?" Anna Knight said as she abruptly peeked in the parlor, shattering Abigail's private thoughts.

Abigail glanced at the leather satchel lying on the chair beside her. She couldn't let Anna take it. She would never be able to explain why Ian had the minister's clothes.

"It's really no bother," Anna continued, walking into the room. "I can do it on my way home."

"No, I'll get it," Abigail said, a bit too quickly. "Tomorrow, I'm delivering some items from the church. I'll add these to it."

Anna stopped in the center of the room, the satchel only feet away. "It isn't much of a donation," she said, eyeing it curiously. "Although every little bit helps, I suppose."

"Yes, I would think so," Abigail said, afraid Anna would check. "Sometimes people donate a single pair of shoes, or even a blouse. Whatever they can part with to help the poor."

Anna stared at the satchel. "What's in it?" she asked, taking a step toward it.

"A hat and a coat," Abigail said, leaning over and taking it from the chair before Anna reached it. She peeked inside and set it on the floor beside her.

Anna paused, looking at her curiously. "Do you know Mr. Blaine well?" she asked. "Friends from when you once lived in the city?"

Abigail tensed. She wondered if Anna overheard them, or caught fragments of phrases, inadvertent gazes—anything that might have made her suspicious. Abigail had to diffuse the situation, erase any doubts before they were planted.

"It just seemed you were a bit familiar, is all," Anna probed.

Abigail laughed lightly. "A bare acquaintance, actually," she said. "Although I did know his father. He's the cabinetmaker."

Anna shrugged. "Not familiar to me, ma'am."

"Oh, I thought you might have known," Abigail said with a secret sigh of relief. "They have a cabinet shop over on Chestnut with a very good reputation."

"I didn't realize. Did you purchase from them in the past?"

Abigail smiled, although it was a struggle to do so. She didn't like lying. But she had to. "No, I actually know the father, Patrick Blaine, through his donations to one of the libraries."

"I can understand that," Anna said. "Every time I see you, there's a book in your hand."

Abigail laughed lightly. "I've been a reader since I was a child."

"My boy reads, too. Almost as much as you do." She turned to leave. "I suppose I best get started with dinner."

As Anna left the room, Abigail hoped she had dispelled any suspicions. But she had to be careful—especially if Ian ever returned to the rectory. Not only should she be wary of Solomon, but now Anna, too. She realized it would be best if she didn't interact with Ian at all.

But she didn't think she could do that, no matter how hard she tried.

27

"I swear she said fifteen thousand," Ian said firmly.

Patrick looked up from the bureau he was building, fitting a delicate piece of molding along one of the drawers. "She actually told you how many troops the British have?"

"Unless she was joking," Ian said. "But It didn't seem like she was."

"Why would she betray the British?"

Ian wasn't sure he knew the answer. "I asked her to warn me if Duncan said anything about me. It seemed like she would, so I took it further."

"And you asked for military information?"

Ian nodded. "At first, she didn't seem interested. But when I was leaving, she told me how many troops Howe has and quickly closed the door."

Patrick paused, pensive. "We need to verify that number."

Ian thought about his excursion to Trudruffrin, the British camp sprawling along Old Lancaster Pike and then merging with the Hessians, their paid mercenaries. "It seems accurate, based on what I saw."

"That was your best guess after a twenty-minute look,"

Patrick said. "I'll talk to Barnabas. He can get the exact number. Then we'll see if she tells the truth."

"If she does, I'll ask her to tell me more. She does have access to information. Maybe we should listen to her."

"If she's willing to share it," Patrick said. "I suppose she overhears Duncan discussing military matters, or maybe he talks during meals, says things he shouldn't."

"I suspect he does. I'm sure they dine together."

Patrick was quiet for a moment. "But I'm reluctant to trust her. I know her well. I like her. I wanted you to marry her. But why would she do this?"

Ian couldn't answer. It hadn't really occurred to him. "I'm not sure," he admitted. "But she must have a good reason."

Patrick wasn't convinced. "I'm afraid it's a trap," he said softly. "Either laid intentionally, with her assistance, or she was given false information to see what she would do with it."

Ian refused to believe it. "She's too smart to be tricked."

"You're probably right," Patrick agreed. "She's one of the smartest people I know—must be all those books she reads. But I also remember her family as staunch Loyalists. That's why they left."

Ian thought for a moment, searching for a reason to justify what Abigail did. "Maybe it's personal, something to do with me."

Patrick gave him a stern look. "She married another man, lad. You need to always remember that."

Ian realized his father was right. But they had also been wronged by her father. Now they both knew it. "Regardless of who she's married to, I doubt she's a British spy."

"No, but her husband may be. Duncan lives with them. It's a dangerous combination."

Ian hesitated, wanting to believe only the best of Abigail. "She could have turned me over to the British at the church, but she didn't."

"No, she didn't. But she still has some feelings for you, she isn't heartless. Just don't expect it to happen again."

Ian was quiet. He might still love Abigail, and he might want her to protect him, to trust him, to work with him, but that didn't mean she would. "I have to see her again," he said. "I need to know the truth."

Patrick studied Ian, the father afraid to let his son make his own mistakes. But he knew, in a city occupied by the British, a mistake could be deadly.

"I'll be careful," Ian promised, observing his father's reaction.

Patrick wavered. "If you approach her, make whatever you say seem vague, so it can be interpreted more than one way. Then if challenged, you can claim you meant something else. We'll see what Abigail can offer."

28

Oliver Hart and Missy Malone knocked on the door to the rectory promptly at two p.m.

"Mr. Hart and his guest, Miss Missy Malone, have arrived," Anna, the housekeeper, announced as she led them into the parlor

"Abigail, it's so good to see you again," Missy said as they entered.

"It's good to be back," Abigail replied as the two women hugged. She whispered in Missy's ear. "Don't ever mention Ian."

"Your secret is safe," Missy murmured. "I'm sure Oliver doesn't remember, if he even knew to begin with."

"Thank you so much," Abigail whispered. They broke the embrace. "Oliver, how are you?"

"Hello, Abigail," Hart said. "All is well. It's nice to see you back in Philadelphia."

"I see you all know each other," Colonel Duncan observed.

"From my life in Philadelphia," Abigail said. "Before I became the minister's wife."

"Welcome to both of you," Solomon added. "We're so pleased you could come."

"It's difficult to get Oliver out of the house," Missy said, smiling. "But he tends to enjoy himself when he does."

Hart didn't reply. He merely shrugged and rolled his eyes—much to everyone's amusement.

Duncan stood by the fireplace, a glass of Madeira in his hand. "We were discussing philosophy," he said. "The ancient Greeks. A favorite topic of the minister."

"I pretend to be fascinated by the discussion," Abigail said. "When actually my mind is far away, wondering what life on a farm or a cottage by the sea might be like."

"Then I shall use the same approach," Missy said.

They all laughed. Missy Malone was just as Abigail remembered—a vivacious, likable young lady with a smile always fixed to her face. Oliver Hart was much the opposite. He was handsome, forty at most, a successful businessman who was allied with Duncan and may have betrayed Ian. That alone was enough for her to dislike him.

"Has the city changed much since you last saw it?" Hart asked Abigail politely.

"We've only been here a few weeks," she said. "But the occupation force is difficult to miss." She cast a wary eye at Duncan. "They seem to be everywhere."

"They are," Missy agreed. "Soldiers camp in every corner of the city. They even commandeered the Presbyterian Church on Pine St. and converted it into a hospital."

"A necessity in times of war," Duncan said. "Our wounded are housed there, along with some rebels."

Abigail frowned, her eyebrows knitted. "Why convert a church to a hospital?"

"Because we had to," Duncan replied. "The church was only used by rebels anyway, so what does it matter?"

"I shall make it a point to visit," Abigail vowed, afraid of what she might find.

"The patients will appreciate that," Solomon said. "They likely get few, if any, visitors."

"I'll issue a pass for your use," Duncan said. "It shall provide unlimited access."

Abigail looked at him curiously. "Why do I need a pass?"

Duncan glared at her. "Because it's a British army facility. You also need a pass to get in or out of the city."

Abigail frowned. "What else has changed?"

Although she directed her question to Missy, Duncan replied. "Mr. Hart has been named director of the city's ports."

"An unenviable position, I assume," Abigail said.

"What makes you say so?" Duncan asked, eyeing her suspiciously.

"When I pass the docks," Abigail said, "many ships sit idle, as if no trade is conducted. The seaman lounge about, playing cards and telling tales that I'm sure cannot be true. I suspect they would rather be sailing the seas."

"I've seen the same," Missy said. "Just traveling to Oliver's house or place of business."

Abigail looked at Hart curiously. "How did shipping come to be your calling?"

Hart hesitated, as if reluctant to share his life. "I was raised by an uncle in Plymouth. He taught me a love for the sea."

"You inherited his company?" Solomon asked.

"Hardly," Hart said with a light laugh. "When I was twelve years old, I served as a cabin boy on a ship to India. I learned everything I could about ships, commerce, and trade routes, and worked sixteen hours a day to build my business."

"I'm impressed," Duncan said, although it didn't really seem that he was.

"There's no need to be," Hart said. "I told the story because you asked. Few know it and fewer care. Because many in Philadelphia have a similar story. And the spirit it drives, the thirst for success, is what the Crown now combats."

Duncan smirked. "It sounds a bit dramatic."

"It is a fascinating story," Solomon said. "I heard similar tales in New York."

"That's why people come to the colonies," Hart continued. "Anything you could possibly want is within reach, if you work hard enough to get it."

Abigail walked to the window and pulled the curtain aside. An empty wagon passed with lettering on the side: *Blaine & Son, Cabinetmakers.* Patrick Blaine held the reins. She smiled. It was so good to see Ian again, even if he was mired in potential disaster. She missed him, whether she wanted to admit it or not. Now a dying ember had been reignited, and she wasn't sure what to do about it. Maybe she would avoid him. Or maybe she wanted to be whisked away from a dull, predictable life to adventures that only the unknown could offer.

Anna announced that dinner was served, and they adjourned to the dining room for ham, the piglet perched in the center of the table, completely intact, its head and feet part of the delicacy to be enjoyed, along with potatoes and cooked vegetables.

"We're honored to have you as our guests," Solomon said to those in attendance.

"My thanks to you, also," Duncan offered, "for housing my officers at the church."

"You're more than welcome," Solomon replied. "The rooms were little used."

"Four officers are lodged in my home," Hart said, glancing at Missy.

"Who might they be?" Duncan asked.

Hart stared at him blankly. "We actually have little interaction."

"Oliver can easily go an entire day without speaking," Missy said, and then smiled. "But fortunately, I talk enough for both of us."

They all laughed. It was hard not to like Missy Malone. It was much harder to become acquainted with Oliver Hart.

"You complement each other well." Abigail said.

"Someone has to look after him," Missy joked. "He's not capable of doing it himself. He would work non-stop if I didn't remind him to rest occasionally."

Hart smiled, as if he enjoyed her teasing.

Abigail watched him, the darling of the occupation, and wondered how he behaved when the colonials ran the city. Had he acted the same, serving a different master, or had his political views changed when most expedient. She sensed he was a dangerous man, one who would destroy what stood in his path if it hampered efforts to achieve his objective.

"Will you be attending Sunday service?" Solomon asked their guests.

"Yes, of course," Missy said as Hart nodded.

"I'm interested in observing the congregation," Duncan said. "I suspect some of the remaining rebels will show their faces. I need to expose them."

Solomon watched the colonel warily. "I don't consider their sympathies. I only hope to unite them in worship."

"You don't, but I must," Duncan said, as he eyed those at the table. "Perhaps we all should. The Crown expects it."

29

The following morning, Abigail took the pass that Colonel Duncan had provided and walked to the Presbyterian Church, which had been converted to a British hospital. It was a two-story stuccoed building on Pine St., just above Fourth, the overhanging front roof supported by eight large pillars. An old cemetery sat beside it, some of the tombstones hidden by shrubs and trees.

Across the street sat three clustered brick row homes, two British soldiers stood just past the steps of the first, eyeing her curiously. No residents walked the streets or sat on stoops—the area was controlled by the military. She observed the soldiers a moment more and climbed the steps to the church entrance.

She walked through the double doors, shocked at the sight she confronted in what was once the sanctity of a church. She had been there before—a beautiful building with large twelve-paned windows, a balcony hugging the exterior walls, rows of varnished wooden pews occupying the first floor. At least, that's what it looked like the last time she had seen it. But that was before the British came.

Most of the wooden pews had been torn out and were

stacked haphazardly against a back wall. Dozens of British soldiers lay on cots along one side of the building, the stench of sweat and sickness stealing the stale air. On the opposite side, where half of the pews remained, rows of colonial soldiers lay on thin blankets, their worn blue uniforms a stark contrast to the red coats of their enemy.

"Can I help you, madam?" a soldier asked, walking to the entrance to greet her.

"Good morning," she said, as pleasantly as she could. "I'm the minister's wife, Abigail St. Clair, and I have a pass from Colonel Duncan to visit the wounded."

The soldier looked at her strangely. "Why would you ever want to do that?"

She smiled. "I like to help if I can."

He scanned the pass and handed it back to her. "I'm Tommy Scanlon, ma'am," he said. "Just a simple soldier. The surgeon isn't here today."

"That's fine, Tommy Scanlon, simple soldier," she said, amused. "I'll just visit with the men."

"Some are beyond help," he warned.

She paused, concerned for infectious diseases. "Were they wounded in battle?"

"Most were, but some are sick."

She eyed the Patriots on the opposite side. "How about the rebels?"

Tommy Scanlon shrugged. "I don't know, ma'am. No one pays much attention to them."

Abigail cringed, her attention drawn to the colonials. "Then I'll tend to them first," she said, ignoring the surprise he displayed. She paused, eyeing the stack of removed pews, the wood split and damaged. "Will the pews be restored when the wounded are healed?"

"No, ma'am," he said. "We'll use them for firewood over the winter."

She grimaced, remembering how beautiful the church had been. "And the church?" she asked. "What do the British intend to do with it?"

"I'm told when the wounded are gone, it'll be used as a stable for the horses."

Abigail's eyes grew wide. "That's a disgrace."

Tommy Scanlon shrugged. "Maybe the plans will change."

She could see in his eyes that he didn't like the plan any more than she did. "This was a beautiful church, Tommy."

"I'm sure it was, ma'am," he said quietly.

Abigail was disgusted, but also powerless to change what the British had done—and still intended to do. She left Tommy by the door and walked down the center aisle, the British on her left, comfortable on cots, the colonials on her right, lying on the floor. She hadn't gone far when one of the Patriots raised his hand weakly, motioning to her. She walked toward him.

"Water, ma'am," he gasped, his voice hoarse, his lips parched. "Please."

She turned, Tommy Scanlon still near the entrance. "Tommy, can this man have some water?"

"Every morning they get a cup," he said. "Those are my orders, ma'am."

She looked at the soldier, his face flush, a soiled bandage wrapped around a bare chest, part of his body covered by a threadbare blanket. "Wait just a minute."

Abigail turned and stormed down the aisle. She glared at Tommy Scanlon, who watched her approach, his eyes wide. "I need a bucket," she demanded. "Show me where the well is."

"But ma'am—"

"Don't make an enemy of me, Tommy Scanlon," she warned. "It wouldn't be wise."

He studied her a moment more and seemed to agree. "I'll show you," he said, leading her toward the back of the church, near the altar.

"I want fresh bandages, too."

"The surgeon won't like that," he said, cringing.

"He'll learn to like it," she said. "I can promise you that."

She got water and returned. She paused, her gaze passing over the rows of sick and wounded Patriots, lying on the floor with dirty bandages, parched throats, and vacant eyes that showed no promise for the future or recollection of the past. Across the aisle, in stark contrast, the British were obviously treated well, most in good spirits, others napping comfortably.

She dipped cups in the bucket and served fresh water to the wounded colonials. For those that needed it, she changed their bandages, horrified by the way they had been treated. She spent over an hour at the makeshift hospital, listening to those that wanted to speak, consoling those that didn't. She suspected many would die, but she promised to make them as comfortable as possible. When she finished assisting the Patriots, she glanced at the other side of the church, where the British and Hessians soldiers lay on cots with straw mattresses, each with water before them, and was sickened at the contrast.

"I'll be back," she said to Tommy Scanlon. "At least once a week."

The young man tipped his hat. "Then I suppose I'll be seeing you soon."

When she left the hospital at Fourth and Pine, she couldn't resist walking a few blocks west to Sixth. When she got there, she stood in front of a stately home, built back off the road, a short front yard with a wrought iron fence around it. The brick building had a slate roof, blue shutters flanking twelve-paned windows. It was a beautiful estate, once home to a prosperous family, and she looked at it lovingly.

"I was wondering when I would see you," said a voice behind her.

She turned to find her cousin James, an older man with

118

curly gray hair, spectacles on the edge of his nose. "Oh, James, it's so good to see you," she said as she gave him a hug.

"Are you missing your family home?"

"I am," she said as she glanced at the residence. "Although I hadn't thought about it until I returned."

"The minister's wife," James said, looking at her grandly. "Your father made the match he always longed to make."

She smiled but felt the hurt inside. Her father had made the match. But only after he had manipulated a daughter he supposedly loved to get her to do what *he* wanted—not what she wanted. "Stop by the rectory and visit me some time," she said. "I would love to see you."

"I shall," James said. "It would be a delightful visit."

"Are you enjoying the house?"

"I am," he said. "It was nice of your father to rent it to me."

"I think he plans to return in the spring, assuming the British are still in control. My sisters may come sooner."

The front door of the house opened, and two British soldiers emerged. They walked down the steps and out the gate, nodding to James and Abigail as they passed.

"I would invite you in," James said with a shrug. "But there are two more inside. Not very nice men, I'm afraid." He leaned closer and whispered. "It really isn't my home anymore. It's theirs."

"You have four officers billeted in my house?" she asked, angry.

He nodded. "I almost had more."

"Did you protest?"

"Vehemently," he said. "And it was clearly explained to me who was winning the war. I was reminded that I always claimed to be a Loyalist, and now was the time to prove it."

The tone of his voice made her suspect he may no longer be loyal to the Crown—or at least he had doubts.

She was beginning to feel the same.

30

Ian walked into the Anglican Church, his father, Patrick, beside him. Even though Patrick was Irish, and raised a devout Catholic as a child, there were no Catholic churches in Philadelphia, and he had attended the Anglican Church since the day he had arrived.

Ian hid a smile as they entered. Only a few days before, the room beside the altar had sheltered him through the night as he hid from the British. Abigail had helped him escape. To him, it was much more than her saving the life of a former lover. It was a new beginning. But he wasn't sure what it meant to her— one last favor, perhaps.

They walked down the center aisle, a family in front of them, the man in his finest jacket, the woman in her best dress and bonnet, two little girls, nicely dressed, tagging along. The pews were quickly filling, many anxious to see what the new pastor would bring to the service. At the far end of the church, the altar was bathed in brilliant rays of light streaming through the arched windows behind it. Ian and Patrick walked halfway down the aisle and sat in one of the pews to the right.

"Quite a crowd," Patrick said, gazing around the room.

"Some will have to stand," Ian said. "There aren't enough seats."

"Oliver Hart is glued to his British masters," Patrick muttered with disgust.

Ian looked to the left. In the front row, General Howe was seated with his staff, Colonel Duncan among them. Oliver Hart and Missy Malone sat just behind them, the rest of the row filled with Loyalists, as if they had to show their allegiance to the Crown. Barnabas Stone was wedged among them, loyal to the British in public, devoted to the Patriots in private.

"I do see some of our friends, though," Patrick added, referring to Barnabas.

Many loyal to the rebellion were still in the city, the colonial capital before it was overwhelmed by British and Hessian soldiers. Ian wondered if the enemy realized how tentative their hold was. If the citizens revolted, joined by a coordinated attack by Washington's army, a bloodbath would ensue, hidden only by the red coats the enemy wore.

Ian studied the parishioners, glancing left and right, up one row and down another. He found it amusing those loyal to the rebellion sat beside some known to support the Crown. But each minded their business, quietly hid their views, even if their neighbors suspected otherwise. It was too dangerous to speak your mind. All knew it.

"There are more British officers than I expected," Ian whispered as they waited for the service to begin.

"Might be enough to support an army of fifteen thousand," Patrick said, gazing around the room. "Just as Abigail suggested."

The minister stepped from the room to the right of the altar, now home to British soldiers, and assumed his position at the pulpit. Murmurs of conversation subsided, and all eyes were trained upon him. He thumbed through a Bible that rested on the podium, collected his thoughts, and looked up at the congregation, ready to begin.

In the front row, a half dozen pews away, Abigail sat quietly. She focused on the minister's sermon, his voice booming through the building, his stature erect, his presentation clear, his manner confident. He was most comfortable in the pulpit, and his personality paled in any other setting. She turned, her gaze resting on Ian. He nodded discreetly, and locked his eyes on hers, but she smiled and looked away.

Solomon St. Clair was a good speaker and the hour passed quickly, almost all in the audience captivated by both the content and delivery of the sermon. At its conclusion, with Abigail and the minister staged at the door, the congregation left in single file, each congratulating the new minister on his presentation.

Patrick and Ian filed out. As Patrick paused to speak with the minister, Ian gave his attention to Abigail.

"Madam," he said with a nod, acting formally for any who might be observing. "Such a wonderful service. I already look forward to the next."

"The minister is a gifted theologian," Abigail said. She leaned closer, making sure no one could hear. "I need to see you."

He glanced at those nearby, his father conversing with the minister. An elderly couple stood behind him, the man watching them curiously.

Abigail noticed the observer and smiled faintly. "I'm in need of some cabinetry," she said loud enough for any to hear.

31

Abigail remained in the reception line as the last of the congregation filtered from the church. Most greeted her briefly, a nod and kind word, but all stopped to speak to Solomon. He had delivered a stunning sermon, beyond what many had ever heard, and most in the congregation paused to offer their thanks and congratulations.

The Loyalists and British officers who sat with General Howe were the last to leave. Abigail was speaking to the candle-maker's wife when Oliver Hart approached. She was leery of the man, knowing he most likely betrayed Ian, even though he was polite and friendly when he dined at the rectory. She found human behavior interesting, how some seemed to have two personalities—a real person and a shadow. She suspected Hart was a complex man. He had a motive for helping the British and, although she didn't know what it was, she suspected he was trying to save his business. But she didn't know him well. When she had lived in Philadelphia, everyone knew of Hart because he was wealthy. Many people knew of her father, Miles Cooper, because he was a renowned solicitor. But not many people knew her.

"Good morning, Mrs. St. Clair," Hart nodded as he reached her.

"Hello, Mr. Hart," she responded.

"Pastor, that was a fabulous sermon," Hart said to Solomon, who beamed with the compliment.

Missy Malone leaned toward Abigail. "Your secret is safe," she whispered.

Abigail looked at Hart to ensure she couldn't be heard. "Did you ask Oliver?"

"Yes, I casually mentioned you," she said. "He remembers your father well, but had little recollection of you, although he did remember your older sister Emma."

"Did he know Ian and I almost married?"

"I got the impression he doesn't even realize you know each other."

Abigail was relieved. "I'm trying to avoid an uncomfortable situation."

Missy grasped her hands and squeezed them. "Even if you get into trouble, I will help you get out of it. If there's anything else I can do, or anything you need, just let me know."

"Thank you," Abigail said, surprised by her warmth.

Missy didn't step away but looked directly at her. "I do mean anything."

Abigail wasn't sure what she meant. Before she could ask for clarification, Missy moved to the minister and a British soldier took her place. Abigail nodded politely.

The British officers passed quickly. Duncan skipped the line, but General Howe stopped to speak to Solomon. Those remaining studied the pair, especially Duncan, wondering what their connection might be. How well did they know each other? Even Abigail couldn't say for sure.

One carriage after another departed, the crowd beginning to thin. Oliver Hart and Missy Malone stood on the pavement, waiting for their carriage. Abigail tried to decipher Missy's cryptic statement—the offer to help, regardless of the request. Could she have assumed, because Abigail mentioned Ian, that their relationship had rekindled? Or was it much deeper. Was she talking about the rebellion? Missy must know she came from a Loyalist family. Anyone watching Solomon converse with General Howe could easily see where their loyalties lay. But it was a statement Missy made twice, almost insisting.

Abigail realized that there was much more to Missy Malone than what she assumed. She had to find out what it was.

32

Ian and Patrick made their way through the crowd that mingled in front of the church. They turned the corner, walked out to Second and went south, headed home with others who attended the service. Once they had gone a hundred feet, and the crowd began to thin, Ian leaned close to his father.

"Abigail asked to see me," he said, ensuring no one was close enough to hear.

Patrick nodded to a woman standing on the pavement with a teenage boy, likely her son. They made eye contact, each smiling. "Good morning to you," Patrick said in his Irish brogue.

"Good morning, sir," she replied, eyes twinkling.

Ian tugged at his father's arm, leading him down the street. "What are you doing?"

"I only stopped to say hello," Patrick protested. "There's nothing wrong with that now, is there? What better place to meet a new friend than at church service?"

"Did you hear what I said?"

"Of course, I did," Patrick said. "Something about the minister."

"No," Ian replied, amused. "Something about Abigail."

"Well, it had better be good. Interrupting your father when he's about to meet a nice lady. What were you thinking?"

"I'm not sure Dolly would like your new friend," Ian said, reminding his father of his lady friend from the City Tavern.

"Never you mind. It's my business now, isn't it?"

"Yes, I suppose it is," Ian said. Patrick was more of a flirt than a rogue and, since he enjoyed it so much, most overlooked it. "Abigail said she needs to see me."

Patrick stopped abruptly. "When exactly did she say that? Because I've been beside you all morning and I heard nothing of the sort."

"She said it just as we were leaving. While we were in line to greet the minister."

Patrick was quiet, eyeing those nearby. The church crowd began to disperse, walking in different directions, while others climbed in carriages and drove down the cobblestone street. British soldiers were mixed among them, walking down the street or riding by on horseback. With an army that equaled the number of citizens, the streets were filled with soldiers, something unlikely to change.

"Wait until the crowd thins a bit," Patrick said. He eyed a nearby redcoat among the pedestrians. "The devils have ears everywhere."

When they reached Market, some of the parishioners turned east, toward the river, while more went west, toward shops and houses that lined the city's main street. Others remained on Second St. walking toward their homes, or perhaps going to the City Tavern for a morning meal.

"What does she want?' Patrick asked, no one close enough to hear.

"She wants me to meet her. She's in need of some cabinetry."

"And you believe her?"

"Why would I not?"

Patrick paused. "I suppose it could be legitimate. But I think you need to be careful. I keep reminding you, she isn't the Abigail who left two years ago."

"She did ask in her husband's presence," Ian said, defending her. "If there was a need for secrecy, she would have created it."

"Yes, I suppose. But I still think you should avoid her. She's a married woman. If you keep seeing her, it'll lead to no good."

Ian suspected his father was right. But the temptation was too great. He couldn't resist.

"She's a Loyalist," Patrick added softly. "Or at least her family is."

"But she would never betray me."

"Maybe not intentionally," Patrick said. "But she only has to make one mistake—say or do something wrong—and you'll be hanging on the end of a rope."

"There's little risk, I assure you. I simply go to the rectory and inquire about the cabinetry she wants. What happens next is entirely up to her."

"Make sure you're not walking into a trap," Patrick said. "I've warned you once and I won't do it again."

"It seems innocent enough, even if her intention is not."

"But someone might be watching, hiding nearby and listening."

"When I returned the minister's clothes, only Abigail and a maid were there."

"Who is the maid?"

"Her name is Anna Knight," Ian said. "I don't know if she served the prior minister or not."

"Where was the minister?"

Ian hesitated. He hadn't considered anyone else listening, other than the maid. It didn't seem that Abigail had, either. "I don't know," he admitted. "I didn't see him."

"Which doesn't mean he wasn't there. Maybe Abigail didn't even know he was home. He could have walked in the back door with no one knowing."

"Yes, I suppose," Ian muttered. It was something he hadn't considered.

"You need to get smarter. You think you're meeting a woman you once loved and still might. Maybe you are. Or maybe you're not. Maybe she moved on and you should, too."

Ian realized he could be naïve, but he doubted Abigail would do him any harm.

"Don't forget Duncan," Patrick warned. "Just because he thinks you're innocent, doesn't mean he's not still suspicious."

"I'll be careful in all I say," Ian promised.

"Be aware of the surroundings," Patrick continued. "What she says and who may be listening."

"I will," Ian assured him. "But I have nothing to lose. At the very least, we may have a new customer. But we could also get information at the same time."

"Keep the conversation limited to cabinetry. It's better that way."

"I will," Ian said. "Unless there's a valid reason not to."

"Make sure you remember that. Don't trust her. At least not yet."

33

Abigail sat in Solomon's office, an opened letter from New York before her. She scanned all of her sisters' messages, and then read her father's response to her inquiry. His reply was very simple: *I did what was best for you.* She was angry and hurt. Why had he lied to Ian and her, destroying their relationship? She could have decided what was best—she didn't need him to do it for her. If she had known the truth, she never would have left Philadelphia. Now she was married to another man, unable to right the wrong.

She was interrupted by a knock at the front door. She put the note in her skirt pocket, her anger not subsiding. Anna Knight, the housekeeper, hurried from the kitchen to answer. Abigail listened, wondering who it might be.

"Good morning Mr. Blaine," Anna said. "Are you bringing more items for charity?"

"No," Ian said with a light laugh. "I was invited to discuss some cabinetry."

"I saw your satchel and thought you might have another donation."

"Not this time," Ian said. "I brought tools to support my trade—rulers. compasses and sketch pads."

Abigail couldn't help smiling as she listened. She had told Ian she needed cabinetry. But she hadn't expected him to come so soon. She considered her father's response, which proved Ian had told the truth. She owed him an explanation. But it wasn't the time or place.

"Who made the inquiry?" Anna asked.

"The minister's wife made mention at yesterday's service."

"Please come in and sit down," Anna said politely, "and I'll go get her."

Anna appeared in the study a moment later. "Mr. Blaine is here, ma'am," she said. "About some cabinetry."

"Yes, of course," Abagail said, acting as if she had just remembered. "I'll see him now."

Anna returned to the kitchen and Abigail went into the parlor. It was an elegant room, smoothly plastered, painted a muted yellow with white crown molding, fluted casing around windows and doors. A brick fireplace was centered for both warmth and function, opening to the kitchen. A couch sat against the back wall, two pleated chairs with an oval table between them just across from it. Ian sat in one of the chairs, waiting patiently.

"Hello, Mr. Blaine," Abigail said loudly, for Anna's benefit should she be listening. It was best to keep everything formal. She couldn't let anyone discover that she and Ian knew each other, let alone that they'd been lovers. Anna already seemed suspicious.

Ian rose from the chair and bowed slightly. "Mrs. St. Clair."

Abigail came closer, glancing about furtively. She wanted to ensure he understood the purpose for the visit, and not see something that wasn't there. "This is business, and don't think otherwise."

"Yes, of course," he said with a slight nod.

She could tell by his expression that he didn't believe her. He suspected there was still something between them. Maybe there was. "I do appreciate you coming."

"I came at the first opportunity. I'm sure I can build something to your liking."

"Good, I am in need." she said. "It's actually a chest, versus a cabinet. But still within your capabilities."

"Yes, of course."

"I'm afraid Anna will have to accompany us."

"Why would that be?" he asked softly, looking to the doorway that led to the parlor, and then the open fireplace.

She watched him curiously, but realized he ensured no one eavesdropped. The fireplace communicated with the kitchen and offered the perfect opportunity.

"Because the chest will go in my bedchambers," she said.

"I understand," Ian said, as if he really didn't.

Abigail suspected he was wary of a trap. A British colonel was lodged in the rectory, absent at the moment. "Anna," she called. "Can you meet us upstairs?"

"Yes, ma'am," came a reply from the back of the house.

Abigail led Ian upstairs and into her bedroom, a canopied bed along one wall, a wardrobe opposite, with hand-carved vines and roses traveling its length, flanked by two twelve-paned windows. The room was painted light blue, the moldings a crisp white. A vase of flowers sat on a bureau, a lavender fragrance consuming the room, with a hairbrush and hand mirror beside it.

Anna came to the door and looked at them curiously. "Do you need something, ma'am?"

"Could you help Mr. Blaine obtain measurements for a chest I would like him to build?"

"Yes, of course, ma'am," Anna said, standing at the threshold.

Ian looked confused, as if it wasn't what he expected.

Maybe he thought they would start where they ended two years before. But now he understood. She had made a simple request. She wanted a chest.

"What would you like constructed?" he asked, admiring the intricate carvings on the wardrobe.

Abigail pointed to the foot of the bed. "I thought a chest that fits here would be nice. For some clothing and personal effects."

"Of course," he said, removing a wooden ruler from his satchel. "Did you have a particular size in mind?"

She used outstretched hands to show what she wanted. "I would think about this wide."

He knelt on the floor to take measurements.

"Should I assist, sir?" Anna asked,

"I think I can manage," Ian replied, as if he knew she was there for another purpose, a chaperone, perhaps. He scribbled dimensions on a piece of paper. "I can sketch the chest and provide an estimate of the cost." He turned to look at the wardrobe. "I'll ensure it's as elegant as the rest of the room's furnishings."

"That would be lovely," Abigail said.

Anna walked into the hallway. "I'll be just a minute, ma'am. I have to check on dinner."

"Take your time," Abigail called, listening as she hurried down the steps.

Ian stood and came close to Abigail. "There won't be any charge."

"No special treatment," she insisted. "It'll plant suspicion where it has no need to grow."

He nodded and sketched the wardrobe, capturing the vine and rose carvings. He could draw beautifully and was duplicating the image exactly as it existed.

A moment later, Anna stepped back into the room. "Do you need my assistance with the measurements, Mr. Blaine?"

"No, I have them," Ian said. "I just want to draw the detail on this wardrobe."

Anna glanced at the sketch. "You can make the chest match the wardrobe?"

"Yes, I think so," Ian said, his drawing almost complete.

"You're an excellent artist," Abigail said, looking over his shoulder. But she already knew that. She just didn't want Anna to know that she did.

"Thank you," he said. "One of my few talents."

"I find that hard to believe, don't you Anna?" Abigail asked.

"I suppose that remains to be seen, ma'am," Anna said lightly. "But we'll know when we see the chest."

Ian grinned. "I won't disappoint you," he said, looking directly at Abigail, referring to much more than a chest. "Not ever."

Abigail smiled but didn't reply. She couldn't. "I suppose we're done here," she said, leading Anna and Ian from the room.

They went downstairs and paused in the foyer, Anna leaving for the kitchen.

Abigail opened the door. "Will you return tomorrow?"

"Yes, of course," he said. "If that's convenient. I'll have everything prepared."

It wasn't the time to discuss her father's note. But she wanted him to know that two years ago, a decision had been made *for* her—not *by* her. Now she made her own decisions. As he crossed the threshold, she was struck with a thought, a way to make amends, to obtain revenge, to keep an ember burning. She leaned toward him.

"I will help you," she whispered.

34

The City Tavern was a spacious restaurant, known more for drink, a quick dinner, and conversation than fine dining. An open hearth sat in the center of the room, a kettle of stew or porridge normally cooking, a bar to the left, the stools filled with men stopping to quench their thirst or those staying for the evening, enjoying a generous intake of beer. The main floor was filled with plank tables of different sizes, holding anywhere from six to twelve guests. A narrow landing stretched three steps up from the lower floor, separated by a railing and holding a half dozen oval tables usually meant for two.

Barnabas Stone sat at a table beside the door, entertaining a British officer, playing the role of one of the city's most devout Loyalists. Their dinner completed, they enjoyed a mug of beer and discussed the occupation.

"I want the names of whoever aids Washington, if you can get them," a British major named Thaddeus Johnson requested.

"I have more than a few suspicions," Barnabas said, "but until I'm certain, I hesitate to reveal them."

"It doesn't matter if you can prove their guilt," Johnson said. "We can do that."

"But why put an innocent man through such an ordeal?"

"General Howe is convinced the city is filled with spies. We've all been asked to prove it."

"I'm sure Washington has eyes and ears on every corner," Barnabas said. "But in time, they'll be exposed."

"Anything you see or hear is best passed on to me," Johnson said. He drained the rest of his mug and stood. "I'll be seeing you shortly."

Just as the major left, Patrick and Ian Blaine came in. They frequented the tavern at least one night a week, sometimes twice. If they came for a meal, they sat in the upper landing, usually in the corner, and watched the guests around them. It was also a private location, if there could be such a thing in a thriving alehouse, and gave Barnabas an opportunity to speak to them while they were served.

"Patrick, Ian, glad to see you," Barnabas said. "We've beef stew today, one of my specialties, as well as shepherd's pie."

"A difficult decision, I'm thinking," Patrick mused aloud.

Dolly Clarke, barmaid, part owner, and Patrick's steady companion, came to greet them. "Your normal table is empty."

"Then that's where we'll be sitting," Patrick said with a wink.

"I'll bring two mugs of beer right over," Dolly said, smiling, as Patrick and Ian walked to their table.

The inn was crowded, more British soldiers than usual. Barnabas looked at each table in turn, trying to determine who minded their own business and who didn't. He waited until Patrick and Ian were seated, and then approached their table, clearing some empty dishes from the table beside them.

"Barnabas, can you join us?" Ian asked.

"For a moment," Barnabas replied. "Let me clear this table."

He leaned closer, nodded to a nearby table filled with British officers, and whispered. "Best watch your tongue."

"I'll get those," Dolly said, referring to the empty plates Barnabas carried as she brought two mugs of beer.

"I can barely lift a finger," Barnabas quipped. "Dolly has everything done before I can get to it."

"I have no choice if I want it done right," she teased as she set down two mugs of beer.

"That's the truth," Barnabas said as they all laughed.

"What'll you be eating?" Dolly asked. "The stew's good and hot."

"I'll have the stew," Ian replied.

"I will as well," Patrick said. "Who could resist it? That's why I'm here."

"Are you here for the stew or the person that made it?" Dolly asked mischievously.

"Maybe a bit of both," Patrick said. "As any good man would admit."

"Coming right up," Dolly said. She paused, leaning closer to Patrick. "If there's anything else you want, Patrick Blaine, anything at all, you just ask."

Barnabas watched Dolly walk away and he then sat beside them, facing the crowded tavern. "Any more problems with Duncan?"

"Haven't seen him," Ian replied.

"Although he could have someone watching us," Patrick said.

"I'll see what I can find out," Barnabas offered. "I've developed a few contacts that should prove useful."

Dolly dished their stew into two large bowls, added spoons, and brought them to the table. "Enjoy your meal," she said. As she walked away, she looked over her shoulder. "I'll be back to see what else you might need, Patrick Blaine."

Patrick smiled. "I'll look forward to it."

Barnabas eyed those in the tavern, sitting quietly as Patrick and Ian began to enjoy their stew. After a moment, he leaned forward and whispered. "Anything to tell me?"

Patrick glanced at those nearby. "Was the number correct?" he asked, referring to the size of the British army.

"It was," Barnabas confirmed. "And validated more than once."

Ian leaned toward him. "I'll be meeting with the source again tomorrow."

"I don't want to know who it is," Barnabas said. "But I want to hear what you learn."

"Are you the proprietor?" one of the British soldiers then asked loudly.

Patrick eyed the soldier. "Looks like trouble," he muttered. "Ignorant redcoats. Somebody needs to put them in their place."

"If they're looking for trouble, they found it," Barnabas said. He rose from his chair. "Yeah, I'm the owner. What of it?"

"This stew tastes like it came from the wrong end of a horse," the soldier bellowed, breaking into a fit of laughter along with his comrades. "I want my money back."

Barnabas left the landing and walked up to the table. "It couldn't have tasted too bad," he said, standing with his hands on his hips. "You ate every drop of it."

Those sharing the soldier's table laughed even harder.

The man looked at his comrades, his face crimson. "Nobody insults me," he declared.

"Then keep your mouth shut," Barnabas said. "And you won't have to worry about it."

"You've no idea what's coming," the soldier snarled, standing abruptly, his fists clenched.

Barnabas remained impassive. He was a good head taller than the redcoat. "I know you're not looking for a fight," he said. "But if you are, you came to the right place."

The soldier eyed Barnabas, knowing it was likely a fight he couldn't win. After a moment passed, his glare softened, and he sank back in his seat. "I only wanted a good meal," he grumbled. "Just like I paid for."

Barnabas suspected the beer was speaking for him and searched for a compromise. "I'll give you a mug of ale on the house. No more."

The soldier looked at him dourly for a moment, trying to save face. "Agreed," he muttered.

"And we stay friends," Barnabas added, thrusting his hand forward.

The soldier stood and reluctantly shook his hand.

Barnabas turned to Patrick and Ian and winked.

35

Abigail was returning from the poorhouse, having delivered donations left at the church, when she met Colonel Duncan waiting at the alley that led to the rectory. She hid a frown. It seemed the colonel, who she was starting to despise, managed to appear wherever she was.

Where have you been off to, Mrs. St. Clair?" he asked, as if he had the right to know everything she did.

"I brought some clothes to the poorhouse," she replied. "Why are you lurking in crooked alleys?"

His eyes widened, startled by her question—or that she had the gall to ask it. "A quick walk to meet one of my captains. Nothing more."

As they turned down the alley toward the rectory, Abigail wondered if they had met by chance or plan. Duncan was cunning, and he normally had a reason for every move he made.

"Solomon's sermon was well received," Duncan remarked.

"I had no doubt that the congregation would be pleased."

"Did you observe those in attendance, as we discussed?"

She hesitated. "I attempted to, but was soon immersed in Solomon's sermon, like all who were there."

Disappointment crossed his face. "You saw no one, from your time as a Philadelphia resident, who supports the rebellion?"

She had no intention of betraying any friends—or even enemies. She avoided the question. "Many soldiers attended," she said. "More than I expected."

Duncan realized she was stalling. "Of course, there were soldiers in attendance. We occupy the city. Now, answer my question."

Abigail showed doubt, more feigned than genuine. "I'm sure there are some," she said slowly. "But if they hide their allegiance and cause no problems, what does it matter?"

"It matters because I say it does," he growled. "We can't risk a coordinated effort with colonial forces."

She paused, considering those in attendance. "There are none that I suspect," she said. "At least from my limited observations. But you must remember, my family left for New York just as the rebellion began. There was no organized effort by residents, at least none that I was aware of, other than the members of Congress who have since fled the city."

"You're taking the wrong approach," Duncan said sternly. "You should suspect them all, then prove their innocence."

Abigail glared at him. "Everyone in the congregation should be assumed guilty?"

"No, everyone in the city."

"If you assume every soul is about to overthrow the occupation forces, I wonder how you sleep at night."

The door to the parsonage opened just as they reached it, and Solomon stepped out. He glanced at them curiously. "Am I interrupting something?"

Abigail eyed her husband. "The colonel was asking who, if any, in the congregation might be aiding the Patriots."

Solomon shrugged. "I have no knowledge or opinions. I only seek to serve their souls, to ensure they do what's right."

Abigail glanced at Duncan. "The colonel claims everyone is suspect, at least until proven innocent."

"A necessity, I'm afraid," Duncan said tersely.

"The colonel trusts few," Solomon observed. "I suspect from experience."

"You're correct," Duncan replied. "I've seen what most have not. I don't intend to repeat mistakes."

Solomon gazed at him thoughtfully. "Perhaps a visit to the confessional would help," he suggested. "If we follow the path that's right and true, we have a much different perspective of mankind."

Duncan ignored him. "There are some who I trust," he said. "But I'm wary of all others."

"Even though they've given you no reason to suspect them?" Abigail asked.

"Until they give me reason to assume otherwise," Duncan said.

"That seems the reverse of what the law requires," she argued.

"I don't have the luxury of learning the law. Nor do I care."

"Perhaps you are the problem, not the residents," she said, her tone laced with humor rather than sarcasm, and her comment did not offend.

Duncan smiled. "I'm told I can trust some, like Barnabas Stone, the owner of City Tavern."

"Have faith, Colonel," Solomon said. "The answers will come, but only when the Lord is prepared to provide them."

Duncan was quiet, his thoughts wandering. "I still suspect the cabinetmaker's son," he revealed. "He may not have spied on our camp, but that doesn't mean he's innocent."

"Ian Blaine?" Abigail asked, knowing she had to convince Duncan otherwise.

"Yes," Duncan muttered. "Although all seem to trust the father. Maybe from prior business dealings."

"I don't know the man well," Abigail said, "but most would say like father like son."

"Most would," Duncan said, eyeing her curiously. "But I would not."

"I spoke to him this morning," she said casually. "I never got the impression he conspired against the Crown."

"What would you speak to him about?" Duncan asked, with a hint of accusation.

"Abigail wants a chest for her bedroom," Solomon interjected.

"Their cabinetry comes highly recommended," Abigail added. "They've always had an impeccable reputation."

"Yes, I suppose," Duncan replied, eyeing her closely. "But be wary of the man."

"I shall," Abigail said. "Even though a word was never said that I would deem suspicious."

"Not that you should," Duncan said, laughing lightly. "He's trying to sell you furniture."

"Approach the man with caution, dear," Solomon advised. "The colonel said some rebels do remain in the city."

"There are many that need to be closely watched," Duncan said sternly. "I put Ian Blaine at the top of the list."

36

―――――――

"I an, I've been waiting for you" Abigail said as she opened the door.

He glanced around the rectory as he entered. "I expected your housekeeper."

"She went to the bakery," Abigail said. She wore a light gray dress, billowing to the floor, which accented her green eyes and the twinkle housed within them. "But she'll be back any minute."

As Ian came in, he considered his father's words of warning, that he should assume someone was listening. "And the minister?"

"He's gone for the day," she said as she led him into the parlor and sat down. "He went somewhere with Duncan."

He sat beside her and leaned close. "You said you would help me," he said softly. He left his request vague, like his father suggested.

She studied him closely, almost as if she was undecided. But then she spoke. "You have to be careful," she warned. "Duncan still suspects you."

"He always will," Ian said, trusting her regardless of what his father said. "Probably due to Hart."

"Duncan dines with us," she continued in a hushed whisper. "Sometimes he reveals military information."

It was just as he had suspected. He could imagine Duncan bragging during dinner, letting secrets slip. "Such as?"

"He might reveal where the main body of troops are located, without realizing it, or where they might be redeployed."

"Where are they now?"

"Camped along the road to Germantown," she said. "They prepare for an attack from the colonials."

He listened closely. "What else?"

"Since I lived most of my life in Philadelphia, he wants me to identify those who support the rebellion and might even ask me to approach them to assess their loyalties."

"He wants you to spy for him?" Ian asked in disbelief.

"Yes, but in secret. No one would know except him and me."

"Do you trust him?"

"Absolutely not," she said. "I suspect he has an ulterior motive—something that goes beyond seeking those that aid the enemy."

Ian hesitated, trying to imagine the ambitions of a man he did not know. "Has he given you any names of those he suspects?"

"Not yet," she said. "He told me he has other avenues to explore."

"I must know everything you discuss," Ian said firmly. "We need to somehow trick him and use it to our advantage."

"He's mentioned several Loyalists," she said. "Bankers, solicitors—but the whole city already knows their allegiance."

"And Oliver Hart?"

She nodded. "They seem close. Hart dines with us occasionally. But he doesn't say much, mostly talks about commerce."

"Tell me all that is said, whether it seems innocent or not," Ian requested. He realized how valuable she could be. She had access to privileged information, military matters, and supply routes that were casually revealed. But he also knew it could be a trap.

"You seem reluctant," she said, watching him.

"We have to be cautious. Duncan could feed you false information. His request that you spy may be a ruse. He might suspect you."

She hesitated. "I didn't get that impression," she said. "At least not yet."

Ian leaned toward her. "It's so good to see you."

"Don't," she said, holding a finger to her lips. She glanced toward the hallway.

Ian was suspicious. "I thought no one was here?"

"No one is," she said. "But Anna is due back. She sneaks in sometimes." She smiled faintly. "Did you bring the drawing of the chest?"

He opened his leather satchel, withdrew the sketch, and handed it to her.

"It's beautiful," she said as she studied it. She turned to face him. "And costly."

"I told you I would build it at no cost. Consider it a gift,"

"Thank you," she said, smiling. "That's very kind. But you know we can't do that. I must be treated like any other customer or Solomon will become suspicious."

He nodded in agreement, even though he wished it was different. "The design is intricate. It'll take much to construct."

"Yes, I'm sure it will," she said, looking at the drawing. "But you don't know the minister."

"He won't spare the expense?"

She shrugged. "We'll see," she said. "He's very thrifty, so it remains to be seen."

"It's the carvings that make it expensive. They match the wardrobe."

She thought for a moment, trying to visualize it. "I'm not sure I know what you mean."

"May I show you?"

She paused. "Anna will be back."

"She's seen us measuring for the chest," he said. "She won't suspect anything."

"All right. But we must be quick."

He followed her upstairs and into her bedroom, again taken by the feminine feel, how much the room defined her. He went to the wardrobe and pointed at the carved vines that travelled along its length. "These are the carvings I matched on the chest."

"Oh, I see," she said, looking at the drawing and then to the wardrobe. "I'm impressed."

He leaned closer, drinking her scent, the faint smell of lavender from her perfume tickling his nostrils. He was so tempted to kiss her, or at least try, but knew he shouldn't.

She turned, her gaze meeting his, knowing his thoughts. "We can't," she said softly.

He moved toward her until they were inches apart.

She almost surrendered, then stepped away. "We have to go," she said. She paused, as if not sure how to proceed. "I'll tell you everything I learn."

He looked at her, so beautiful, her green eyes bright, her face flawless. "How will we communicate?"

She walked to her bureau and picked up a piece of red ribbon. "If I have something to share, I'll attach this ribbon to the window sash at 8 a.m. The window faces the alley that leads back to Second St."

"If the ribbon is attached, what do I do next?"

"Meet me in the Northeast Square at 9 a.m. I walk or run errands every morning, weather dependent, so no one will be suspicious when I leave the house."

"I'll get there before you arrive and wait on a park bench."

"Just beware," she said. "British soldiers are camped in every open space of the city. But much of the square is still wooded. No one would suspect that we meet there to trade secrets."

"I'll be careful," he said. He paused, looked in her eyes and stepped closer. "Maybe we can start where we ended."

The front door slammed closed. "Abigail," the minister called. "Are you up there?"

"It's Solomon!" she hissed. She hollered down the steps. "Yes, I'm upstairs."

"I have to speak to you," the minister said, his footsteps on the stairs.

Ian's eyes grew wide. "This doesn't look good."

"No, it doesn't! Find someplace to hide. Leave as soon as it's safe."

"Leave, how?" he asked, eyes wide as the minister's footsteps came closer.

"Eight 8 a.m.," she whispered. "Look for the ribbon."

She took the plans for the chest from his hands, stepped from the room, and closed the door behind her.

37

"What are you doing?" Solomon asked as Abigail closed the door. He looked at her curiously, as if he caught her doing something she shouldn't be doing.

"I thought you were gone for the day," she said. She lightly touched his arm and walked toward the stairs, hoping he would follow. She couldn't let him find Ian, or any hint that he had been there. It would be too difficult to explain—drawings for the chest in hand or not.

He turned to face her but didn't follow. "Duncan changed our plans."

"Are you coming?" she asked, pausing.

He looked at the closed door, as if a lingering question had to be answered.

"I have the sketch for my new chest. Mr. Blaine stopped by a little while ago."

"Oh, I didn't know you were expecting him."

"I wasn't actually," she said, still at the top of the stairs. "But I did tell him to bring the proposal when he finished it."

"Why don't you let me see it?"

She started down the steps. "It is dear, but very beautiful. I'll show you."

"Wouldn't it be easier if I knew where it was going?"

She stopped, three steps from the top. "I was going to put it at the foot of the bed."

"But if we look at the drawing in your bedroom, I can more easily visualize it," he said. He turned the doorknob and opened the door.

Abigail tried not to panic. She continued down the steps, slowly, looking up at him through the railing. "Yes," she said. "Just let me see if Anna is back first. I want to talk to her about dinner."

"There's no need for her to cook dinner," he said, poised in the doorway. "Colonel Duncan asked us to meet him at Fox and Demayne. Oliver Hart was also invited."

"Oh, I wasn't aware," she said. "What's the special occasion?"

"He didn't say. But we're soon to find out."

She had to keep him out of the bedroom. But she wasn't sure how to do it.

"Are you coming back up?" he asked. "I would like to see what the chest will look like."

"Yes," she said. She took the drawing from the pocket of her dress and dropped it, hoping it would flutter down the stairs. But it didn't. It fell on the next step.

Solomon stood at the threshold, the door open. "Careful," he said. "I wouldn't want you falling down the stairs."

"No," she said. She picked up the paper and came towards him. "Here's the sketch."

He met her at the top of the stairs and took the drawing. He started walking to the bedroom but paused. "It's very well drawn," he said. "But I wasn't expecting the cost."

"Mr. Blaine is a good artist," she said, ignoring talk of price. Her heart was racing. Ian was only feet away. "If they build as well as they draw, it should be a charming addition to my bedchambers."

"But it is expensive," he said, frowning. "I don't know that it's worth the money."

"It's hand-carved," she protested. "It matches the wardrobe." She pointed to the vines traveling along the chest, roses sprouting in symmetrical form. She eased between him and the bedroom.

"Can we do without the carvings?" he asked. "That should reduce the expense."

"I'm sure it will," she mumbled. "And make it like every other chest in Philadelphia."

"It's just an expensive trinket," he scoffed.

"Something I will have for the rest of my life—even pass down to a daughter someday."

"Perhaps," he grumbled, although he didn't seem convinced.

"What shall I tell him?" she asked, acting cross. "I'm sure there's a waiting list. They do have other customers."

Solomon sighed. "I have no desire to starve you of what you hold dear."

"Thank you," she said. "It's much appreciated."

"But it is a horrid expense."

"But one you can easily afford."

He frowned. "Yes, I suppose," he said. "But I'll have to sell more copies of my dissertations if I'm to support this type of lavish lifestyle."

"It's only a piece of furniture. You act as if I purchased the American colonies."

"It seems like you did," he muttered.

She grabbed the sketch and hurried down the stairs, feigning anger to distract him. "Think about it," she said. "I'll tell him we haven't decided."

"There's no need to go off in a huff."

"Come on," she said, secretly sighing with relief. "We don't want to keep Colonel Duncan waiting."

38

Ian stood flat against the wall, hidden behind the opened door. If Solomon took only a few more steps, he would find him.

Abigail tried to distract her husband, doing whatever she could to keep him away from the bedroom. Once their discussion degraded to an argument, she stormed down the stairs. Solomon meekly followed, his footsteps echoing off the hardwood floor.

When Ian was sure they were gone, he stepped into the hallway and peeked into the foyer below.

"Maybe if you show me where you want to put the chest, and how it matches the wardrobe, I'll understand the need," Solomon said.

"Not now," Abigail replied. "I've no desire to keep arguing about it."

"But we're not arguing," he protested. "I only questioned the cost."

Ian stepped back into Abigail's bedroom. They might come back. He needed someplace to hide. The bed was high, so he knelt, looking underneath it. Boxes were stored there, probably filled with dresses or coats.

He hurried to the wardrobe and opened the doors, hoping he could squeeze inside. It was filled—dresses, blouses and skirts hanging on hooks and folded in piles at the bottom. The faint smell of lavender, perhaps from her perfume, drifted from the wardrobe and for a moment he paused, enjoying it. He wondered what a woman did with so many clothes—the wardrobe, boxes under the bed, and a bureau with six spacious drawers. He was beginning to understand the need for a chest.

Abigail and Solomon were still on the first floor, but he didn't know how long they would stay there. He crept to the windows. Both looked out over the alley that led to Second St. But nothing along the building provided a path to climb down —no ledges or chimneys or staggered brickwork. Trees surrounded the house, but no limbs were close enough to use as an escape. He crossed the room to a door beside the bed, suspecting it led to a neighboring room, a nursery perhaps. Very slowly, he opened it.

It was another bedroom, with an oak frame bed, a wardrobe and bureau, nothing else. Sparse, but functional. He stole into the room, still able to hear the muffled conversation below. He opened the wardrobe, finding it filled with the minister's clothes. He paused. Abigail and the minister had separate bedrooms. But then, he supposed many couples did.

He went back into Abigail's bedroom and softly closed the interconnecting door. He tiptoed to the entrance. Just as he was about to turn the knob, he heard the front door close. He crept into the hallway and stood at the top of the stairs. Solomon had mentioned going to dinner. Maybe they left. He slowly started down the stairs, pausing to listen at each step.

He was halfway down when the front door opened.

"Wait there," Abigail said as she entered.

"I can get it," Solomon replied.

"No, I will," she insisted. "It's no bother. You don't have to come."

She stepped into the foyer and stopped abruptly when she saw Ian halfway down the steps. She shook her head vigorously, eyes wide, and motioned for him to go back upstairs.

Seconds later, Solomon entered. "I think I left it in my study."

"I told you I would find it," Abigail said as she went down the hall beside the stairs.

Solomon followed her through the foyer, never looking up. If he had, he would have seen Ian nearing the top of the stairs.

Ian hurried into the hallway, peeking into the foyer. He could see the open front door but not much more.

A moment later, Abigail appeared, the minister behind her, now carrying a cane. It seemed more for show than support, a brass lion's head on its top, but was apparently precious since the minister wouldn't leave the house without it. Ian waited a few more minutes to ensure they were gone, and then came down the steps, pausing every few seconds to check if anyone was in the house.

When he got to the foyer, he thought the front door risky and went down the hall and into the kitchen. He was just about to exit when he saw Anna, the housekeeper, coming up the walkway. She carried cloth satchels in each arm, bread and produce sticking out from the top.

Ian turned and raced through the kitchen. He could hear Anna fumbling with the back door. It opened seconds later.

"Abigail," she called as she entered.

He had no option but the front entrance. He crept to the foyer while Anna was putting her bags down in the kitchen.

"Abigail, are you here?" Anna called.

He gently opened the door, stepped onto the alley, and

closed it softly behind him. A young couple passed, a toddler with them, but no one else was nearby. Ian hurried down the lane towards Third, getting as far from the rectory as quickly as he could.

39

Abigail and Solomon entered Fox and Demayne and were led to a table overlooking the Delaware River where Hart and Duncan were already seated. Duncan was in uniform —a red coat and white shirt, his powdered hair in a short ponytail—while Hart wore a brown coat and white ruffled shirt, his black hair short, his brown eyes inquisitive.

"Our thanks for your invitation to dine," Solomon said, as they were seated.

Duncan smiled. "Just an example of how I treat my friends."

"As opposed to his enemies," Hart added. "Who fare far worse."

Abigail wasn't sure if Hart offered a threat or a stumbled attempt at humor. After no reaction from Duncan and Solomon, she chose to ignore it. "What's the special occasion?" she asked, skeptical of their gathering.

"It's not a celebration, I'm afraid," Duncan said sternly, eyeing each in turn.

Abigail knew something was wrong. She only hoped Ian wasn't involved. "What happened?" she asked.

"Colonial interference with the occupation has become dire," Duncan said.

Abigail eyed him curiously. "I've heard no mention of anything nefarious."

Duncan leaned closer, as if sharing a secret. "There's a powerful spy in the city. Someone providing information to Washington's army."

Hart looked at him strangely. "You occupy the former colonial capital. You don't control the countryside. I would think there is more than one spy in the city."

"Someone is sharing military secrets, regardless of how they collect it," Duncan explained. "I need your help to identify the culprit."

"What am I to do?" Solomon asked. "I only seek to serve my congregation."

"Every citizen must be watched," Duncan replied. "We can't allow this to continue."

Abigail was skeptical. "That seems harsh, Colonel. Why take such drastic action?"

Duncan sipped his port. "It's warranted," he said grandly. "I have undeniable evidence."

Hart wasn't convinced. "But Colonel, the residents know more than you might think. Your secrets could be common knowledge."

"I'll provide an example," Duncan said. "The colonials launched an attack on Germantown. They were soundly defeated. But they knew where our troops were positioned prior to the battle."

Abigail moved her hand to her mouth, covering an audible gasp. She had just given Ian that information. Too late to impact the battle—she had only told him hours before—but she now knew how critical what she learned could be.

"How do you know someone in Philadelphia warned

them?" Hart asked. "Even a nearby farmer can observe British troop movements."

"You might be correct," Duncan admitted. "But I still think spies in Philadelphia are more likely. And so does General Howe. Maybe they're much closer than we think." He leaned forward, as if sharing as secret. "If I arrest one of the ringleaders, I'll be promoted to the rank of general. Long overdue, but certainly warranted."

Those at the table eyed Duncan warily, so intent on proving misconduct, even if none existed—perhaps for personal gain. It was a dangerous road to travel, a route that shouldn't be taken at all.

"We'll assist however we can," Solomon said, trying to ease the tension. "But I must admit, I feel uncomfortable doing it."

"I'm afraid I will have little to contribute," Abigail said. "I don't remember what anyone said or did when I lived in the city."

"The colonel made the same request of me," Hart added hastily. "In regard to employees and acquaintances. But I, too, struggle to identify any loyal to the rebellion."

Abigail suspected Hart tempered his message. But why? Was it to build a trust he would later betray?

"Yes, perhaps," Duncan muttered, eyeing them warily. "But we do have suspects. The cabinetmaker, for example."

"Ian Blaine?" Hart asked. "I thought his innocence had already been proven?"

Duncan ignored him. "Blaine is our most likely candidate," he said, and turned to Abigail. "Is he building the chest you requested?"

She glanced at the minister. "Solomon has yet to give his permission."

"It's very costly," Solomon said. "I'm not convinced of the need."

Duncan sipped his wine. "It would be an opportune time to observe him more closely."

"The chest would be built in the shop and delivered to the rectory," Solomon said. "But I do need an additional pew at the church. I can ask him to build it."

"That should work nicely," Duncan said. "You can observe him while he works."

"I suppose I could," Solomon said reluctantly. "But I've no experience in rooting out subversion."

Duncan glared at him. "Pastor, I'm asking for your assistance. Will you provide it?"

Solomon's eyes widened. "Yes, of course. I'll have Blaine build the pew."

Abigail had to warn Ian that Duncan wasn't merely suspicious, he was determined to prove him guilty. And she had to do it quickly. Before he made a mistake from which he couldn't recover.

"If Blaine is a spy," Solomon said, "and he thinks we're watching him, won't he simply flee?"

"We have ten redoubts circling the city," Duncan said smugly. "No one can enter or leave without a pass—even those bringing produce or product into the city."

"A process soon to be extended to the ferries," Hart added.

"British gunboats are on their way upriver," Duncan continued triumphantly. "Which eliminates another escape path."

"If only more could be done to obtain supplies," Hart mumbled, broaching a topic that seemed self-serving.

Duncan eyed those at the table, as if wondering whether he could trust them. "A dilemma soon to be remedied. We have an attack planned on the river forts."

"Then we'll soon control the river," Hart said, failing to hide his glee.

Duncan looked at them smugly. "Yes, we will. There's little chance that Ian Blaine, or anyone else, can escape."

"Not unless we want them to," Hart added.

Duncan sipped his port and gazed at the river. "I've just had an interesting thought," he said, as if all should recognize his brilliance. "Why don't we lay a trap for Mr. Blaine. And see what we might catch."

40

"The British should not expect the church do their bidding," Abigail complained as they left Fox and Demayne and walked back to the rectory.

"I think it best that we comply with Duncan's request," Solomon countered. "At least in regard to Blaine."

"We don't even know the man," she said. "We're now supposed to help the British expose him as a spy—whether he's guilty or not?"

Solomon was quiet for a moment. "We may have no choice," he said softly.

Abigail realized she was in a delicate situation. She had to warn Ian about Duncan's plot without arousing Solomon's suspicions—if she hadn't already.

"You're quiet," Solomon said. "You don't agree?"

"I don't think Duncan should force you to hire Blaine, simply to ensnare him in some insidious trap."

"You make it sound far worse than it is," he scoffed. "We're only to interact with the man, hire him to build the pew or the chest."

"He's been to the rectory twice to discuss the chest. We can't keep wasting his time."

"I'm still inclined to purchase it," Solomon muttered, as if he feared upsetting her.

She knew he would agonize over the expense—it's just the way he was. Unless the expense was related to him. Solomon had the finest of everything, even the ridiculous cane he insisted on carrying, which he didn't need at all. But any expense for her was most difficult to obtain. She had little hope that the chest would ever be purchased. If it was, it would only be after weeks of indecision.

"If nothing else, Duncan asks that we get closer to Blaine," Solomon continued. "And either the chest or the pew offers that opportunity."

"Neither does," she argued, "because they're both business transactions. We aren't the man's friends, and we never will be." She had to avoid letting Solomon and Ian engage in any social setting. It would be too hard to maintain the lie—that she didn't know Ian very well—and too easy to make a mistake.

"But I suspect Duncan will want to lay this trap for Blaine while he works for us, assuming he agrees to do so."

"I'm not sure what this trap will be, but is it really something a man of God should be executing? Do you even know what they want you to do?"

"No, I don't," Solomon said. "But I don't think they do, either."

Abigail suspected Duncan had private discussions with Solomon, just as he had with her. He was a dangerous man who seemed intent on getting everyone to spy on each other—husband watching wife, friend watching friend, stranger watching stranger. All for the good of the Crown. Or maybe for personal reasons—so he could become the general he believed he should be.

"I'm sure that, when the time comes, Duncan will tell us what he wants," Solomon said.

Abigail was leery of the whole situation. "I don't want to be involved in this."

He looked at her suspiciously. "We haven't heard his request, or even if he'll make it."

She noticed the look he gave her. It seemed Duncan had already planted seeds of doubt in her husband. "Isn't it a treacherous path for the church to take?"

Solomon was quiet. "I'm in no position to oppose Duncan."

"He can't hurt you," she said, knowing secrets from New York shouldn't be revealed in Philadelphia. "Especially since Howe is your friend."

"But I can't take that chance," he said. "I must do as asked."

Neither spoke for a few moments as they turned onto Second St., carriages and wagons passing on the cobblestone streets beside them.

"It's a precarious position for Duncan to put you in," she said, trying to temper his suspicions. "You're a man of God, not a British spy. I refuse to participate—especially if former friends or acquaintances are targeted. They don't deserve to be treated that way, and neither do I—war or not."

"I have too much to lose, as you well know," he insisted softly. He stopped walking and turned to face her.

She smiled weakly, his secret too painful to discuss, and lightly touched his arm. "Yes, you do," she agreed. "But Duncan doesn't have the power he claims, nor can he cause you any harm."

"But he said General—"

"Howe never ordered Duncan to have a minister spy on his congregation. You know the general, go and ask him."

"I couldn't impose."

"Then do as Duncan asks," she said simply. "But try to maintain your principles."

"I'm not sure how," Solomon mumbled as they started walking again. "But I'll do the best I can."

"Would you like me to visit Blaine's shop to inquire about the church pew?"

Solomon thought for a moment as they walked down the lane that led to the rectory. "No, I think I should make those inquiries."

41

Abigail tied a red ribbon on her window sash, a signal to Ian that she had information. It was too important— Germantown, the British redoubts, the Jersey attacks, the trap that was being set—and she couldn't risk waiting. She was wary of Duncan—and Solomon, too. It seemed that the colonel wanted to control everyone—through blackmail if he had to. Duncan was cunning, he had an agenda, and he would use whoever he wanted, as long as it led to his success. The damage inflicted, the lives destroyed, really didn't matter to him.

She readied herself to leave, planning to meet Ian at the Northeast Square. But as she reached the front door, Duncan entered the parlor.

"Where are you hurrying off to, Mrs. St. Clair?" he asked curiously.

She smiled, pretending to be embarrassed. "Nowhere in particular. I like to walk in the morning, usually for pleasure but sometimes I run errands for the church."

He studied her for a moment, as if struck with an idea. "A walk sounds inviting," he said. "I think I'll join you. It's a pleasant morning."

She hesitated, hoping to avoid him. "I don't want to keep you from your duties."

"Nonsense," he said. "I have time for a walk. Even with the responsibilities I shoulder."

She couldn't go anywhere near the square. If Ian saw her with Duncan, he would assume the worst. But if he saw the ribbon on the sash, went to the square to meet her and she never arrived, he would at least know something was wrong.

"You seem preoccupied," Duncan said, observing her closely. "Is anything wrong?"

"No, not at all," she replied as she opened the door and stepped out.

"Do you have a friend who might be waiting?" he asked with just a hint of accusation. "I wouldn't want to interrupt anything."

"No, it's fine," she said, forcing a smile.

As they left the house, Abigail led Duncan toward the docks, opposite the Northeast Square.

"Why the river?" he asked, as their route became clear.

"The view is beautiful, and the water has a soothing effect."

"Be careful near the docks," he warned. "Unsavory characters lurk about."

She laughed. "Colonel, that's nonsense. The riverfront is beautiful—restaurants, stately trees, benches with views of the water or city."

"I don't see the attraction," he muttered.

"I watch the ships, too," she added, wondering why he didn't want her near the river.

"Most ships are docked."

"Because of the rebel forts?"

He looked at her suspiciously. "What do you know about rebel forts?"

"Only what we discussed at dinner," she said, recovering quickly. "Both you and Mr. Hart have mentioned them."

"Oh yes," he mumbled, as if he remembered their discussions. "We have to capture the forts to clear the channel so ships can get to sea. But it won't be long."

Abigail innocently displayed an interest. "How do we get supplies now? I see ferries loaded and produce coming into the city, but many stalls at the open market are empty."

"Once we take the forts, commerce will flow again. In the meantime, we get what we can from New York, across Jersey, and then downriver."

"I'm sure Anna will be pleased," she said, referring to their housekeeper. She made a mental note of what she just learned —the supply route the British were using. "She has such a hard time getting food. As do many others."

They walked down the block and crossed the street. A few pedestrians passed, dressed in fine clothes, like solicitors, or working men: carpenters, tanners, and blacksmiths. Women held babies in baskets, some with toddlers walking beside them.

"I think it's time we started meeting privately," Duncan said abruptly. "I want names and addresses of friends and acquaintances, with an assessment of their loyalty to the Crown."

She hesitated. She had to stall him if nothing else. "I'm afraid I won't be much help."

"Why is that?"

"I come from wealth," she told him. "My family has a strong allegiance to the king, as did almost all of those I associated with. Some left for New York or Canada. Others returned to England."

He frowned but wasn't deterred. "You seem friendly with Missy Malone. I'm sure you have other friends like her."

"I did know Missy before I left. An acquaintance more than a friend."

He was quiet, plotting his next move. "Your morning walk

provides an opportune time for you to offer the information I'm looking for. I plan to accompany you when I have the time."

She laughed lightly. "I'm afraid you'll quickly become bored," she said, trying to dissuade him. "I often go to the library or different bookstores."

He gave her a smug smile. "Except on the days I go with you," he said curtly. "I'm determined to find the spies in this city. My promotion depends on it."

"Of course, Colonel," she said softly. "I only hope my memory serves me."

"It shall, Mrs. St. Clair, I'm sure." He lightly grasped her elbow, as if to guide her along the pavement. But he was also giving her a subtle message. "All will be our secret, known only to you and me. You do understand that, don't you?"

"Yes, Colonel," she replied, suspecting he trusted no one. She waited a moment and gently pulled her arm from his grasp. She turned down Market to Second, making the walk as brief as possible.

Duncan pointed to a sign affixed to a lamp post. "Remember our dinner discussion? I told you trouble was brewing. A warning for residents."

She walked closer to the poster. "A warning for what?"

"Spies," he said. "We know they exist. We just have to find them."

"Oh, my," she said as she read the announcement. "It says if caught, they'll be hung."

He grabbed her arm, rougher than the first time, and glared at her. "They will be, Mrs. St. Clair, I promise you. Whether man or woman."

42

Ian was working in the shop, building a bookcase with fluted trim for a solicitor that lived on Tenth St., when his father came in with an anxious expression.

"The minister is here to see you," Patrick hissed.

Ian looked at him curiously. "What minister?"

"The minister of the Anglican Church."

Ian put down the awl he held and looked at his father with arched eyebrows. "Abigail's husband?"

"Yes," Patrick said, leaning toward him. "You had better hope he's here for furniture."

Ian glanced in the showroom, disaster looming. Had the minister overheard a conversation with Abigail? Or had he learned they were lovers, almost married, barely two years before? Was he wary—suspecting Abigail revealed military secrets? What if he demanded Ian never see her again?

"Don't keep him waiting," Patrick urged. "See what he wants."

Ian approached the minister, who was admiring a buffet on display. He turned as Ian neared.

"Mr. Blaine?" he asked.

"Yes, sir," Ian replied, sighing with relief. It seemed the visit would be friendly. "We met briefly, Mr. St. Clair. I was at your welcoming party as well as your last service."

"I do remember," Solomon said, studying him through round spectacles. "I appreciate your support for the church."

"I've been a member for many years," Ian said. "As has my father." He motioned to Patrick, who stood on the shop threshold, watching curiously.

"My wife Abigail informed me of your reputation," Solomon said.

Ian was nervous, wondering how much the minister knew and where the conversation would lead. "I hope she was complimentary."

The minister chuckled. "Yes, she was. By all means."

"What can I do for you, good sir?" Ian asked, hoping to stop the chatter and determine the minister's motive.

"Since you were at last week's service, I'm sure you noticed it was well-attended, and some were left standing."

"Yes, I did," Ian said, relieved the discussion related to business and nothing more. "A testament to your skills as an orator."

Solomon laughed lightly. "Thank you, I appreciate that. But I suspect the attendance was more curiosity—who is this new pastor?"

"I think not," Ian assured him. "Your reputation preceded you."

"That's nice to know," Solomon said. He paused, as if collecting his thoughts. "But, given the attendance, I've come to inquire about adding another pew on the side of the church."

"Is there enough space to support one?" Ian asked. He couldn't help but assess the man. He wondered what Abigail saw in him. They seemed very different. But he knew they must have much in common. They loved each other enough to marry.

"Yes, I think there's adequate room," Solomon replied. He frowned, as if struck with a thought. "Although I am concerned with cost. The church has few funds for expenditures, but the need for more seating is substantial."

Ian glanced at Patrick, who nodded discreetly. "Let me see what you want built," Ian said. "If it's not significant, we can do it as a voluntary effort, donating material and labor."

The minister seemed relieved. "I would be so grateful," he said. "As would others in the congregation."

"But we would like mention at the service," Patrick called from the shop doorway. "Just to recognize our efforts."

"Yes, of course," Solomon said hastily. "I would be more than happy to do so. On multiple occasions."

Ian hid a grin. He realized, as Patrick did, that the acknowledgement would lead to more customers, making the voluntary effort more than worthwhile. "When can I visit the church to see what your needs might be?"

Solomon thought for a moment, considering his schedule. "How about tomorrow morning at 9 a.m.?"

43

Oliver Hart tapped on the carriage wall, signaling the driver to stop. As the carriage came to a halt on the side of Chestnut, just past Third, he opened a small partition so he could communicate.

"Is everything all right, sir?" the driver asked.

"Yes, just sit here for a minute," Hart requested. He leaned to look from the window.

"Is there anything you need?"

"No, not right now," Hart said as he closed the partition.

Missy Malone gave him a confused look. "Oliver, what are you doing?"

"I want to see something."

"See what?" she asked. "It's almost dark. What are you looking at?"

"Ian Blaine is outside his cabinet shop."

Missy leaned toward the window and looked out. "Is there a British law against standing on the pavement in front of your own establishment and talking to another resident of the city? Because if there is, I'm not aware of it. I suspect many others aren't, either."

Hart hid a smile. Missy could be very abrupt sometimes, witty at others, but always sarcastic. "No, of course not."

"Then why are we sitting here watching Ian Blaine?"

"Because I don't know the man."

"Who cares?" an exasperated Missy said. "Are you supposed to know every citizen in the city?"

"No, of course not," he replied. "But Duncan wants Ian Blaine observed."

She shook her head, eyes wide. "Are you serious?"

"I'm trying to prove something."

"You're not proving anything," she insisted. "If Duncan wants Ian Blaine watched, then let him do it."

"I'm not necessarily watching Blaine."

"You're not necessarily making sense," she said. "Can we be on our way?"

"Just a minute more."

"Oliver, it took weeks to persuade you to see this play. That's how difficult it is to get you out of the house."

"I do enjoy my home," he mumbled, his attention diverted.

"I'm sure you do. I do as well. But I am greatly anticipating this performance. I refuse to miss it because you prefer to watch Ian Blaine talk to a stranger."

"I want to see who the man is and if it's anyone I know."

"It's probably a customer," she said, leaning in his lap to see out the window.

The man talking to Ian Blaine turned abruptly and walked away, headed toward the river. His face wasn't visible and, with dusk approaching and his quick gait, his identity would never be known. Ian went back into the cabinet shop, the door closing behind him.

"Should we go around the block and try to catch a glimpse of him?" Hart asked.

Missy leaned back in the coach and looked at him strangely. "No, we shouldn't."

"It'll only take a minute."

"Oliver, what is wrong with you?"

"Nothing, I'm just curious," he said. "I want to see who Blaine associates with. Duncan would be interested."

"Maybe it's none of Duncan's business. Or yours, either."

"But it is our business," he stressed. "We need to know what they're doing. It may be entirely innocent. Or it may not be. There could be danger."

Missy laughed. "Oliver, are you joking?"

He looked at her, a bit hurt. "No, I'm not."

"I've known Ian Blaine my whole life," she said. "He poses no danger to anyone, believe me—except for an unsuspecting young lady, perhaps."

Hart hesitated, the image of the spy's face at Trudruffrin clearly in his mind. "Duncan is convinced he's a colonial spy."

"Half of Philadelphia are colonial spies of some sort," she said. "Tell the driver to continue, or we'll be late for the play."

Hart tapped on the wall of the carriage and the driver once more guided the carriage down the cobblestone streets.

"Who cares what Duncan thinks," Missy continued. "You should stay out of it."

Hart paused. "Yes, maybe you're right."

"What are you trying to find out anyway?"

"I only hoped to prove innocence or guilt."

"Stick to ships," she said. "At least you know something about them."

44

Ian arrived at the church shortly before 9 a.m., carrying a
leather pouch with a ruler and some basic tools. He only
planned to measure and lay out what the minister wanted, not
actually start construction. He went inside, but didn't see
Abigail or the minister, only soldiers in the rooms adjacent to
the altar. He looked over the church, the location where the
minister wanted the additional pew not obvious and went
outside to wait.

He worried about Abigail and wanted to make sure she was
safe. She had left the ribbon on her window sash, but never
came to the Northeast Square. He assumed something had
gone wrong, but he didn't know how serious it was.

He sat on a bench by the entrance, watching pedestrians
pass down the alley that led to Second St., enjoying a brisk
October morning. Two British soldiers came by on horseback,
not paying any attention to him—if they saw him at all. In the
distance, probably from the Northeast Square, he could see a
pole with the British flag unfurled, announcing to all that King
George controlled the city, on the slim chance that anyone still
doubted that he did.

A few minutes later, Abigail came from the rectory, crossing the cobblestone street and glancing over her shoulder. When no one followed, Duncan or the minister, she sat on the bench beside him, but left space between them.

"I was wondering if you would come," Ian said.

"I have to talk to you," she said softly, furtively glancing around. "I have important information."

"Hush," Ian whispered.

A British soldier appeared from the side of the church, one of the orderlies using a room beside the altar. "Good morning," he said. "It's a beautiful day, isn't it?"

"Yes, it is," Abigail replied, smiling sweetly.

The soldier paused at the pavement, just past the bench, and gazed up and down the lane that ran in front of the church. He was young, late teens or early twenties, and seemed as if he waited for someone. But they couldn't speak freely. He was too close.

Abigail leaned towards Ian, eyeing the redcoat. "I couldn't come to the square. Duncan followed me."

"Duncan?" he asked, alarmed.

"Yes," she whispered. "He suspects you, and I think he suspects me, too."

Ian glanced at the soldier and then looked at her strangely. "Why would he suspect you?"

The soldier took a step closer and casually paced the pavement.

"We must talk," she murmured. "I have so much to tell you."

Ian kept his gaze on the redcoat. "Trust no one."

She leaned closer. "I saw signs posted. They intend to hang spies. Men or women."

"I have no interest in hanging."

"Nor do I," she said. "But you have to be careful. You're in danger. So am I. Don't underestimate Duncan."

He sat up straighter, not expecting a warning. He studied

the soldier, who still looked up and down the street. "How do you know?"

"Both Hart and Duncan are watching you," she said. "They plan to trap you and somehow prove guilt."

"It's Hart," Ian hissed. "He's trying to convince Duncan."

"Just beware," she warned. "Duncan still wants me to identify the locations and loyalties of former friends."

Ian looked at the soldier. He could be close enough to listen but acted as if he didn't care what might be said. "You can use that to our advantage," he said. "Protect those that need it; implicate those that don't."

"I don't want to implicate anyone. Duncan has an evil agenda, all tied to his own advancement."

He glanced at her, the woman he once loved and probably still did. He couldn't let her risk her life. Not for him or the cause. "Maybe you should avoid me."

"I can't," she said. "The information I get is too valuable."

The British soldier took a few steps farther away.

Ian rose, paced for a moment, and stood in front of Abigail, blocking her from the soldier. "Whisper," he said softly.

She looked down the street, to the rectory. "The minister will be here any minute."

"Then hurry," he said. "What did you learn?"

The soldier waved to a young woman coming down the alley and briskly walked away. Like many redcoats, he was interested in a local girl. Abigail waited until they were gone.

"Tell me," Ian said. "While we're alone."

"I have to get information to you faster. I knew about Germantown."

"It's all right," he said. "We had other sources. It didn't help, though."

She glanced around nervously. "The British are building ten redoubts, forts around the city. The passes needed to get in or out of the city are just the beginning. Soon you'll need the same for ferries or any other ship on the river."

Ian was quiet, listening, studying the street, glancing back at the church doors, ensuring they were alone. He already knew what she just told him, as did others—Barnabas and his father. But it showed she had legitimate sources.

"I may be able to get the exact locations for the forts," she continued. "But I'm not sure."

"What else?" Ian asked. "I'm listening."

"They're getting supplies from New York. Across Jersey and down the river. But they intend to gain control of the entire river."

"That's unlikely," Ian said. "We have two forts just south of the city, in Jersey and Pennsylvania. There's nothing they can do."

"Yes, there is," she said firmly. "They have—"

The rectory door opened, and Solomon stepped out. He walked across the cobblestone street. "Oh, there you are darling," he called. "I thought you would wait for me."

"It was such a fine morning, I thought I would walk," Abigail replied with a nervous smile. "But Mr. Blaine was waiting so I've been chatting with him until you arrived." She stood and pulled her shawl tighter around her bosom.

"Good morning Mr. Blaine," Solomon said as he crossed the street.

Abigail turned, her face not visible to Solomon. "They're about to attack the forts."

45

It was almost dusk when Barnabas lifted the last crate of potatoes from the back of the wagon. He glanced up and down Second Street, made sure no one was near, and leaned close to the driver. "What else do you need?" he asked.

The man wore shaggy clothes, as if he had worked a long day, a wide brimmed hat pulled low. "Anything you can get on the river forts," he said. "We know the attacks are coming. But we don't know when or the strength of their forces."

Barnabas eyed a pair of British soldiers coming toward them. "Carry this around back with the rest, and I'll get your money," he said loudly so the soldiers could hear.

The driver followed him down a narrow alley and they set down the last two crates by the back door to the tavern. "It's going to get much worse," the man warned. "Especially supplies. There's less every day."

Barnabas removed a roll of bills from his pocket and peeled a few from the stack. He handed them to the driver. "If we starve, the British starve, too," he said. "We may not need guns to defeat them."

They walked back down the alley to Second St. "Try to find

their supply routes," the driver said. "Maybe we can steal what they're bringing."

"At least get them to the people instead of the redcoats."

The driver climbed on the wagon and took the reins. "I'll have another load on Tuesday," he called.

Barnabas waited while the wagon pulled away, the wheels rattling on the cobblestone. The occupation was about to take a drastic turn. The enemy's success depended on supplies. Their chances were precarious at best.

He entered the tavern, the tables filled with patrons, most enjoying a mug of beer or a light meal, supper served in the afternoon. A few ate bowls of stew, a kettle over the open-hearth fireplace. On the landing at the edge of the room, where a few empty tables remained, Ian and Patrick sat in their usual location, watching the customers while they enjoyed their drink. Barnabas filtered through the crowded tavern to their table.

"Join us," Patrick offered.

"For a moment," Barnabas said as he moved a chair and sat so he could see the entrance and those who were gathered around the room.

"More redcoats than usual," Ian muttered.

"I'm glad they're here," Barnabas said. "It's good for business and it keeps them from looting."

"The looting will only get worse," Patrick said as he sipped his beer.

Barnabas eyed each table near them—the patrons and what they were doing—ensuring they couldn't eavesdrop. When satisfied it was safe, he leaned forward. "Anything to share?"

Ian quietly provided the information he had—forts around the perimeter, travel passes, supplies from New York, an upcoming attack on the forts along the Delaware, and a trap being set for him. Barnabas knew most of it. But it showed Ian was linked to someone closely tied to the British.

"Do you trust this source?" Barnabas asked.

"I do," Ian said. "She has as much to lose as I do."

"It's a woman?" Barnabas asked.

Ian paused. "Is that a problem?"

Barnabas hesitated, but then slowly shook his head. "Not if she's smart. The redcoats are less likely to suspect a woman."

"She's very smart," Ian said. "But she's afraid the British might be watching her."

"Why is she doing it then?" Patrick asked with his Irish accent. "She comes from a Loyalist family."

"Best be careful," Barnabas advised

"I hate to disparage the woman, I really do," Patrick continued. "But I don't think she can be trusted."

They were quiet for a moment, watching the crowd while they weighed the risks. After enjoying a few swigs of beer, and eyeing the redcoats warily, Ian leaned forward. "Is there anything you need to know?"

"I need more about the river forts," Barnabas requested. "Dates, troop strengths and routes the British will take to attack. Fort Mercer in Jersey and Moultrie in Pennsylvania."

"The more she can learn, the better we'll be," Patrick added. "But we need to make sure whatever she says is true."

Barnabas was quiet for a moment, thinking. "How do you know she isn't working for the British?" he asked. "Feeding you false information to prove you're a spy. Maybe that's the trap."

Ian paused as if it wasn't something he considered. "I don't think she would do that."

"Duncan's trap could be for her," Patrick warned. "But she doesn't know it and neither do you."

46

Abigail, Duncan, and Solomon waited in the parlor for dinner, enjoying a glass of wine, when Oliver Hart arrived, minus Missy Malone. Abigail was about to inquire as to her absence when she realized there was a pattern to her attendance. When Missy was present, it was a social event, and conversation rarely strayed to military matters. But when Missy wasn't, the discussion focused on strategy. If she was correct, she might hear some secret worthy of sharing with Ian.

Missy's absence made Abigail wonder if she shared Hart's political views, which made her offer to help, no matter what the need, far easier to decipher. But it did leave a lingering question. Why would she assume Abigail was a Patriot? Due to her prior relationship with Ian? Or was it something she overheard? Abigail would have to approach her cautiously.

"I accompanied Mrs. St. Clair on a walk the other day," Duncan said, interrupting her thoughts. "She has an interesting perspective on the city and its residents."

Abigail wasn't sure what Duncan implied. There was nothing spectacular about their walk. But she pretended there was. "It was a nice stroll along the riverfront."

"Abigail goes out every morning," Solomon said, and then added mysteriously. "Supposedly on walks. But I've stumbled upon her in several different locations."

Abigail paused, wondering what he inferred. Had he followed her, or was he joking? "I visit the hospital once each week," she clarified. "The poorhouse, too. I deliver donations received by the church."

"And bookstores and libraries," Solomon added. "Her favorite haunts."

"She is an avid reader," Duncan said. "She sometimes reads several books at once. It's a curious habit to watch."

Hart's expression changed. "It seems we have much in common."

"Really?" Abigail asked. "Is Missy a reader, also?"

Hart hesitated, then smiled. "Missy is a talker. That doesn't leave time for much else."

They all laughed, then were interrupted by Anna. "Dinner is served," she announced.

They moved into the dining room. Duncan's orderlies had delivered a quarter round of beef and Anna and her teenage helper prepared it along with potatoes and squash, rolls used to sop up the gravy. The meal was served with Madeira port, although cider and water were also offered.

"A fine meal, Anna," Solomon said. "You've exceeded your usual excellence."

"My privilege to serve," Anna replied as she filled their wine glasses. She lingered near Duncan, leaning lightly against him.

"Thank you for such a fine dinner," the colonel echoed.

Anna smiled and went into the kitchen. As she passed through the doorway, she glanced back at Duncan, which did not go unnoticed by Abigail.

"I've developed a plan to trap Blaine," Duncan announced.

"Any action taken should be carefully considered," Hart

warned. "If we trap someone who is innocent, it could persuade those neutral to join the rebellion."

"Our plan, and its execution, will be flawless," Duncan promised.

"What do you intend to do?" Abigail asked as casually as she could.

"I think we should give him false information," Duncan said.

"And see if the rebels act?" Hart asked.

"Yes," Duncan replied. "It's a method proven throughout history."

Abigail hesitated, but couldn't help defending Ian, even though she knew she shouldn't. "Has it occurred to anyone that Mr. Blaine might be innocent?"

Duncan shrugged. "I don't really care. General Howe wants spies arrested. Blaine is a likely suspect. The court can sort out his innocence or guilt."

"We can't approach him directly," Hart said. "It will only make him suspicious. It might be better if he overheard it."

"We should use someone we trust," Duncan said. "Like Barnabas Stone."

"Maybe Abigail and I can assist," Solomon offered. "Blaine is working at the church."

"Will he be there tomorrow?" Duncan asked.

"Yes, at 8 a.m."

"I think I have a suggestion," Hart said. "Why not say I have rebel sympathies, and if the right man approaches me, I will turn."

Duncan put down his wine glass. "Splendid!"

"But who would believe it?" Abigail asked. "You led the British march into the city on the first day of the occupation."

"Which makes him all the more valuable to the rebels," Duncan said.

"It's also easy to verify," Hart continued. "The rebels will try to enlist my support."

"At which point we arrest Blaine," Duncan said. "Simple and effective."

47

When dinner ended and Hart had gone, Abigail settled in the parlor with Solomon and Duncan, enjoying a late afternoon tea. The men were soon immersed in political discussions, comparing different governments in history to the British Empire.

Abigail listened while they talked, should any information slip that might be valuable to the colonials. She scanned a poetry book by Thomas Gray, the pages opened to the poem, *Elegy Written in a Country Churchyard,* but she couldn't focus. She had to warn Ian. He was walking into a trap, about to over-hear utter nonsense—that Hart was ready to join the rebels. She doubted he would believe it, given Hart's loyalty to the Crown. But with the loss of their capital city, the Patriots might grasp at anything that could lead to victory. If a man wrapped firmly in the enemy's embrace wanted to leave it, they might welcome him. And hang in the process.

She slept restlessly, suspecting the trap could just as easily be laid for her. She lay awake for hours, wondering what she should do. When she finally did sleep she had horrid dreams, images of shoes dangling in midair.

As soon as she awakened, she went through her morning routine and discussed household chores for the day with Anna. All the while she eyed her pocket watch, knowing Ian would soon be at the church. If she got there before Solomon, she could warn him of the treachery underway—before he was tangled within it and strung up on the gallows.

It was just before eight a.m., when Solomon emerged from his study. "Are you ready to go to the church?"

She hesitated, annoyed she hadn't left earlier. "Are you sure we should do this?"

"The colonel asked us to trick Blaine. We're honor bound to do so. I'm only trying to do what's right."

"I'm not sure what role I play," Abigail muttered. "If there's any at all."

"It's very simple. We'll say Colonel Duncan is suspicious of Oliver Hart and thinks he's trying to contact the rebels."

As they left the rectory and crossed the street, Abigail had a feeling of dread. Each day that passed pulled her deeper into the conflict. What had at first been only a burning curiosity became a flame she couldn't extinguish. At some point she had to make a decision, even though the correct choice might not be the safest.

They entered the church, and Solomon showed her where Blaine would be working. "We can stand here," he said. "Just around the corner."

"How will we start the conversation?"

"Talk about last night's dinner party. I'll make the statement about Hart."

"We can only hope it satisfies Duncan," she said, warily watching for Ian.

He arrived ten minutes later, his wagon loaded with planks of wood. Solomon was at the altar, fussing by the pulpit, but as soon as Abigail started for the door, he hurried down the aisle.

Ian came in, carrying a wood box filled with tools—chisels, hammers, and planes. "Good morning," he said, looking first at Abigail and nodding to Solomon who was just behind her.

Abigail widened her eyes and mouthed silent warnings, trying to get Ian's attention. But at first he didn't notice and, when he finally did, he only looked at her curiously.

"I have a sketch with dimensions," Ian said.

Solomon studied the drawing. "Will it be built into the wall, like the other pews?"

"Yes, I'll make it look the same, just as you requested."

Abigail again tried to warn Ian, but he was focused on Solomon, gauging his reaction. She had to get him alone, but without taking risks. Duncan's plan was too dangerous; she couldn't delay telling him. But if she was caught warning him, she could hang beside him.

Ian set his toolbox down and withdrew a wooden ruler. He took measurements of the existing benches and the space where the new pew would go. He was kneeling, with his back to Abigail, when Solomon led her around the corner, still within Ian's earshot.

"I enjoyed our dinner party last night," Solomon said. "I'm still shocked by the upsetting news, though."

"What news was that?" she asked. "With all the talk of war and rebellion, I'm afraid I stopped paying attention."

Solomon frowned, annoyed she hadn't cooperated. "Oliver Hart is not to be trusted. He sympathizes with the rebels and will join them if ever asked."

"But he led the British into the city on the first day of occupation," Abigail said. "I would think he made his loyalties quite clear."

Solomon glared at her. "Every man has his price. Hart only searches for his."

"What does he hope to gain?" she asked.

"Who knows? Money, love. Maybe Missy Malone persuaded him. We can only guess what his motive might be."

Solomon peeked around the corner and motioned for Abigail to do the same. Ian had his back to them, taking measurements, but seemed to listen intently.

The minister smiled slyly and winked at Abigail.

48

"But I heard it clearly," Ian said to his father when he returned to the cabinet shop.

"It makes no sense," Patrick said. "The British just put Hart in charge of the port."

"Do you think it's a trap?"

"I wouldn't act on it," Patrick said. "Especially after what Abigail told you."

"But if true, it could be a great opportunity. I'm sure he knows many British secrets."

"I'm sure he does, too," Patrick agreed. "But why would he be willing to share them?"

Ian was quiet for a moment. "They did hint that Missy Malone may have persuaded him."

Patrick hesitated. "The Malones are a fine family. I've known them for years."

"Are they Loyalists or Patriots?"

"They're businessmen, just like us," Patrick said. "They work hard and keep their mouths shut."

"But the pastor didn't know I heard him, which makes it all the more believable."

"If Hart wanted to work with the colonials, we would already know. Did you forget that Duncan came in the middle of the night looking for you?"

"No, I didn't," Ian said, his memory of hugging the chimney still fresh.

"Who do you think told Duncan about you?" Patrick asked. "It had to be Hart."

Ian remembered how close he had been to getting caught at Trudruffrin. "You're right," he admitted. "Hart was the only one who saw me."

"Of course, it was Hart," Patrick said, his voice getting louder. "He led the enemy on their parade through the city. What other proof do you need?"

Ian hesitated. "But it didn't seem staged. Abigail said nothing suspicious. Only the minister."

"Just because you overheard part of a conversation, doesn't mean we should believe it. And it doesn't mean we should trust Abigail, either."

Ian was quiet. He still loved Abigail. And she still loved him —he was sure of it. Only he could express it and she couldn't. At least that's what he kept telling himself.

"Assuming it is true, what turned Hart?" Patrick asked. "It can't be Missy Malone. They've been together for months. A year or more."

"I don't know," Ian admitted. "But you're right. It is too risky."

"Hart is a Loyalist, even if it's only come out since the occupation."

"He could only seek an opportunity."

Patrick shrugged. "He might need money. I'm sure his business is failing, especially with his ships stuck at port."

"What should I do?"

Patrick paused, pensive. "See what Abigail tells you. But

don't let on that you overheard anything. And definitely do not approach Hart."

"I'm sure she'll tell me the truth."

"You better be careful, son," Patrick warned. "She could be tricking you."

"She would never do that."

"Ian, you don't understand what I'm trying to tell you. They could be forcing her to do it."

49

The Indian Head Tavern, a competitor to both City Tavern and Fox and Demayne, was located at Front and Spruce, overlooking the docks. It wasn't as large as other taverns, and was smaller than the restaurants, but it had a nice view of the ships on the river, the sails unfurled for clippers that cut through the water, furled for larger ships, idle until the route to the sea was open, free of colonial interference.

Oliver Hart sat at a window table, looking past the street to the water, a dark blue jacket hugging his fit frame, a ruffled white collar sticking from it. Missy Malone sat beside him, her black curls spilling to her shoulders, blue eyes that twinkled in the light.

"Oliver, you look like you're in pain," Missy said as she studied her brooding companion.

"Not at all," he said. "You preferred to dine out, so we will."

"Do you intend to make it a miserable experience or can you try very hard to enjoy yourself. I know it's difficult, that you disdain social settings, but perhaps this once you can at least pretend you like it."

He smiled. "I will enjoy myself," he promised. "How can I not? I'm in your company."

"Very sweet," she said. "That was a very good try. If you continue with that behavior, we might still salvage our dinner and make it a pleasant experience."

Oliver sipped his wine. "I have nothing against dining out," he said, glancing at the docks as he spoke. "I'm only more comfortable in my own home."

"Yes, I know," she said. "You make that quite obvious. But it does no harm to leave it once in a while."

Hart looked away from the window and gazed around the room. A dozen couples were seated for dinner, most well-dressed, some of the city's wealthy. Others were tradesmen, wearing the best clothes they had, but not competing with the bankers, solicitors, and businessmen who formed the core of the city's elite.

"There's a British officer sitting in the back with the daughter of a man who runs a stall at the open market," Missy whispered.

"That didn't take long," Hart said. "The British have only been here a few weeks."

"I suppose it's likely. A city with a shortage of men, besieged by an army. Nature is bound to take its course."

The waitress arrived with their meal, steak with peas and potatoes. She set their plates down and placed some bread beside it. "Will you be needing anything else?"

"No, not right now," Hart said, but stopped her as she turned to go. "I do have a question."

"What might that be, sir?"

"Are you having problems getting supplies?" he asked. "Meat and potatoes, bread or beer?"

She leaned closer to him. "We are," she said, as if admitting something she shouldn't. "If those eating dinner only knew."

"How bad is it?" Missy asked. "I know there's less at the

market every time I go."

"Bread and beer are still available," the waitress said. "But everything else is growing scarce."

Hart looked at those around the room, the wealthy unaware while working families felt the shortage. "I think it'll ease soon."

"I sure hope so," the waitress said and left to serve other customers.

"I don't see how it can get better," Missy whispered.

"The British need to open up the river," he said, taking a forkful of food.

"If they don't do something soon, people will go hungry. Some may even starve."

"It's food now, which will get worse, but when winter arrives it'll be firewood."

"Unless something gets done," she said and sipped her wine.

Hart continued eating, occasionally glancing at the docks across the street.

"Are they your ships?" Missy asked abruptly.

He looked at her, startled, as if she broke his concentration. "Sorry?"

"Are they your ships?" she asked again.

"Yes," he muttered, looking out the window.

"Is that why you keep looking at them? You've been distracted since we got here."

He studied her for a moment, wondering whether to share what he had seen. Finally, he decided to do so. "Lean closer to me," he said. "Look at the largest ship, the one with the highest mast."

She moved toward him and looked across the road. "What are all those British soldiers doing by your ship?"

He turned to face her. "I've been wondering the same thing."

50

Abigail waited until just before eight a.m., put a white shawl over her blue dress, and left for the rectory. She had to warn Ian that everything he overheard about Hart was false, a trap laid by Duncan. She crossed the street, admiring the leaves changing to orange and red, painting a fiery portrait that complemented the urban landscape. Just as she reached the church, Ian pulled up in his wagon.

"Good morning," he said as he climbed down from the bench seat.

The church door opened abruptly, and Solomon stepped out. He looked at Abigail curiously and turned to Ian. "Mr. Blaine, how good to see you. I thought I would stop by and check your progress."

"Good morning, Pastor," Ian said.

Abigail tried to hide her surprise, wondering when Solomon had left the house. She thought he was in his study, working on his sermon. He must have gone out the back door.

"How is the new pew coming along?" Solomon asked.

"It's going well," Ian said. "Although it's challenging to duplicate the existing panels, built into the wall with such ornate moldings. But I'm sure you'll be pleased when it's completed."

Abigail tried to get his attention, but Ian turned and went to the rear of the wagon to remove several pieces of oak.

Solomon turned to Abigail. "What brings you here?"

She quickly thought of an excuse. "I came to get the donations to take over to the poorhouse."

"I didn't expect to see you," Solomon said, without saying why.

Ian approached, carrying the wood.

"Let me get the door for you," Solomon said.

"Thank you, sir," Ian said as he carried the wood inside.

"How long will it take to build?" Abigail asked, still trying to get Ian's attention.

"Three or four days," Ian said. He set the wood down in the space allotted.

"If you need assistance carrying anything, I could ask the soldiers lodged next to the altar," Abigail said. "I'm sure they would be willing to help."

"No, I'll be fine," he said. He took one of the boards and laid it on the floor. "That's how long the new pew will be."

Solomon studied the plank. "I think it will fit nicely."

"Mrs. St. Clair?" Ian asked.

Abigail made eye contact, giving him a frantic look. "It'll look quite handsome. I can imagine myself sitting there, enjoying one of Solomon's sermons."

Ian nodded slightly, perhaps to show he understood her subtle message. "It'll be the same height as the other pews."

"A splendid addition to the church," Solomon added.

"I think so," Ian said, eyeing the space. "Now if you can hold open the door, I'll bring in the rest of the wood."

"Of course," Solomon said, moving a few steps ahead.

Abigail leaned toward Ian. "We have to talk," she whispered.

"Did you say something, darling," Solomon asked, turning as he opened the door.

"I only warned Mr. Blaine to be careful," she said. "We wouldn't want him to injure himself."

Ian caught Abigail's gaze and winked subtly. He went to the wagon, removed more wood, and carried it into the church. He made a second trip for the remainder.

"There is something else I wanted to discuss," Solomon said when all the wood was inside. "After the new pew is finished, could I persuade you to do a little more volunteer work?"

Ian hesitated, but then smiled. "I would be delighted. What do you need?"

"I'm sure you have ointment or wood treatment," Solomon said. "Could you possibly polish the remaining pews?"

"Yes, of course," Ian replied. He glanced to the room beside the altar, housing the soldiers, almost as if he wondered why they couldn't do it.

"I think it will greatly add to the appearance," Solomon said.

"I'm sure it will," Ian agreed, as he opened the door. "I'm going to the shop now. I'll bring the polish back with me."

"I do appreciate it," Solomon said as they followed him outside.

Abigail moved close to Ian. "Meet me at the square," she whispered.

Solomon turned quickly, giving her a curious look.

51

Solomon glared at Abigail while Ian guided the wagon down the lane. "What did you say to Mr. Blaine?"

She shrugged. "I don't think I said anything."

"Just now," he said, his tone harsher. "As he was leaving."

She hesitated, appearing perplexed. "Goodbye, Mr. Blaine," she said. "Why, what did you think I said?"

"I thought I heard you say square."

Her heart thumped against her chest. How could she be so careless? "You heard me say bye or Blaine, rather than square," she said, trying to recover.

He stared at her for a moment, waiting for a reaction that never came. "Where are you going now?"

"To the poorhouse," she said and paused, as if struck with a thought. "Why don't you come with me? It's such a pleasant morning."

"I think I shall," he said, his gaze fixed on hers.

She lightly touched his arm. "How nice. I'll just be a minute. Let me collect the donations."

Abigail went inside the church and hurried down the aisle. It wasn't as bad as it seemed. She could collect the donations and take them to the poorhouse, chatting innocently with Solomon as she did so. Ian would wait at the Northeast Square, but when she didn't arrive, he would know something was wrong. Placating Solomon was most important, regardless of how much time Ian wasted.

She opened the lid to the wooden box that housed donations, finding several sets of children's clothes, two pairs of worn shoes, and a pair of spectacles. Canvas bags were left in the box with the donations, and she managed to fit everything into them. A moment later she stepped out of the church, Solomon standing by the entrance.

"I'm ready," she said as she started walking. She took a few steps and stopped. Solomon hadn't moved. "Are you coming?"

He stared at her curiously, a cynical glint in his eye. But a moment later he seemed to dismiss his suspicions. "I think I'll remain here. I want to prepare the altar for Sunday's service, and then go back to work on my sermon."

"Are you sure?" she asked. "It won't take long."

He considered her request. "No, thank you. But when you return, perhaps we'll take a stroll by the river."

She forced a smile, knowing she had little time to meet Ian. Solomon would be waiting. "I'll leave you to your work then," she said. She took another step and paused. "Solomon?"

"Yes," he said, his mind already on other matters.

"Are you sure you want to walk later?" she asked. "If not, I may stop at the hospital to see if I can offer any assistance,"

He hesitated. "Perhaps not. But I'll decide when you return." He went back inside, showing no interest in her activities.

She left the church and hurried down the street, destined for a quick stop at the poorhouse and then the square. She assumed Ian would take his wagon back to the shop, so she did have time. She acted as casual as she could to erase Solomon's suspicions, but just as she turned the corner on the narrow lane beside the rectory, cutting through to Third, she looked back and saw Solomon abruptly exit the church. He paused on the pavement, arms crossed, and watched her, but she wasn't sure why. She kept walking and, a few seconds later, could no longer see him.

The poorhouse was located at Fourth and Arch, which was on her way to the Northeast Square. Run by the Religious Society of Friends, they took donations from throughout the city, including many of the churches, and housed, clothed, and fed the poor, their numbers increasing with the occupation.

"Two satchels of clothing today," she said as she entered and gave the items to an older woman in a simple black dress.

"Every little bit helps," the woman said.

"I'll do better on my next visit," Abigail promised as she headed for the door. She meant it. Even if she had to donate some of her own belongings, which she had already done on several occasions. Many people needed assistance. The British favored those who supported them, ensuring they received most of the dwindling supplies. It created three tiers of society: the wealthy Loyalists, British officers, and the remainder, many of whom struggled to survive.

She hurried out the door and walked directly into Oliver Hart.

52

"Mr. Hart, how are you?" Abigail asked. She was confused. Was he following her? "I'm surprised to see you."

"Hello, Mrs. St. Clair. I brought some articles to donate," he said, pointing to his carriage. "These are trying times."

She thought his behavior odd but wasn't sure why. "Yes, they are indeed," she agreed. "I just donated some clothing left at the church."

"It's comforting to know our residents care for each other."

She hesitated. It was a cryptic statement. Was he criticizing the British, or complimenting the citizens? Or was he only showing a different facet of himself—one she had never before seen? "I come at least once a week. Sometimes twice. If no donations are left at the church, I tend to bring something of my own, so great is the need."

He looked at her for a moment, as if he wanted to say something but wasn't sure he should. "That's very kind—and much appreciated, I'm sure. Would you like me to take you back to the rectory?"

"Oh, no, but thank you," she replied. "I have errands to run."

He tipped his hat, bowed slightly, and started up the walk to the poorhouse entrance.

She wasn't sure if he told the truth. He carried no donations but did claim they were in the carriage. Maybe he posed a question to the staff before he brought them in. She waited until he was inside, made sure the carriage driver wasn't watching, and continued up Arch to Sixth.

She was wary of being followed—Duncan was watching her, Solomon was suspicious, and now, a chance meeting with Hart. She had to be cautious. As she walked, she checked for Hart's carriage, but didn't see it. Just to be sure she wasn't followed, she mingled among the soldiers that wandered near the square, paused to gaze in shop windows and, when convinced it was safe, she hurried to meet Ian.

When she arrived, she found more British tents than her prior visit. Rifles stacked in tripods were ready for use, soldiers sat beside smoldering campfires, some playing cards, others reading newspapers. Along Race St., beside the trees that bordered the pavement, a group of soldiers marched under an officer's watchful eye, their steps in unison, their heels thumping the cobblestone. But much of the square was filled with trees, and she wandered along the path that led to the interior.

Ian waited on a bench, watching people as they passed. He seemed like anyone else who visited the park, enjoying the fall day. He stood when she approached, and they walked together, furtively glancing at anyone nearby.

"I can only stay a minute," Abigail said. "It's safer that way."

"Agreed," Ian said. "Too many soldiers. Is Duncan still watching you?"

"I'm not sure," she said. "But I just saw Hart at the poorhouse. A coincidence, I suppose."

He stopped, eyes wide. "There are no coincidences."

She shrugged. "He was making a donation. He didn't follow me."

"Did you actually see him make the donation?"

She hesitated. "No, I didn't."

They were quiet as a British soldier came toward them, walking quickly and passing by.

"I think Solomon is suspicious, too," she said. "He heard me whispering to you at the church when I told you to meet me here. But he didn't hear what I said."

Ian frowned. "Maybe we need to avoid each other for a few days."

"I think it's wise," she agreed, as reluctant as he was. "Maybe while you build the church pew. Unless I stumble upon something significant."

They walked in silence, came to the end of the block, and turned, walking down a different path that intersected the square. Children played on a stretch of grass, running beside the white tents of the British soldiers.

"Whatever you overheard about Hart is wrong," she said. "It's the trap I warned you about. Do not approach him. They're waiting for you to do so and will immediately arrest you."

"I suspected as much," he said. "But why all the bother? Why are they so worried about me?"

"It's not from spying on the encampment," she said. "They seem convinced you were in Jersey. But they think there's something else. They just don't know what it is. Apparently General Howe is pressing his officers to identify colonial spies and he's promised Duncan a promotion if he finds one. Be wary of Solomon, also. I think they enlist his aid."

"All the more reason for us to be careful," he said, glancing around furtively "Do you have anything else?"

She paused, making sure no one was nearby. "Did you understand what I said about the attack on the Jersey fort?"

"Yes, but I need more details. And whatever you know about Fort Moultrie, which is on this side of the river, just south of the city."

"Duncan never speaks of Moultrie. I don't think he's involved. But he does talk about Mercer, the Jersey fort. I think he's planning the attack."

"Try to learn when it is, what troops will be sent, and the route they plan to take."

She was quiet for a moment, trying to interpret fragments of conversations she may have overheard. "I'll see what I can find out."

"Just be careful," he said. "If the minister, Hart, and Duncan are all watching you, they have a reason for doing so. Something you said or did."

"I've done nothing to arouse suspicion," she said. "I'm more concerned about you. They're determined to trap you. Hart is just the beginning. Something else will follow. Another trick, more sinister."

"They're wasting their time," he assured her.

"But they won't give up. They're convinced you're guilty. Even if you're not, Duncan is not above insisting you are, so he gets what he wants."

He was quiet for a moment, assessing risk. "The slightest mistake will doom us."

"We still need to communicate. Especially if I find you're in danger."

Ian paused as two soldiers approached. They nodded at Abigail, but only glanced at Ian. They stopped a few feet away and spoke in German.

"Hessians," Ian whispered. "German mercenaries."

"They might speak English," she hissed. "Be careful."

He eyed the pair, within earshot. "It's too dangerous for us to come here."

"Where else can we meet?"

He hesitated, as if trying to think of a safe haven in a city overrun with British soldiers and residents loyal to the Crown. "Anyone could be watching us," he said. "Duncan, Solomon, Hart, British soldiers, Loyalists. Even people both of us know."

"I fear the residents as much as the redcoats," she admitted. "Especially after seeing the posters warning citizens of colonial spies."

Two soldiers came down the path towards them. "We have to find someplace safer," he said. "I'm nervous with all the activity."

She glanced at the soldiers. "Let's meet at the library. I go there often. On Chestnut."

"It's close to the shop," he said warily.

"Just the next time, while we find other locations."

The soldiers walked down a narrow path between trees and shrubs and were soon gone, but Abigail noticed two gentlemen, well-dressed, standing near Ninth St., about forty feet away. They stared at her curiously. She realized many people knew her, even though she didn't recognize them. She was the minister's wife.

"Do you know those men?" Ian asked. "They keep looking at us."

"No, I don't. But I should go. I'm afraid I'm being watched."

As she turned to leave, he lightly grabbed her arm. "Why are you doing this?"

"Not now," she said and walked away.

53

It was late, the streets bare except for an occasional carriage, its wealthy owners returning from private parties or some other form of entertainment not available to most. Oliver Hart had attended a few, crammed with high-ranking British officers and the Loyalists who wanted to ensure they treated their occupiers well, assuming a new day had dawned. But Oliver Hart was a private man, and he preferred to be alone. These eccentricities made him mismatched for the social circuit and, a few weeks after the British arrived, he was no longer part of it.

Even when he did attend, depending on who hosted, he sometimes went alone. Many looked down upon Missy Malone, daughter to a carriage builder. If she wasn't with him, the inevitable matchmaking began, and well-meaning partygoers would try to find some available, aristocratic young lady— company he didn't want. A man more interested in work than family, at least for now, he didn't need another lady friend. He was quite happy with Missy and assumed, at some point, maybe once the war was over, they could easily end as man and wife.

He walked along Front St., observing idle ships rocking

gently with the current as a cutter passed close to the wharf, disturbing the tranquil water. Some of the smaller ships were still active, traveling the northern part of the Delaware River, moving commerce from farms and towns to the city. But it was minor compared to the burgeoning trade conducted when access to the ocean wasn't impeded by colonial forts.

An occasional British soldier passed on horseback, patrolling the streets, making their presence known. Most of the residents tolerated them, whether they agreed with the occupation or not, knowing their survival depended on it. Hart eyed the soldiers curiously, wondering where they came from —England, Scotland, Wales, or were they recruited from Canada.

He continued for several blocks, staying in the shadows. He then stopped and looked in all directions, ensuring no one was nearby, and went down a weathered wharf. Several times he stopped, waited a minute, and ensured he wasn't being watched. When satisfied he wasn't, he stole to the end of the pier where a two-masted ship was docked, its sails furled. Only a faint glimmer of light from the moon bathed the river and all around it.

Hart stood by the gangplank and waited, his gaze shifting from the wharf to Front St., an occasional carriage or horseback rider passing by. None noticed him and, even if they did, wouldn't recognize who he was or what he was doing.

After a moment, a man appeared on the ship. He wore black breeches, a black coat with a white shirt, only the collar showing, and a black tricorne. He came down the gangplank, his black hair dropping below the hat that crowned his head. As he approached Hart, he glanced down the dock, as if wary of intruders.

"Hello, Mr. Hart," he said, once he reached the wharf and stood in the shadows.

"Mr. Geraghty," Hart replied. "Was the route from upriver traveled with no opposition?"

"None took me for an enemy, and I blended easily with others under sail."

"Good," Hart said, pointing to the ship. "What does she carry?"

"Squash, corn, peas, and some wheat."

"Well done," Hart replied. He moved closer, ready to share a secret. "Soon the river will be clear, and a route to the sea available."

Geraghty looked down the dock. "How long before that occurs?"

"Shortly," Hart said. "By the end of the week."

"I had best be ready then."

54

Barnabas Stone stood on the corner of Walnut and Second with his British contact, Major Thaddeus Johnson. They had enjoyed a delicious dinner of shepherd's pie and two mugs of ale, their discussion focused on colonial spies—also an obsession of Colonel Duncan.

"I appreciate your assistance," Johnson said, as he prepared to leave. "As does General Howe."

"I'll have more when we meet again," Barnabas promised. "But those I named should lead to others."

Johnson tipped his hat and climbed into a waiting carriage. "Good day, Mr. Stone."

Barnabas hid a smile as the major drove away. He had given Johnson a nugget that would never be gold, just enough to preserve his reputation as a devout Loyalist and treasured contact. He had done the same with other British officers, whatever was needed to convince them he was a valuable source.

As the carriage hurried down Second, Barnabas saw Patrick and Ian Blaine walking along Walnut. Although they were coming for dinner, it gave them the opportunity to exchange information. The tavern offered a safe location, a public place where discussion went unnoticed or was assumed innocent. Even though the British knew the Blaines were acquaintances, Barnabas still minimized their public contact to avoid arousing suspicion.

"You're just in time for a fine dinner," Barnabas said loud enough for any to hear as he led them across the threshold.

They entered to find most tables occupied, the patrons enjoying a good meal. Noise from murmured conversations, laughter, and an occasional cough, drifted through the room, accented by the aroma of a freshly cooked meal. They hesitated, acting as if they couldn't decide where to sit, but eyed the table at the rear of the upper landing, against the back wall.

Dolly, Patrick's lady friend, approached while they stood by the entrance. "Hi, love," she said to Patrick and gave him a quick hug. "Hello, Ian. Your usual seats?"

"That would be nice," Patrick said. "Gives us some privacy."

Dolly gave him a light kiss on the cheek. "Quite a crowd tonight."

"Better full than empty," Barnabas said, scanning the room to locate the British soldiers. "I'll join you for a moment."

They followed Dolly to the landing and sat at the end table, facing the room.

"We're serving shepherd's pie and bread," Dolly said. "With beer or cider."

"I'll have the cider," Ian said.

"The same for me," Patrick added.

"Anything else?" she asked.

"Not just yet," Ian said.

"Coming right up," she said, and then paused. "I get off at eight, Patrick Blaine. Just in case you were wondering."

They laughed as Dolly walked away.

Barnabas leaned close. "I've only got a minute," he said, watching the entrance as more customers came in.

Ian studied those nearby. None posed a threat. "The information on Hart was false. It was the trap my source described."

"Just as we suspected," Patrick added.

Barnabas nodded, wondering what Duncan was doing. "Why all the effort to catch Ian?"

"Howe promised to make Duncan a general if he caught a major spy," Ian said.

"But why you?" Patrick asked. "They must have a reason." He hesitated, then looked at Ian warily. "Unless someone betrayed you."

Ian ignored him and leaned closer. "I think it's Hart. He has Duncan convinced I'm a threat."

"Whatever the reason, we need to outsmart them," Patrick said.

"We will," Barnabas promised. He paused as two Hessian soldiers came in and sat just below the landing, watched them a moment, and then continued. "Is there anything else I should know?"

"My source promised more on the Jersey attack," Ian said. "Routes, troop strengths—whatever she can find out."

Barnabas nodded. "That's good. We'll likely be outnumbered, so anything she provides will help."

"Assuming we can trust her," Patrick said.

Ian frowned. "I trust her. I have no reason not to."

"Just be cautious," Barnabas urged. "Especially since they suspect you. Be careful where you meet. Use different locations at different times."

"Assume the British are close, about to capture you at any moment," Patrick advised.

"It's safer to be afraid," Barnabas added.

Dolly came with their shepherd's pie, putting their plates on the table. "Here you go. There's plenty more if you're hungry."

"Thank you, ma'am," Ian said.

"Can you join us?" Patrick asked.

Dolly scanned the room, noticing some who waited for service. "Maybe for a minute," she said. "Let me wait on those soldiers by the door first."

As she scampered away, Barnabas looked at those nearby and leaned closer. "I've been thinking," he whispered. "If Hart can lay a trap for Ian, why can't we lay a trap for Hart?"

55

Abigail sat in the parlor doing needlepoint, another hobby she sometimes pursued, a talent surpassed only by her skill with a chessboard. The pattern showed two women in colonial garb, one blonde, the other brunette, and she smiled subtly as she worked it, thinking it resembled her and Missy Malone. She decided to give it to Missy as a gift when completed.

It was the first brisk evening of fall and, even though a light fire might be warranted, no effort was made to start one given the shortages that plagued the city. When winter arrived, if conditions didn't improve, firewood would become more precious than gold. She eyed Duncan and Solomon, glasses of port in their hands while they discussed British colonies around the globe and how different they were from America. She decided to broach the supply shortage, to see what response she might receive.

"With supplies already scarce, how much worse will it get before winter?" she asked, wondering if Duncan would reveal any secrets. "I fear firewood will be most difficult to obtain."

"You have nothing to fear, madam," Duncan said. "Nor do you, good sir."

"I rest assured," Abigail sighed, and turned her attention to needlepoint, acting as casually as she could. "It seems the Crown has plans to supply the city,"

"As soon as we take control of the river, supplies will again be plentiful," the Colonel said. "I promise."

"That day can't come soon enough," Abigail remarked, acting as if she only made casual conversation. "Because there certainly isn't enough. I must increase my efforts to obtain donations for the poor, for they surely need it."

"A temporary situation, I assure you," Duncan said.

"I don't understand your optimism," Solomon said. "If the problem was that easy to address, it should have already been solved. The citizens grow restless, as I'm sure you're aware. They fear starvation."

Duncan hesitated, giving the threat some thought, and sipped his wine. "The British navy sends gunboats up the Delaware as we speak," he boasted. "An attack on Fort Mercer in Jersey is imminent. We're using the Hessians, German mercenaries. Professional fighters."

Abigail was quiet, pretending to be absorbed in her needle-point, studying the pattern carefully, as if she sought perfection. But she listened intently, knowing what Duncan revealed could turn the tide of battle and ultimately determine who controlled the city.

"I haven't seen many Hessians in the city," Solomon said. "Certainly not at service."

"Most are camped on the road to Germantown," Duncan revealed. "But with the colonial threat minimized, we can divert them to Jersey."

Abigail looked at Duncan curiously. "Isn't there a good deal of coordination involved in an operation like that?" she asked, knowing his ego would make him explain it.

"Yes, there is," he said. He paused, as if to add drama. "I'm heavily involved."

"A talent few possess, I suspect," Solomon said.

"You are quite correct," Duncan replied, "Which is why General Howe entrusted me with the operation. But the tactics are quite simple. The Hessians march to the river, where Oliver Hart will have ferries and boats to transfer them to Coopers Ferry."

"But what of the horses and wagons needed to support them?" Abigail asked.

"Not much is needed," Duncan said. "Mercer is only a day's march from the ferry. Fortunately, a good road is available, aptly named the King's Highway."

"We shall anxiously await the results," Solomon said, glancing at Abigail, impressed by Duncan's explanation. "As will the citizens of the city."

"A single battle will clear the river?" Abigail asked.

"Minor skirmishes may follow," Duncan said. "But victory provides the access needed."

"And the city will then be fed and clothed?" Abigail asked.

Duncan nodded. "The army and our friends will be fed and clothed," he clarified. "I don't care about anyone else."

56

A bigail fixed the red ribbon on her window sash, even though it was risky. But she knew if Ian was seen in the area, he could claim he was working at the church, or getting measurements for work in the shop. Even though she had seen him two days before, they had to meet again. The information she had, an imminent attack on Fort Mercer, had to be shared.

She peeked from the window but didn't see if he came by. Just before 9 a.m., she hurried from her room and eased down the steps. She was careful leaving the house, creeping up to Solomon's study, listening to him moving about, either at his desk reconciling church business or working on his sermon. When satisfied he was occupied, she tiptoed to the front door and stepped out, gently closing it behind her.

Once out of the house, and wary of being followed, she took a different path and turned toward the river. She went down to Front St. walked past the docks, stacks of crates sitting on the shore, boats harbored, their sails down. When she reached Chestnut, she turned away from the river, having almost completed a full circle, while cautiously looking behind her, and hurried to Carpenter's Hall, the library on the second floor.

It was more than a house for books. It was also a small museum. Bookshelves were complimented by displays of antique glass, coins, old maps, fossils, a fauna exhibit—much of which had been donated by members of the Continental Congress. She strolled through, eyeing the exhibits, and found a section devoted to ancient history. She took *Plutarch's Lives* from the shelf, a popular work that compared the lives of ancient Greeks to Romans. After only a few moments, she became so immersed in the pages that she neglected to notice Ian as he cautiously crept up beside her.

"This is too dangerous," he hissed. "There's a British officer in the next row."

She kept her eyes trained on the book. "I had to see you."

"What happened?"

She put the book back on the shelf, gauged their distance from the officer, and walked farther down the aisle.

Ian followed, a few steps behind her. He approached casually, removing a book from the lower shelf, just behind her.

"An attack on Fort Mercer is imminent," she whispered. "By both land and sea. They're using the Hessians, German mercenaries."

"This isn't a trap, is it?" he asked.

A woman in a red dress and a white bonnet came toward them, eyeing the volumes on the shelves. She walked between them and continued, pausing at the end of the aisle. Abigail glanced at her curiously. Anyone could spy for the British, man or woman. She eyed the woman a moment more and, when she showed more interest in books than them, Abigail focused on Ian.

"No, it's not a trap," she said. "It was discussed at the rectory, a solution to the supply shortage."

"But it could have been intentional, like the trap laid for me."

She hesitated, reliving the conversation. Most of the discussion had been Duncan describing his skill in preparing attacks. "It's valid information," she assured him. "I'm certain."

He seemed satisfied. "We still have to be careful."

The woman who had passed came toward them again. She stopped, fifteen feet away, and studied Abigail, almost comically, as if suspecting she did something she shouldn't be doing. When Abigail met her gaze, the woman turned and left, moving to a different section.

"This is as dangerous as the square," Abigail muttered. "Many know me as the minister's wife."

Ian scanned the aisle. "We should hurry. What else do you know about the attack?"

She took a book from the shelf and opened it, leaning close to him as if showing him something. She spoke softly. "The Hessians camped on Germantown Road will march to the river. Oliver Hart will organize an assortment of ships to take them to Coopers Ferry."

"Do you know the date?"

"No, but it's very soon," she said. "I didn't want to delay, like I did with the information I had on Germantown."

"Do you know their route to Mercer?"

She paged through the volume. "They intend to march down the King's Highway."

"I know it," Ian said, pausing, as if the image of the road passed through his mind. Someone moved about in the aisle behind them. "We should go. Anything else?"

"I saw ammunition stockpiled on Front St. I don't know it's purpose."

"It's either staged to defend the city or will be used in the upcoming attack."

They were interrupted by footsteps, boots thumping on hardwood floors. A British officer turned the corner at the end of the aisle and walked toward them. He paused a few feet away, scanning the shelf.

Abigail froze, not sure what to do. If she walked away and Ian followed, it might seem suspicious. Or maybe the officer would assume they were a young couple visiting the library. But she couldn't take that chance. She moved a few feet away, bent to the bottom shelf, and removed a book about economics —commerce between nations.

Ian remained where he was, scanning the shelf and then selecting a book. To any observer they seemed to innocently search for something to read, maybe together, maybe not.

She glanced at the officer. He seemed to look for a specific book, but how could she know? His right index finger traveled the spines that graced the shelf. He removed a volume, fanned through it briefly and returned it. He took a few steps more, removed another book from the shelf, and studied it more intently than the last.

Abigail glanced at her book. She was certain the soldier was watching. Even if he wasn't, it was still a risk she shouldn't take. She returned her book to the shelf and casually walked toward the soldier, passing Ian as she did so.

"I have to go," she whispered.

She went to the end of the aisle. "Excuse me," she said, the soldier blocking her path.

"Sorry," he said, looking up from the book. He moved forward and, as she walked by, he returned to the book.

She walked around the end of the aisle, toward the exit. Nodding to the librarian as she left, she started down the steps. She then paused, waiting to see if Ian followed.

He arrived a moment later.

"I didn't expect so many people," she said.

"We can't come here again. Where else do you go? Any shopping?"

"Rarely," Abigail said. "Anna usually goes."

"Do you have a routine?"

She hesitated, walking down the steps. "Saturday, I planned on stopping at the bookstore."

"Which one?"

"Bells or Honey & Mouse."

Ian looked at her curiously, perhaps seeing something he hadn't seen before. "Doesn't Bells have books for men?" he asked. "Mainly military history?"

"Woman can read, too," she said. "Regardless of the topic."

"I'm impressed."

She smiled. "I also go to the poorhouse on Fourth St. and the hospital at the Presbyterian Church."

"I'll meet you at Bells on Saturday."

"What time?" she asked. "We have to ensure we don't see the same people when we meet."

Ian nodded, realizing she was right. "Ten a.m."

She was leery. "We should meet in different places on different days. If we develop a routine, someone will notice."

He leaned closer. "I want to see you in private."

She smiled, more from the memory than the offer. "Aren't those days behind us?"

57

The following morning, just past 8:30, Abigail walked to Pine Street and went to the Presbyterian Church, now serving as a hospital. She had stopped to see the baker on the way, and carried several loaves of freshly baked bread, still warm, and one of the few items still readily available.

As she entered the church, she found conditions similar to her last visit. Pews removed, the broken wood stacked near the entrance, wounded and sick British to the left, comfortable on their cots, Patriots laying on threadbare blankets on the right. The number of afflicted was about the same, although a few spaces were empty among the colonials.

She had barely taken a dozen steps when Tommy Scanlon, the young redcoat she had met on her initial visit, came to greet her. "Good day, Mrs. St. Clair."

"Hello, Tommy, how are you?"

"I'm well," he replied. "Did you bring bread for the men?"

"I did," she said. "I suspect whatever they get is not as fresh as this. Can you help me hand it out?"

"Yes, of course."

She gave him some of the loaves. "You tend to the British, I'll hand them out to the colonials."

Tommy started breaking bread, handing chunks to the British.

Abigail eyed the sick and wounded lying on the hardwood floor, probably close to thirty, and broke a piece of bread for each. Some men were asleep, or barely conscious, and she skipped them. She was sad, knowing some might be gone by her next visit—not strong enough to survive, or recovered and sent to a prison ship. After she had given fresh bread to all who wanted it, she fetched a bucket and went to the well for water. She was filling the Patriots' cups when a man in uniform approached. He was tall and thin, his white hair long and curly, round spectacles perched on his nose.

"Who are you, and what do you think you're doing?" he asked.

She rose, not intimidated, and faced him. "I'm Abigail St. Clair, the minister's wife. I come once a week to see the wounded."

"Ah, yes, so Scanlon told me. I'm the surgeon, Dr. Wheatley."

"I'm pleased to meet you," Abigail said, amused by the doctor's frosty demeanor. "I do have a pass from Colonel Duncan, should you need to see it."

The glare on his face faded, and his tone got softer. "No, that won't be necessary. But please refrain from changing bandages, as I'm told you did on one occasion."

She studied him for a moment before she replied. "Dr. Wheatley, I changed the bandages because they were badly soiled. Otherwise, I would not have interfered."

"Yes, of course," he said, not expecting to be challenged. "It's just that there's a limited supply."

She leaned closer. "Should you not have enough, please

advise me," she said. "I will ensure you get what you need. Even if accomplished through church donations."

His eyes widened, surprised by her determination. "Thank you, Mrs. St. Clair," he said. "I do appreciate your efforts."

She left the hospital thirty minutes later, resisting the urge to go farther west on Pine to see her childhood home. She had walked less than half a block when a carriage pulled to the side of the road. The window was opened, and Colonel Duncan's head appeared.

"Mrs. St. Clair," he called. "Allow me to take you back to the rectory."

She hesitated, having no desire to ride with him. But she knew she couldn't decline. "Thank you, Colonel," she said as she approached the carriage. "That's very kind of you."

She stepped in and sat on the seat across from him, even though he had moved to one side, expecting her to sit beside him.

"Visiting the wounded?" he asked.

She nodded. "I try to come at least once a week."

"I'm sure it's appreciated."

"I think so. If I can make a difference in their lives, even a small one, then it's a morning well spent."

"I'm sure it is," he said. He leaned toward the window and pointed to a three-story brick townhouse. "Who lives there?"

She glanced out the window and shrugged. "I don't know."

"Who do you know that lives on this street?"

She hesitated and decided not to share the location of her childhood home. As they continued, brick and wood-frame houses passing, she realized she had to identify some former acquaintances or risk both anger and suspicion.

"As I recall," she said, pointing to a brick house, "Mr. Telford who works at the post office lives there."

"Friend or foe?"

She smiled, acting as innocent as she could. "Colonel, I

really don't know. When I left the city, politics wasn't counted as a major interest. I can identify individuals who I remember, but likely won't know their allegiance."

"Keep showing me," he grumbled.

As they reached the next block, she pointed to a wood-frame house, squeezed between two brick buildings. "An old friend of mine, Lizzy James, used to live in that house," she said, reminiscing for a moment. "But I haven't seen her since my return. I suspect she probably married and moved away."

Abigail identified those she knew for the remainder of the ride to the rectory. When their journey came to a close, she had named seven or eight people from her past but provided little information that Duncan could use. But she knew it was only the beginning. Their efforts would continue. He would demand much more the next time.

58

Barnabas entered the cabinet shop, saw the showroom empty, and called to the back room. "Patrick, Ian. It's Barnabas."

A few seconds later, Ian appeared in the doorway. "Hello, Barnabas. Come on back."

Barnabas went to the shop, ducking slightly to get in the doorway, his height equal to the frame.

"Is something wrong?" Patrick asked as he set a wood chisel down on a work table and wiped his hands with a rag.

Barnabas came closer. "Given the information that Ian provided, we warned those at Fort Mercer to prepare for an imminent attack."

"Is someone watching the Hessians?" Patrick asked. "If what we learned is true, we'll know the assault is underway as soon as they march to the river."

Barnabas nodded. "The Hessians on Germantown Road were preparing to march this morning. I have men watching the river to see where the ferries are sent."

"Will they use the Arch St. terminal?" Ian asked.

"I suspect they'll use the ferries and any other ships they can muster."

"Then they'll likely land at Cooper's Ferry," Patrick said. "Just as Ian said."

"What about the British ships?" Ian asked.

"We've confirmed gunboats coming upriver," Barnabas said.

"An attack by land and sea," Patrick muttered. "It'll be a difficult fight."

"We're ready," Barnabas said. "We have men stationed up the coast, runners to inform those at Fort Mercer when and where the Hessians land."

"Can anything else be done in Jersey?" Ian asked.

"We're dismantling the bridge on the King's Highway at Timber Creek," Barnabas said. "That should make a mess of things for the redcoats."

Patrick turned to Ian. "I hope we can rely on your source, and that this isn't a trap."

"It was detailed information," Barnabas interjected. "Much better than we normally get."

"But men are risking their lives based on what she said," Patrick countered. "She had better be right."

"Preparation is no crime," Ian said. "We know an attack is coming, whether timed as described or not."

"But can we trust her?" Barnabas asked.

"Yes, I think so," Ian replied. "This will prove it."

"She still hasn't provided a motive," Patrick said. "Which makes me suspicious."

"No, she hasn't," Ian admitted. "But it must be a good one. She's at risk, too. Even more than we are."

"So far, everything she said seems likely to happen," Barnabas said. "Hessians on the march, British gunboats. But we won't know for sure that the attack is coming until we see the Hessians board ships to Jersey."

"Has she mentioned anything else?" Patrick asked.

Ian thought for a moment. "She did see ammunition stock-piled on Front Street."

"Could that be for the invasion?" Patrick asked.

"I don't think so," Barnabas replied. "It's for the defense of the city, should the colonials launch an attack. I've seen stock-piles in other locations as well."

Barnabas stepped to the threshold and looked to the front of the shop, out the window onto Chestnut. A handful of British soldiers were standing on the pavement. "There's a group of redcoats in front of the store."

Patrick stepped beside him. "Looks innocent."

"Not that it is," Ian muttered.

"I had best be going," Barnabas said, eyeing the soldiers warily. "I'll use the back door. Is there anything else?"

"Are we setting a trap for Hart?" Ian asked.

"We should," Barnabas said. "I have a plan we can use."

"What are we going to tell him?" Patrick asked.

"I thought we could create fake orders, with maps, that direct Washington to leave Valley Forge and attack New York. Then we'll feed it to Hart."

"How do we get it to him?" Ian asked.

Barnabas was quiet for a moment. "Let's make sure we can trust your source. If we can, we'll deliver the information through her."

59

Two days later, Abigail was sitting in the parlor, reading *The Vicar of Wakefield* by the Irish writer Oliver Goldsmith, a second book lying on the couch beside her, when Colonel Duncan stormed in the front door, slamming it closed behind him. He wore an angry scowl and cast her a look of disdain.

She was alarmed. She had never seen him so angry before. "Is everything all right, Colonel?"

"No, it isn't," he growled. "Where's the minister?"

"Working on his sermon."

"Solomon," he called.

A moment later the minister appeared, holding some papers in his hand, and peering through his glasses. "What's wrong?" he asked warily.

"The Hessians were badly defeated at Fort Mercer yesterday," Duncan said.

Abigail looked at Solomon, her eyes wide, and then to the colonel. "Were our forces not prepared?"

"Our forces are always prepared," Duncan replied bitterly.

"How did a misfit band of farmers defeat them?" Solomon asked with amazement.

"Obviously, the rebels were warned," Duncan said. "The main bridge on our attack route was dismantled before we got there, causing a significant detour that added to our defeat."

"Had a trap been set?" Solomon asked.

Duncan was quiet for a moment. "No, not a trap," he said. "But those in the fort were prepared. The rebels even had gunboats staged along the river."

"Our navy was also defeated?" Abigail asked.

"Yes, "Duncan replied with disgust. "Several ships were lost."

"What a tragedy," she said softly, although she was secretly pleased.

Duncan glared at her for a moment, as if struck with a thought, but seemed to dismiss it. "It was almost as if they were waiting for us," he muttered.

"It does seem that treachery was afoot," Solomon said.

"It was, I'm sure," Duncan replied. "Now I only need to determine who's responsible. Not only was our army beaten, but my promised promotion is impacted by our defeat. Someone will pay the price for that, I assure you."

Abigail debated joining the discussion, risking Duncan's wrath, to plant doubt where it was needed most. "Colonel, wouldn't you expect them to be prepared?"

"Not to that degree."

"But, Colonel," she continued, perhaps overstepping her bounds. "If even a military novice like me can see the importance of the fort, and its impact on getting supplies to Philadelphia if lost, don't you think the colonials would defend it vigorously?"

"It was more than that," he mumbled. "Especially with the bridge dismantled. They knew when we were coming and how we were getting there."

"Maybe your troops were observed," she said, continuing the debate to remove any suspicion he might have of her. "Especially when they crossed the river."

Duncan looked at her curiously. "Are you schooled in military matters, madam?"

She wasn't about to permit a condescending lecture. "No, Colonel, I'm not. Certainly not as learned as you."

"Then perhaps—"

"But I do read books," she said, interrupting him. "It's an obsession. Unfortunately, much of the available reading material has a military theme."

Duncan snatched her book from the table, looking at the title. "*The Vicar of Wakefield* is not military material, madam."

Abigail looked at him crossly and picked up her second book, lying on the cushion beside her, and held it up for him to see. "*Marlborough at Blenheim*," she said. "The War of the Spanish Succession"

Duncan was surprised. He nodded with respect. "My apologies, Mrs. St. Clair," he said. "I'm impressed."

"It's the natural move to make," she continued. "Like chess. You do play chess, don't you, Colonel?"

"Occasionally," Duncan mumbled. "But I'm hardly a master."

"Abigail and I play frequently," Solomon said. He winked at Duncan. "Although she always wins."

"The strategy is much the same," she explained. "Your forces took Philadelphia. But you must supply both the residents and your army. Your next move would be to take control of the river. You really have no choice."

Duncan studied her closely, seeing more than a minister's wife. "Perhaps, you are correct, madam," he conceded.

"Just as I suspect the British would like to gain control of the Hudson River in New York," Abigail continued.

Duncan eyed her suspiciously, as if she might be more connected to British leaders than he was.

"Why do you want the Hudson?" Abigail asked rhetorically. "Because you can split New England from the rest of colonies."

"I'm quite impressed, Mrs. St. Clair," Duncan admitted. "I should make you an advisor. You may know more than those I have."

She laughed lightly. "I might like that," she replied, knowing it wasn't possible. "But I would only suggest, sir, that the enemy prepared for your most obvious action."

Duncan eyed her warily, as if he had severely underestimated a potential adversary.

His expression didn't go unnoticed by Abigail.

60

On Saturday morning, Abigail went to meet Ian at Bells book store. Solomon was immersed in a theological paper and showed no interest in accompanying her. He never did. Even though he had many religious and philosophy books that he seemed to enjoy.

She walked to the store quickly, occasionally stopping to gaze in shop windows. When she passed the cobbler, she remembered that her shoes were in need of repair, and she made a mental note to stop when she had time. Philadelphia was a pleasant city—cobblestone streets, brick buildings, trees along the pavement that showered the streets in shade, the orange and red leaves that remained gradually falling to the ground. She was glad to be back. She had missed it, and she liked it much more than New York.

She entered the book store, a small shop with fifteen or twenty rows of books and greeted the clerk. "Good morning," she said to the middle-aged man who sat behind the counter, reading the *Pennsylvania Ledger*.

"Good morning, ma'am," the clerk replied.

Abigail went further back in the store, acting as if she knew exactly what she was looking for. She took one book off the shelf that she intended to purchase, having seen it on a prior visit, and started to examine what was on the shelves, looking at the spines to search for titles she might be interested in reading. She was there about five minutes when she heard the door open and close.

Ian came in, greeted the clerk, and wandered around the store before entering the same aisle as Abigail. He paused, looking into the adjoining aisles. When satisfied no one was nearby, he approached her.

She watched as he came near, his eyes always bright when he saw her. "I suppose you know what happened at Fort Mercer," she whispered.

"Yes, thanks for your help. It may have turned the tide."

"The army was probably prepared anyway."

"I'm sure they were," he said. "But your warning let us disable the bridge."

"Do you suspect another attack?"

Ian nodded. "It'll get much worse now."

"What do you mean?"

"The British will put all their resources into taking the fort," he said. "Since an attack from the north was defeated, I suspect they'll land forces in the south, but in overwhelming numbers."

The door opened and someone walked in, an older man, who started a discussion with the proprietor. Given the way they were chatting, they seemed to be friends.

Abigail paused, listening. "Where can we meet?" she asked. "We can't come here too often."

He paused for a moment, listening to the conversation at the front desk, ensuring it was genuine. He was about to speak when the door opened again.

"Wait a minute," she whispered.

She walked down the aisle and into another, the bookshelves arranged like a maze. When she got closer to the counter, she saw a British soldier a few aisles over. She pretended to browse the books on the shelves but made her way back to Ian.

"British," she whispered. "I should go."

He lightly grabbed her arm. "Can I see you tomorrow?"

She hesitated. "We shouldn't see each other too often. It's bad for both of us."

"Just to say hello," he coaxed. "Maybe you'll have more information."

She held her finger to her lips, signaling for him to be silent. The British soldier was asking the proprietor for help. They talked for a moment, and then went to the other end of the store.

"Just for a few minutes," she agreed. "Like today."

He waited, listening to the discussion on the other side of the store. "Come to my carriage house tomorrow at 9 a.m. I'm sure you remember it. Go down Third but use the alley between the watchmaker and the baker. I'll have the door open, waiting for you."

She turned and her gaze met his, each showing what shouldn't be seen, feelings that never waned, even though they should have. "Ian, it seems dangerous, meeting there."

"No, it'll be all right," he assured her. "Just make sure no one sees you."

She was quiet for a moment, considering the risk, the alibi she would have to invent should Solomon question her. "I'll only come for a few minutes," she decided. "What about residents or shopkeepers looking from windows?"

"They won't pay any attention," he said. "But I'll check anyway, and you should, too. If you see anything suspicious, just walk past."

"All right," she said, turning to go. She reached for his hand and squeezed it tightly. "I'll try to get more information."

"We want to set a trap for Hart. If I give you false information, can you somehow convey it?"

She frowned, a bit reluctant. "I'm not sure. It depends what it is."

"But a possibility?"

"I have to think about it," she said, uncertain. "Is there anything else?"

He paused to scan the store. The proprietor had returned to the counter and the soldier wandered the aisles. He looked at Abigail, as if he remembered something. "I need to know why you're doing this," he said. "What's your motive?"

She hesitated, gazed in his eyes for a moment, but decided it wasn't the time. "I'll tell you tomorrow," she said and briskly walked away.

61

Oliver Hart walked down Front St. toward Global Shipping, his company's office, when a carriage escorted by British soldiers on horseback came to a halt beside him. The redcoat driving got down from the bench and opened the door.

Colonel Alexander Duncan stepped out. "Good morning, Mr. Hart."

"Colonel," Hart said tersely, reminded of the British soldiers searching through his cargo when he dined with Missy Malone.

"A word please," Duncan said, nodding to a woman who passed.

"Of course," Hart said, walking from the pavement onto a nearby pier. He went to the railing and leaned on it, watching the water wash the shore.

Duncan stood beside him. When he was sure no one was near, he spoke. "We attacked the Jersey fort that controls the river. By both land and sea."

Hart turned to face him. "And the result?"

"A devastating defeat."

Hart looked back at the water. He wasn't a military man, and he knew there were a dozen things that could have gone wrong, but nothing was more important than gaining control of the river. The whole city would starve if they didn't—including the British army.

"Another attempt is already planned," Duncan continued.

"Why did the attack fail?"

"They either knew we were coming or were better prepared than we anticipated."

"Or both," Hart said. "Regardless, the outcome is devastating to the city."

"And to your business," Duncan said coldly. "Is that what has you most concerned?"

Hart turned to meet Duncan's gaze. He was tired of his arrogance. "What has me most concerned is a partner that searches my cargo."

Duncan gave him a confused look. "What are you talking about?"

"I was having dinner the other day, across the street from one of my wharfs."

"What does that have to do with me?"

"Your soldiers searched cargo offloaded from one of my ships," Hart said. "Scribbling notes like they took inventory."

Duncan was quiet for a moment, but then shrugged. "Only keeping a partner honest. As I told you once, my family came close to bankruptcy because the colonials stole a ship's cargo. I won't be robbed again."

"My business is based on trust."

"Verification is good for all involved," Duncan countered.

"Understood," Hart replied curtly. "Then I suppose we should complete our transaction."

Duncan looked at his carriage, soldiers waiting for his return. The ships on the wharf were idle, no one walked the pier. He wasn't concerned about passing pedestrians.

Hart reached into his pocket and withdrew a folded stack of money. He meticulously counted some bills under Duncan's watchful eye and handed them to the colonel. "Is that what you've been waiting for?"

Duncan took the bills and counted them. "Yes, it is," he said. "The amount received matches the inventory my soldiers recorded. You're an honest man, Mr. Hart."

"What are you two gentlemen doing on this fine day?" a female voice called

Hart turned abruptly to find Abigail approaching. "Mrs. St. Clair," he said with a nod. "It's nice to see you."

"What are you doing here?" Duncan asked, his eyes showing anger, even though a smile was pasted on his face.

She looked at him curiously and held up a book. "I'm returning from Bells," she said. "I thought I'd take the long way back and stroll along the river."

"It is a pleasant morning," Hart said, gazing up at a cloudless sky.

"A bit brisk perhaps, but enjoyable just the same," she replied.

"How did you manage to find us?" Duncan asked sharply.

"I saw Missy on Locust St., about to enter a clothing store," Abigail said. "She asked that if I saw Mr. Hart, to tell him that she's slightly delayed."

"Thank you, Mrs. St. Clair," Hart said. "For delivering the message."

"You're most welcome," she said, eyeing them strangely. "I'll be on my way. Good day gentlemen."

62

A bigail left Hart and Duncan on the dock. She wasn't sure what she interrupted, but Duncan didn't appreciate it. Apparently, she saw something she shouldn't. She just didn't know what it was.

She walked to the end of the pier and onto Front St. and saw Missy Malone approaching, her black curls blowing in the breeze. "Hi Missy, I gave Oliver your message."

"Thank you, I wasn't detained as long as I expected." Missy said. "I considered buying the dress in the window, the green one, but chose not to." She looked at the British carriage, the soldiers standing beside it, and then farther down the dock.

"It's Colonel Duncan," Abigail said, answering the unasked question.

"Is Oliver in some sort of trouble?" Missy asked warily.

"I don't think so," Abigail replied. She looked back at Hart and Duncan, still where she had left them. The colonel then started walking to his carriage.

"Duncan is leaving," Missy said. "Should I stay here until he's gone?"

"No, I don't think so. They were only talking when I got there. Something about validating cargo."

"Stay with me a minute," Missy requested. "I'll wait until Duncan leaves."

They watched while Duncan approached his carriage. He stepped in and continued north down Front St., soldiers on horseback flanking him.

"Thank you," Missy said, lightly touching Abigail's arm. "I don't like Duncan much."

Abigail wanted to clarify Missy's cryptic messages from other meetings, but she wasn't sure what to say. She leaned close and started by sharing a secret. "At least you don't have to live with him."

Missy smiled. "I can't even imagine. Nor would I want to." She started to walk away, but paused and returned, as if she had something to share.

Abigail watched her curiously. "Is something wrong?"

Missy furtively glanced in all directions and leaned close to Abigail. "Be very careful," she whispered. "They're all watching you, even those you wouldn't suspect. They're watching Ian too." She abruptly walked away.

Abigail watched as Missy went down the dock. It was an ominous message, probably something Hart had shared. Abigail just wasn't sure what to do about it.

She watched Hart as he greeted Missy. They hugged, Hart smiled, and Abigail realized there was much more to him than the cold man who came to supper. He lived, he loved, and he enjoyed life, just as everyone else did. He just sometimes acted as if he didn't.

She made her way to the rectory, cutting through the open market. Many bays were empty or had few goods due to supply shortages. Only two-thirds of the stalls were stocked, but shoppers still milled about, purchasing fruit and vegetables, flour and meat, and even some live animals—goats and chickens. She realized if the British didn't soon take the Jersey fort, as Hart often discussed at dinner, it would be a long cruel winter. She continued on, turning down Second to the rectory.

Solomon was leaving as she arrived. "There you are," he said as he came down the steps. "I was wondering where you were."

She held up her book. "I got this for you," she said. "I thought it might be a nice addition to your collection."

He looked at her with surprise. "Abigail, that's so kind of you," he said as he took the book, *A History of Ancient Philosophy*. "I can't wait to read this."

"I'll put it in your study."

"Yes, please do," he said. "I'll be over at the church."

"Is anything wrong?" she asked, noting his expression. He looked distant, consumed with a thought he couldn't dismiss.

"One of the British officers made a startling observation," he stammered. "I'm going to speak to him now."

"What did he see?"

Solomon hesitated, as if fact might seem like fiction. "The officer claimed that, on the day they moved their belongings into the church, he saw a minister outside near the window, who then walked through the cemetery."

She hesitated, knowing it was Ian in disguise. But she had to make Solomon think it was innocent. "It was likely you exploring the grounds."

"No, he's certain it wasn't me. He thought the church had two ministers."

"Who else could it be?" she asked.

"I don't know," he said. "It makes no sense at all."

She acted confused. "How could he be so certain it wasn't you?"

Solomon touched his curly hair. "He claimed the minister

wore a hat with a broad brim, but he clearly saw that he had brown hair in a ponytail. Nothing like mine."

"Curious," Abigail said, acting perplexed. "I don't know who it could have been."

"It's a mystery we need to solve," Solomon said gravely.

63

Shortly before 9 a.m., Ian left the shop and walked onto the rear of his property, passed the lean-to, a long narrow building with a short roof and open front where they stored lumber. A quick glance at neighboring buildings showed no one watching, so he continued. The carriage house sat on the edge of the property, off the alley that ran to Third and skewed to one side so wagons had access to deliver wood and furniture.

He entered the rear, through a narrow stable that housed two horses, and into the main part of the building. A wagon for their business was against the far wall, a rarely used carriage beside it. Sometimes Patrick took the carriage out for rides with Dolly, but Ian couldn't remember the last time he had used it.

He walked through the building, opened the door that led to the alley, and stepped outside. He could see Third St. from where he stood, and he scanned the windows of nearby houses and shops. A wagon passed on the road, carrying produce, and two British soldiers galloped by on horseback. A few pedestrians approached, a man who went into the watchmaker's shop, and a family that paused to look in the bakery window.

A moment later, Abigail came down Third. She moved at a

normal pace, gazing to her left and right, as if admiring the townhouses, shops of various businesses on the bottom floor. She paused a few doors down and looked in the window of a store that sold lace—from doilies to shawls—and then continued, eyeing stores across the street. She pretended not to care about passing British soldiers, nodded to a man who walked by with a young boy, maybe his grandson, and strolled down the street as if she had no specific destination.

When she reached the alley, she turned abruptly and walked briskly to the open door of the carriage house. She made eye contact with Ian as he waited, turned to scan the area one more time, and quickened her pace. Once she was inside, Ian closed the door.

The building was spacious and, although it housed both the wagon and carriage, there was ample room remaining. They could hear the horses shuffling in the stable behind it, and beyond that, where another set of doors exited off to one side, they could see the lean-to housing wood, stretching all the way to the shop.

"Come to the back," Ian said, guiding her to the rear of the building. "Was anyone watching you?"

"No," she said, glancing around nervously. "I've been checking since I left the rectory."

He was tempted to hug her but didn't. He grasped her hand and squeezed it to show how happy he was to see her. "I was afraid you wouldn't come."

"I shouldn't have," she said, not making eye contact. "It's risky. I'm only staying a minute."

Ian came closer. He touched her chin lightly, turned her face to his, and looked in her eyes. "This is more than spying, isn't it?"

"Ian, don't," she said, turning away. "We can't act like lovesick teenagers. We're spying on the Crown and risking our lives to do it."

He backed away. She was right. Even though he didn't want to admit it. He kept stepping into yesterday. But he needed to remain in the present. Especially if he wanted to stay alive.

"A soldier at the church saw you dressed as a minister on the day you made your escape," she said.

Ian was alarmed. "He knows it was me?"

"No, he doesn't know anything. He thought there were two ministers and mentioned something to Solomon."

"Is Solomon suspicious?"

"I'm sure he is," she said. "But he'll never know who it was. It's the least of our worries, I would think."

Ian relaxed. "Do you have anything else?"

"Duncan is certain the Patriots knew about the attack on Fort Mercer. He thinks he was betrayed. Missy Malone warned me that I'm being watched. So are you. But not by those most obvious."

Ian frowned. "It's Hart," he said. "He probably told Missy."

She paused. "It's more than Hart. She's cryptic, afraid to commit without knowing my loyalties, but my impression was that it's someone we would never suspect."

Ian was quiet for a moment, thinking. "She's suggesting someone close?" he asked, thoughts drifting beyond Hart and Duncan to friends and associates.

"I think that's what she was trying to tell me," Abigail said. "But Duncan suspects us. I'm sure he's convinced one of us had something to do with the Jersey fort."

"Does he have any proof?"

"No, not that I know of," she said. "I told him an attack on the fort was expected, as anyone versed in military matters would know."

He smiled. "Are you versed in military matters?" he asked, moving closer.

She hesitated. "I could ward off an enemy, if I had the need."

"And unwelcome advances?" he asked.

"Should any be offered."

He kissed her lightly on the lips. Then more forcefully, lingering.

She pulled away. "I must go," she said. "We shouldn't be doing this."

He noticed it was a weak denial. But he didn't press it. Another time, perhaps. "We should probably avoid each other for a few days. Unless something substantial arises."

"I think that's prudent," she agreed. She looked at him, a vulnerable look in her eyes, one he hadn't before seen.

"Why are you doing this?" he asked.

She paused, as if she wasn't sure he would understand. "It's about freedom," she said, not really making sense. "And all I've learned in the last few weeks."

"I don't understand," he said. "You can do as you please. No chains bind you."

She looked at him for a moment, her gaze searching his, and then turned away. "If you only knew."

Horses' hooves clicked on cobblestone, close, at the end of the alley. A horse neighed as it came to a halt. Ian cast a worried glance, hurried to the end of the building, and looked out the window.

"What is it?" Abigail asked.

"It's Duncan!" he said, running toward her. "With soldiers."

64

"Hurry!" Ian said. He took her hand and led her out the back door.

"Where are we going?" she hissed, eyes wide.

"The shop. Quickly! Before they see us."

They sprinted through the yard to the lean-to, hiding behind the building.

"Open up!" the soldiers yelled, banging on the carriage house door.

"This way," Ian whispered. He steered her around the corner of the lean-to.

Redcoats crept down the alley, rifles drawn. They moved slowly, expecting combat, slithering around both sides of the carriage house, converging around back, near the stables.

"Wait," Ian said as he peeked around the edge of the lean-to. "We'll cross the yard and run right in the shop."

"We're coming in!" one of the soldiers yelled.

Soldiers swarmed the carriage house. They barged in the front and back doors.

"Where are you, Ian Blaine?" someone called.

"Now!" Ian said. He raced for the back door, holding Abigail's hand.

They dashed across the yard. Ian opened the shop door, rushed Abigail in, and looked back. He didn't see soldiers, and he doubted they saw him. But he knew they were coming.

Patrick was just past the door, working on a wardrobe, a plane in his hand. He looked at Abigail curiously, his gaze shifting to Ian holding her hand. "What are you two doing?"

"The redcoats are right behind us," Ian said, breathing heavily. "In the carriage house."

Patrick frowned and glanced out the window. "What have you done?"

"I met Ian in the carriage house, Mr. Blaine," Abigail said. "But just to talk."

"A minute later, Duncan came with soldiers," Ian explained.

"He must have been watching you," Patrick muttered. "Snake that he is." He put the plane down and moved to the window, pulling the curtain aside and peeking out. "I told you to be careful."

"I can't help that now," Ian said. "Where are they?"

"They're coming out of the carriage house," Patrick said, "searching the stable."

"What should we do?" Abigail asked, frantic.

Patrick hesitated, his gaze shifting from the store to the back window. "There's a chest near the front door. I know you talked about getting one. Go up there and look at it."

"I'll act like I'm buying it," Abigail said.

"And stay calm," Patrick urged.

Ian led Abigail to the front of the shop where furniture was displayed. Beside the front door was a wooden chest, not as large or elaborate as what he had planned for her, but the enemy didn't know that. He opened the lid and pretended to show it to her.

"They must have been following me," Abigail said, her face pale.

"It doesn't matter now. Act like you're interested in the chest."

A moment later the back door burst open.

"Hey! What's the meaning of this?" Patrick asked.

"Where's Mrs. St. Clair?" Duncan demanded.

Ian listened to the commotion. "You have to be convincing," he whispered to Abigail.

"Have you gone mad?" Patrick asked the British.

"Where is she?" Duncan asked harshly. "Tell me or I'll throw you in jail."

"She's in the front of the store," Patrick said, giving the colonel a confused look. "Why, what's wrong?"

"It's not your concern," Duncan said, rushing past him.

"Did something happen to the minister?" Patrick asked, inventing a cause for the apparent frenzy. "I hope not. I enjoy his sermons. He seemed in good health. A little portly—"

"The minister is fine," Duncan insisted angrily. "Stop your nonsense."

"Here they come," Ian murmured. "Just stay calm."

They stood beside the chest, studying the construction. Ian opened and closed the lid.

Duncan hurried to the front of the building, flanked by two soldiers. They wound their way through the shop and into the store.

"What are you doing?" Duncan demanded as they approached.

"Oh, hello, Colonel," Abigail said. "Are you looking for me?"

"Yes, of course, I am," Duncan said. "Why are you here?"

She looked at him oddly, as if he lost his sanity. She knelt in front of the chest and opened and closed the lid. "Don't you think a chest like this would work well in my bedchambers?" she asked. "I want one for the foot of my bed."

65

"Mrs. St. Clair, I'm glad you're safe," Duncan said curtly as he eyed Ian suspiciously.

Abigail looked at him strangely. "Why wouldn't I be?"

"I saw you enter the alley," Duncan explained, "and assumed you were lured there for nefarious purposes."

Abigail laughed lightly. "Nefarious purposes?"

"One can never be too careful," Duncan offered, looking a bit sheepish.

"All a misunderstanding, I'm thinking," Patrick said in his Irish brogue, standing behind the soldiers.

Abigail cast one last glance at the chest and turned toward Duncan. "Why were you following me?" she asked, looking at him curiously.

"I wasn't actually following you," the flustered colonel replied.

"Then why are you here?" she asked.

"For your protection, madam."

"Really?" she asked, feigning confusion. "You barged into an establishment to claim I'm in danger. How are you protecting me?"

"No, it's not like that at all," Duncan insisted. "My men and I were inspecting ammunition supplies when we saw you on Third St."

"Why is that such an issue?" she asked, realizing that she controlled the dialogue. "I'm not permitted to walk down the street?"

"Yes, of course," Duncan stammered. "But when I saw you vanish into the alley, I feared for your safety."

She feigned a gradual understanding, her expression changing from annoyance to appreciation. "I think I understand now, Colonel. Thank you so much. I appreciate your concern. But you forget I've spent most of my life in Philadelphia."

"Yes, madam, I'm well aware," Duncan said, irritated.

She continued, beginning to enjoy the charade. "I know the streets and alleys well—including any dangers that might exist. But I feel quite safe entering the back entrance of a city icon, with an impeccable reputation, that has been in business for almost forty years. I should be able to do so without the British army rushing in, assuming I'm under attack."

Duncan nodded in respect, his face crimson. "Of course, Mrs. St. Clair," he grumbled, trying to recover. "But if I may ask, what are you doing here?"

"My good Colonel," she said, changing her tone, turning their joust to truce. "Surely you remember me discussing the chest I wanted to purchase."

"Yes, of course," Duncan replied. "I vaguely recall."

"I went to the rectory the other day to take measurements," Ian said. "At Mrs. St. Clair's request."

"That's why I'm here," Abigail continued. "To see what Mr. Blaine has to offer. It was difficult to visualize from the sketch he provided."

"My apologies, Mrs. St. Clair," Duncan said with a slight nod. "I didn't mean to alarm you."

"That's quite all right, Colonel," she replied. "No need to apologize."

He started to go but paused. "Why did you enter from Third St.?" he asked. "The entrance is on Chestnut."

"My visit wasn't planned, Colonel," she said. "I was on my way to the hospital, to visit the wounded, when I decided to stop in. Since I had already passed Chestnut, I merely came through the alley."

"We have a wonderful selection of wardrobes and tables," Patrick interjected, further defusing the situation. "Is there anything that interests anyone? I can easily be persuaded to part with them at more than a fair price."

"We'll build to suit," Ian added. "Should you not see what you want. Designed specifically to your request."

Duncan's face was taut. "No, thank you. Not right now."

"We're more than happy to accommodate," Patrick offered.

Duncan turned to his men. "Come, we must go."

"Good day to you, Colonel," Abigail called as they walked through the shop and went out the back door.

66

Ian followed the redcoats to the back of the store and watched from a window to ensure that they left. He waited a moment more, just to be sure, and returned to the front. "They're gone," he said. "They went down Third toward Market."

"I still don't know why they were here," Patrick said, eyeing Ian.

"Duncan must have been following me," Abigail explained. "Although I was sure no one was behind me."

"You handled him well," Patrick said. "I'm impressed, Abigail."

She smiled. "It's not my nature. It took some acting."

Patrick touched her lightly on the shoulder. "Then you should stand on the stage."

"But I don't think Duncan will soon forget," Ian warned.

"No, the man is dangerous," Patrick agreed. "Today's embarrassment will only increase his determination."

"We should have been more careful," Abigail said. "I don't know how I didn't see him."

"Because he didn't want to be seen," Patrick said. "The

man's a liar. He wasn't inspecting ammunition. He was following you. But you need to determine why."

Ian realized how fortunate they had been. He didn't want to make the same mistake again. "We need to get much smarter. We're citizens trying to be spies. Duncan is an expert."

"Assume every move you make is being watched," Patrick said. "You can't be too careful."

"We only planned to meet for a few minutes," Ian said, trying to explain.

"Just to share information," Abigail added.

Patrick eyed them skeptically. "The two of you need to stop whatever it is you're doing. Before you get caught. Don't think I can't tell. Or anyone else, for that matter."

"But we only meet briefly," Ian protested. "Just when we need to."

Patrick was quiet, studying them closely. "Abigail, tell us why you're doing this. Because not only do you betray the Crown, but you also betray your husband."

She hesitated, as if wondering how much to say. "It started just before I left New York," she said softly. "I learned a secret that was never meant to share. Philadelphia opened my eyes even more."

"I'm not sure I understand," Patrick said, glancing at Ian.

She paused, trying to put thoughts into words. "Like the Presbyterian Church, destroyed and made into a hospital, soon to be a stable. I have many more examples. But when summed with what happened in New York, they show a world I won't walk in."

Ian was drawn to the secret she mentioned. "Has your father replied to your message?"

"He has," she said. "He lied to both of us. He thought it best for us to live our lives apart."

They were quiet, each dwelling on how a few words uttered by one man had so drastically changed their lives.

"He had no right to do that," Patrick said softly.

"No, he didn't," Abigail agreed, a mist masking her eyes.

"I've always liked you," Patrick said. "But I was skeptical when you returned. I thought you were too closely tied to the British."

"Six weeks ago, I was," she said. "I don't deny it."

Patrick looked at the two of them, compassion and understanding flickering across his face. "I know nothing turned out like you planned. But that can't be changed. Not now."

Ian and Abigail glanced at each other, listening to Patrick, knowing he could see what they wouldn't admit.

"The redcoats are smarter than you think," Patrick continued. "Duncan found something that he's not about to forget, maybe the same secret you're talking about. But he's not going to let go of it, or whatever suspicion it fostered."

"We can't stop what we started," Ian said. "It's too valuable to the cause."

Patrick wasn't fooled. "This isn't a second chance, lad," he said softly. "Abigail is a married woman."

Ian thought of the kiss in the carriage house, Abigail's reluctance. Maybe he thought they could start over, but she didn't. His father was right. He was fighting a war, but the British weren't the enemy. He fought the battle with himself.

"If you truly are doing it for the rebellion, you're not very good at it," Patrick continued. "Duncan is watching you. So is Hart. Whether you want to admit it or not."

"We do need to be more careful," Ian admitted.

"Duncan is more dangerous than you know, I'm thinking," Patrick continued. "He may have been nice and polite to Abigail, but his eyes were on fire. He thought he caught you doing something. He just wasn't sure what it was."

"It's more than Duncan," Abigail said. "Missy Malone told me we're both being watched. But she hinted that it wasn't who we think it is. Someone we trust but don't suspect."

Patrick frowned. "Now there's another mystery to solve. We could all be at risk."

"What do you suggest we do?" Ian asked. "We're gathering valuable information."

"I did learn the details about the attack on Fort Mercer," Abigail offered.

Patrick studied her for a minute, doubt housed in his eyes. "First, before anything else happens, I need to know what motivates you, stolen secrets or not. Because it's much more than your father's lies and the redcoats destroying a church that can be rebuilt. You left Philadelphia a devout Loyalist. Something changed you drastically. What is it?"

67

Abigail hesitated, wondering how much of her life should be shared. "Isn't it enough that I help?" she asked. "You don't need to know why I do it."

"If we knew, we might not be so suspicious," Patrick said, almost apologetically. "With Duncan showing up at the door, you don't have a lot of credibility. It could have all been staged."

"And you're married to a well-known minister who has a close relationship with General Howe," Ian added. "Why would you betray him and all he stands for?"

Abigail almost relented. She had known them her whole life, had been in love with Ian and probably still was. They deserved an explanation. But it wasn't the time to provide it. "Trust me," she said. "I do it for you, I do it for all the Patriots, and I do it for myself."

Patrick was skeptical. "You're a good woman, Abigail, and I've always said so. But why should we trust you?"

"I have a very valid reason," she assured him.

"Do you understand our concern?" Patrick asked, his tone harsher. "Your father is a devout Loyalist who fled Philadelphia when the rebellion started—after destroying any chance of you marrying Ian. Rumors are that your husband is here because General Howe personally intervened and requested his presence."

"The church sent him," she said. "They had good reason. But Howe is a close friend. I understand your concern."

"Why would the church send him?" Ian asked softly. "Especially when he's so revered in New York."

She looked at the two of them, wondering whether to share her secret. But she realized it wasn't the time, not yet, maybe not ever. "The church leaders wanted Solomon to experience a different congregation."

Patrick wasn't convinced. "With all due respect, Abigail, and regardless of how we both feel about you, that sounds like utter nonsense."

"Solomon spent his whole life in London, just two years in New York," she continued, knowing they weren't likely to believe her. But it was all she could offer. At least now. "It was time for a change."

"We don't doubt a word you say," Patrick said. "But if you add it all up, it's not a convincing explanation. And our lives are at stake."

She looked at Ian but spoke to Patrick. "Sometimes things aren't as they seem."

"You're talking in riddles now," Patrick said. "It's hard to believe any of it."

Abigail knew they deserved more. They feared for their lives. They also cared about her and were worried for her welfare.

"You can understand our concern," Ian added delicately.

"I know," she said. "It's difficult for all of us. In time, I will confide in you. But I can't do it now."

"Just tell us enough to trust you," Patrick suggested. "That's all we're asking. If you need help, we'll provide it."

She knew they were sincere, that they would do anything

for her. She did owe them an explanation, even if incomplete. She paused for a moment, wondering how much to reveal, and then spoke. "Edward and Alice Walker."

Ian had never heard the names. He looked at Patrick, who was as confused as he was.

"They're in New York," she added.

"What do they have to do with all of this?" Ian asked. "Or did I miss something?"

"They have everything to do with it," she replied.

Patrick shrugged. "But we don't even know who they are."

Abigail watched them trying to solve a puzzle without all the pieces.

"Tell us more," Ian urged.

She knew she had already said too much. "I must go. I've already been gone too long."

"Abigail," Patrick said as she walked to the door. "You can't leave with just the hint of a clue."

"It's all I can offer right now," she said. "I'm sorry." She went to the entrance, her hand on the door knob.

"Wait," Patrick said. "You two can't see each other for a while."

"But we need to communicate," Ian objected.

"We have the library, the bookstores, and the poorhouse," Abigail said. "I won't go to the square again."

"Still public places," Patrick said. "Too dangerous. Eventually someone will see you together more than once and know something isn't right."

"But I need time to find the right location," Ian protested.

Abigail was quiet for a moment, thinking. "I know what we can do," she said. "Tomorrow, I'll put a message in a book at Bells book store. You can retrieve it."

"What if someone finds it?" Patrick asked.

"They won't," Abigail assured him. "There's a book that's been untouched since I arrived in the city."

"Where is it?" Ian asked.

"In the back row, bottom shelf," she said. "All the way on the right."

"What's the title?" Ian asked.

"*Naval Battles of the Ancient World,*" Abigail said.

Patrick laughed. "I can see why no one has touched it."

"I'll put a note in there tomorrow," Abigail said. "As a trial. Leave a note for me when you retrieve mine, telling me where to meet. Now I must go."

68

Abigail never should have let Ian kiss her. But it happened. Even though she had pulled away, all the memories returned with it—all that could have been and what should have been. If only she had resisted, but she let the kiss linger and meekly moved away. Now Ian would be wondering why she didn't. It would be best to never see him again, not exchange a single word, avoid each other no matter what the ways of war. It would be safest. But she wasn't interested in what was safe, she never had been. Neither was he.

They should have been able to meet in the carriage house without any risk. It was sheltered, off the road at the end of a slender alley. No one would have noticed her going there and, even if they did, they wouldn't have cared. She had been certain no one followed her. But it seemed someone did. It couldn't have been Duncan—she would have seen him—or any of his soldiers, even though several had passed. None had noticed her. But someone did—someone was watching her and providing the information to Duncan.

She had to convince Duncan she was a loyal Tory, dedicated to the Crown. If the British colonel doubted her fidelity to the minister, she had to prove otherwise. That might be harder than proving she wasn't a traitor. But she had to earn his trust, and then she could safely relay information the Patriots needed most.

She hurried home, quietly entered the house, and listened for any activity. When she didn't hear anything, she went into the kitchen. Anna wasn't there, perhaps out shopping. She went in the minister's study, an excuse for her absence prepared, but found the room empty. A quick check of the second floor showed no one was home.

She had no idea where Solomon was. It wasn't like him to leave with no explanation. But she had been gone for some time. She left the house and went to the church, walked to the front door, and quietly opened it, peering inside.

It was a beautiful site from the entrance. The altar was at the far end, three huge arched windows behind it, bathing the pulpit in light. She never failed to notice it as she entered, as if God sent a signal from heaven, assuring all of his warm embrace. She paused for a moment, thankful for blessings received, and walked into the church.

It was empty, no sign of the minister. She turned to the right, the alcove beside the entrance, and saw the pew that Ian was building. He was a talented carpenter. She had been impressed with the chest she had seen at his shop, the pretense to convince Duncan she was there for a purpose, and she made it a point to again ask Solomon's permission to purchase hers. She never asked for anything. He should grant this one wish.

She walked down the aisle to the altar, only to see if Solomon might be fussing with something while getting ready for his next sermon, when she heard voices. They came from the room next to the altar, off to the right, where the British officers were housed. She couldn't quite hear what they were saying, and she couldn't risk going any closer. If anyone opened the door, they would find her suspiciously standing there.

Off to the right, in a darkened corner, past the door to the officers' room, was the box for donations left for the poor. Abigail opened the lid and saw a few items, garments and shoes, worn but better than nothing, a broken pair of spectacles that someone could use. She started to collect them so she could bring them to the poorhouse. As she folded the clothing, she could hear the officer's conversation on the other side of the wall

"The Jersey fort will fall," someone was saying. "This is a much larger assault, coming by land and the river. The rebels will never survive."

"When is it?" someone asked.

"In days, I believe. Not more than a week."

"How do you know?"

"General Cornwallis is leading the attack. His orderly told me."

69

"Where were you?" Solomon asked. He stood by the rectory door with his arms folded across his chest. "I've been looking for you."

"I went to the church to pick up donations left for the poor," she said. "Then I brought them over to Fourth St."

He frowned. "But you've been out all day."

"I went for a walk this morning."

"I know," he said. "But you were gone so long I was afraid something happened. I went looking for you."

"Where did you go?" she asked, wondering if he could have seen her and Duncan in the cabinet shop.

"I went to the Northeast Square. But I saw nothing but soldiers. I don't know why you walk there."

"I haven't lately."

"I couldn't find you anywhere," he said, eyebrows arched behind his spectacles.

She knew she had created doubt that, once planted, would be difficult to uproot. "I went down Chestnut," she said softly, almost apologetically. "I intended to go to the hospital but stopped at the cabinetmaker's shop."

"Whatever for?"

"I wanted to see if they had any chests on display," she said. "I'm so hoping you'll permit a purchase for my bedchamber."

His glare softened. "I suppose I've delayed that decision long enough," he admitted. "You may get what you want."

"May I get the original design?" she asked, surprised he consented.

He sighed, as if making the greatest decision of his life. "Yes, I suppose. Not that you need any more furniture."

"Thank you, Solomon. I do appreciate your kindness. Should I let Mr. Blaine know?"

"I'll tell him," he said, eyeing the grandfather's clock. "You had best get ready for dinner. Both the colonel and Mr. Hart will be joining us."

She hesitated, started to speak, but stopped.

"What is it?"

"We often have Mr. Hart for dinner," she said. "At least weekly."

"I enjoy his company. As does Colonel Duncan."

"Can we request that Miss Malone accompany Mr. Hart?"

Solomon shrugged. "Of course," he said. "The thought never occurred to me. But I'll ensure Mr. Hart knows she is welcome."

Abigail went to her bedchambers and breathed a sigh of relief. Whatever suspicions Solomon may have had were dispelled—or at least they seemed to be. But she had to be more careful. She couldn't risk getting caught. She brushed her hair, freshened up, and went back downstairs.

Colonel Duncan arrived with Oliver Hart a few moments later. Missy Malone had made plans with her family and couldn't come on such short notice. They sat in the living room, all enjoying a glass of port while Anna finished making their meal.

"Abigail bought me a book on ancient philosophy," Solomon told them.

Hart looked at Abigail, a rare twinkle in his eye. "It sounds exciting," he said. "Mrs. St. Clair is quite fortunate it was available. I would think it would have sold quickly."

"Yes, I had the same thoughts," Solomon said, not realizing he was being teased.

"Mr. Hart, I do have a request of you," Abigail said.

"And what might that be, madam?" Hart asked.

"From this day forward, any dinner invitation we offer, is also extended to Missy. I do apologize that today's invitation was offered so late."

"Thank you," Hart said, the hint of a blush on his cheeks. "She'll appreciate your kindness."

Duncan was surprised. "Hart, I had no idea the relationship was that serious."

"It's a private matter," Hart said. "I don't discuss it."

"The same invitation is extended to you, Colonel," Abigail said. She wanted to find out who Duncan had following her. Maybe a dinner guest would show who it was—a lady friend Abigail might never have suspected.

"That's very kind, Mrs. St. Clair," Duncan said. "But I prefer that the dining arrangements remain as is, at least in regard to me."

Anna summoned them for dinner, and they were seated in the dining room. Chicken, supplemented with potatoes and corn, was served with port and water. The meal was superbly prepared, as it always was. Although few families in the city enjoyed the same.

"Thank you so much, Anna, for another fine meal," Col. Duncan said.

"I'm pleased you enjoyed it, Colonel," Anna said.

Abigail watched the expressions on their faces—Anna's eyes twinkling, a sly smile from Duncan, and she wondered if prior suspicions she had were justified. Maybe Duncan couldn't bring his lady friend to dinner. Maybe she was cooking dinner. She knew several officers were engaged in secret relationships with servants in homes in which they were lodged. Maybe she observed another example.

Anna noticed Abigail watching and hurried back to the kitchen. Abigail guessed she was correct. She would observe their interaction more closely.

Dinner conversation centered on the city's commerce, the failure of the Hessians to take the Jersey fort, and the growing shortages of food and supplies—nothing was said about the imminent attack Abigail overheard at the church. She listened for any clues regarding future military engagements, but none were voiced.

She watched Hart, wondering why the Blaines were so certain he posed Ian such a threat. Hart seemed close to Duncan, but was cautious, very guarded in any opinion he voiced, the response to any question carefully measured. His expression was always gloomy, as if he would prefer to be alone and it was very painful, or boring, to be with others. Abigail wondered how he ever got paired with the vivacious Missy Malone. But then, opposites did attract.

Dinner was uneventful, no information gathered, and by the time the day ended, Abigail was certain any questions regarding her morning whereabouts had been forgotten. When the day ended, and she was secure in her bedchambers, she prepared the note she would leave at Bells bookstore the following morning, hidden in a book for Ian.

It read: *Another visit is planned shortly for our Jersey family. Much larger than last. And I am definitely being followed.*

70

Ian went to Bells bookstore around 11 a.m. He still wasn't sure how Duncan appeared at the carriage house so quickly. Maybe he was inspecting ammunition stockpiles, as he said, and thought Abigail was in danger. Or maybe he wasn't. Maybe he was watching her—or had someone doing it for him. And maybe the trap Duncan was setting wasn't for him, but for her.

He couldn't stop thinking about her, his lips on hers, at first as light as a feather, then more insistent until she reluctantly pushed him away. It was almost as if the last two years, and all the changes they had brought, had vanished. The kiss hadn't been planned. It was unexpected and welcomed. He wasn't sure why he did it. Impulse most likely. He never expected her to reciprocate. But she did. He realized there was so much more to Abigail than he would have guessed, a mystery to solve, a riddle to unravel. She said her life wasn't as it seemed. And now he wondered what secrets she kept, and how he could persuade her to reveal them. She had provided the names Edward and Alice Walker. But she gave no hint how they contributed to her decision to spy for the Patriots after life as a Loyalist.

Ian entered the bookstore and nodded to the proprietor, a young man browsing through a newspaper. He walked up and down the aisles, pretending to scan the shelves, finding only two other customers, both of whom were nowhere near him.

As he went to the back row, he waited, looking at books on the shelves, making sure no one watched. After a few minutes he knelt down, withdrew the book about ancient naval battles that Abigail had referenced, and pretended to scan through it. He found the note midway, glanced at it quickly, and stuck it in his pocket. He reviewed the book a moment more, inserted his note for Abigail, and put it back on the shelf. He stood, selected another book, pretending an interest that didn't exist. A moment later, he returned it to the shelf and went to the counter.

"This is a wonderful store," he said to the proprietor as he picked up a copy of the *Pennsylvania Ledger* newspaper and paid for it.

"I'm glad you like it, sir," the proprietor said.

Ian left and went back to the shop. As he came up Chestnut, crossing Third, he saw Missy Malone across the street, entering a store that displayed several stylish shawls in the shop window. He wondered if she was loyal to the Crown, like Hart, or did she support the rebellion, as he suspected her family did. Why didn't she tell Abigail who was watching them? She was far more complex than she seemed, and he wanted to know more about her—and Abigail did, too. But it carried too much risk. Suppose they made the wrong assumption, and Missy was tied to Duncan, through Hart. It wasn't worth it. The safest path was to assume everyone was a Tory, even if they weren't.

When he entered the cabinet shop, he found his father in the back, carving the legs to a dining room table. "I have a note from Abigail," he said as he approached.

Patrick stepped away from his work. He went to the

doorway and scanned the store, ensuring it was empty. "Were you careful?"

"I was," Ian said. He handed his father the message.

Patrick quickly read it. "Interesting," he said, looking up. "Another attack, which we expected. But why claim she's being followed? We know she is."

"I took it differently," Ian said. "She's being followed, but not by Duncan."

Patrick thought for a moment. "Then how did Duncan get here so quickly yesterday?"

"He could have been nearby," Ian replied. "And whoever is following Abigail got word to him. Maybe they were on horseback."

Patrick sighed. "Another mystery. Just like the Walkers."

"We'll solve it."

"We shouldn't have to. She should tell us."

Ian didn't know why Abigail was so secretive. He didn't want to discuss it. "How do we find out who's following her?"

Patrick thought for a moment. "I can follow her to find out who it is."

"The next time I meet her, you can wait at the rectory and then follow her when she leaves," Ian said. He looked at the note in his hand. "What should we do about the attack?"

"I had best warn Barnabas," Patrick muttered, putting his tools down on a bench.

"I was on my way to the church. We can stop along the way if you'd like to come."

"Is the pew finished?"

"Almost," Ian said. "It has to be painted and stained. But I also promised the minister I would polish the remaining pews."

"Then I'll go with you," Patrick said. "Between the two of us, we can finish most of it."

They put supplies in the wagon—tools, stain and paint, rags and polish for the pews—and got the horses ready. When they left the carriage house, they went to the corner of Second and Walnut, and Ian stopped in front of City Tavern.

"I'll just run in for a minute," Patrick said.

Ian waited, his thoughts drifting to Abigail. What did Edward and Alice Walker have to do with her allegiance to the Crown? Maybe if he saw her at the church, he could ask her.

Patrick came out a few minutes later and climbed up on the bench seat.

"Barnabas knows?" Ian asked.

Patrick nodded. "He'll deliver the message. And he'll get information on this Walker couple in New York. Although it would be much easier if Abigail just told us."

Ian guided the horses to the church, stopping in the front, and tied them to a hitching post along the pavement. They removed the supplies from the back and carried everything into the church, setting it all down in an empty space in the alcove.

Patrick surveyed the new pew, built in a cramped cavity against the wall. "You did a fine job," he said, running his hand over the bare wood.

"I have molding to add to the legs," Ian said. "And then it'll match the other pews."

"The minister will be pleased. As he should be."

"I'll get started," Ian said. "I only have a couple hours of work for today."

Patrick looked at the empty church. "I'll polish the pews."

They went about their work, Ian focused on the new bench, Patrick polishing the many pews that made the church. The two worked well together. But they always had.

An hour later, the minister came in. Ian had just finished the bench and was adding stain to the seat. Patrick was halfway done polishing pews.

"This is absolutely beautiful," Solomon said as he looked at Ian's work. "Better than I imagined."

"I'm glad you're pleased," Ian said.

"I am," Solomon replied. "You'll be highly recommended should anyone ask."

Patrick stopped what he was doing and came over. "We'll have the pews polished before we leave today," he said. "But the new pew needs a second coat of stain, and we'll paint the legs white to match the others. We'll likely finish late tomorrow, but still in time for Sunday's service."

"Thank you so much," Solomon said. "I do appreciate it."

Patrick and Ian went back to work, while Solomon went to the altar and looked through some papers on the podium. A few moments later, he came down the center aisle and approached Ian.

"I forgot to mention, Mr. Blaine," he said. "I would like you to proceed with the chest for Abigail."

"Splendid," Ian said, holding his brush. "Which size would you like?"

The minister frowned, trying to recall his discussion with Abigail. "I'm not sure," he said with a sigh. "I suppose you'll have to stop by and ask her."

71

The following morning, Abigail went to Bells bookstore to retrieve Ian's message. She came in, nodded to the clerk, and walked down one of the aisles, pausing to scan the shelves. After a minute had passed, she noticed the clerk watching her.

She nodded as their gazes met and cast a disarming smile. "A wonderful assortment," she said pleasantly. "This is my favorite place in the entire city."

"And we're pleased you come so often," he said. "Can I help you find anything?"

"Not just yet," she replied. "I think I'll browse the shelves a moment."

She turned away and ran her finger along the spines on the shelf, feigning interest. She and Ian could no longer use the bookstore to meet or exchange messages. She was too familiar to the clerk, perhaps one of his better customers. If ever asked by authorities, he would remember her well, revealing how often she came to the store, sometimes making no purchase. They needed another place to meet, somewhere private.

She had to buy something to dismiss the clerk's suspicions. She would have to befriend him, prove they shared a love of books and all the imaginary worlds they offered. She strolled through the aisles, pausing when she got to topics she found interesting, removing books from the shelves to scan through them. A second glance at the proprietor proved he was no longer interested in what she was doing, or at least he pretended he wasn't, and had returned to reading his newspaper. She hurried to the rear aisle, knelt to access the bottom shelf, and retrieved Ian's note. It read:

Presbyterian Cemetery tomorrow at 10 a.m. Who is Walker?

She put the note in her pocket. The cemetery was at Fifth and Arch, near the Northeast Square. It was isolated, surrounded by a brick wall, littered with trees that cast shadows on the graves. But it couldn't be a permanent place to meet. They could never explain why they were there. They could only meet briefly to pass information and move on, pretending to visit the graves of former friends or loved ones.

Ian wanted details on Edward and Alice Walker, and she would provide them—she just wasn't sure when. The cemetery wasn't the place to do it. It was a detailed discussion, one held in private, and she didn't see that opportunity arising—at least not in the near future. She would provide just enough information to keep his trust, but still not reveal a secret that must be kept at all costs—even as it started to unravel.

She left the aisle, scanning the books that lined the shelves. To avoid the proprietor's suspicions, she selected a book of Shakespeare's sonnets with a beautiful leather binding that she had admired on a prior visit and approached the counter.

"You'll enjoy that one, ma'am," the man said.

"I'm sure I shall," she replied. "I've always liked Shakespeare."

"As do many," he said. He paused a moment, taking her money and providing change. "You've become a frequent visitor."

He was probing, probably wondering why she was there so

often. "Yes, I love books," she said. "If I'm not here, I'm at one of the libraries." She leaned closer as if sharing a secret. "I read constantly. Even when I should be doing other things."

He laughed. "Many do, ma'am, including me. Even more so since the British occupation."

She hesitated, wondering if he was trying to tell her something, or only making an innocent statement. Or maybe he was laying a trap. No one could be trusted.

"Sales have been good," he continued. "Even soldiers read, I suppose."

She relaxed; the conversation seemed innocent. "I often come while doing my errands. Even if only to check for new manuscripts."

The proprietor smiled. "Thank you, ma'am. You're welcome any time. Keep coming. And tell your friends to come, too."

She left the store, confident she had convinced the clerk she was just an interested customer and started back to the rectory. She was always wary of being watched, especially since Duncan had appeared at Ian's carriage house, so she took a less direct route home. It would serve as a diversion should anyone follow her and show that her behavior was far from routine. She walked all the way to Front St. and turned, strolling past docks and ships sitting at the wharfs, crates stacked on the docks, sailors lounging by their ships. Even with little traffic along the river, the waterfront was always busy.

British soldiers patrolled the street, looking for something that never seemed to exist. The mix of docks, restaurants, parks, businesses that supported the ships, and a stray residence or two, only served to show a kaleidoscope of buildings and activity, none of which threatened the occupation. Civilians strolled the pavement and walkways, much as she did, women in long dresses, some with shawls now that autumn had arrived, children playing, a man sitting on a bench, enjoying his pipe.

After walking a block along the river, she saw Oliver Hart standing at the end of a wharf that jutted into the water, Colonel Duncan beside him. They glanced furtively at those that passed, the seamen moving to and from their ships, merchants delivering or receiving crates that sat on the pier. She stopped by a large oak, standing beside its stout trunk, and watched them curiously, having seen them huddled along the waterfront only days before. After a moment, she thought their behavior unusual and stepped behind stacked crates and peeked around the corner.

They kept looking in the distance, studying a ship sitting in the middle of the river. It moved in no direction, not north or south or to Jersey. Hart looked back toward the street, almost as if to ensure no one watched them. When satisfied no one did, he removed a mirror from his pocket, caught the sun's rays, and flashed it toward the boat.

Abigail knew the mirror was some sort of signal, but she didn't know what for. As she continued observing, the cutter lifted anchor, shifted its sails, and steered toward the wharf. Duncan and Hart faced each other, discussing something that seemed important, at least based on their expressions. When the conversation ended, Hart removed bills from his pocket, meticulously counted them, and gave them to Duncan.

Hart was making a payment, apparently concerning the ship they signaled, although she wasn't sure why.

But she was starting to understand, the mystery almost solved.

72

"It's barely worth the effort," Duncan grumbled as he put the bills in his pocket.

"There's no profit in shipping," Hart said. "Not now."

Duncan frowned. "Then do something about it."

Hart was irritated, wondering why Duncan couldn't understand simple economics. "There's limited trade on the northern half of the river. I told you that before."

"Expand it."

"It's at full capacity. Only a handful of villages, and fewer farms, are located to the north. Every shipping company on the waterfront is fighting for the little trade that exists."

"Hence no profit," Duncan muttered. "Too much competition for too little goods."

"Exactly," Hart said. "We need to open the river to the sea and let larger ships sail."

"It won't be much longer," Duncan assured him as he went back toward the street. His carriage sat along the pavement, flanked by two soldiers.

"Let's hope a second attack proves more successful," Hart said, walking beside a man he was forced to do business with, just to save his company. He wondered if Duncan was ignorant of Philadelphia's plight, a shortage of supplies worsening by the day, or if he really didn't care. The army had what they needed. So did the wealthy. But very soon, a few weeks at most, people would starve. He had known that since the British arrived. But now, the residents knew it, too.

"The forts will be gone in days," Duncan continued. "I promise you."

Hart didn't know whether or not to believe him, but he knew it was useless to argue.

They reached Front St., pausing at Duncan's carriage. "I'll instruct the minister to invite you for dinner," he said. "We can continue the discussion then."

"I'll look forward to the invitation," Hart said, even though he had no interest in attending. But he knew it was a necessity.

"And bring Missy," Duncan added. "Abigail seems to enjoy her company."

"I will," Hart said, grateful for the suggestion. He would rather bring Missy. She could talk for both of them, and he could merely endure the evening.

Duncan paused before climbing into the carriage. "We need to watch Abigail."

Hart eyed him skeptically. "Why should we fear the minister's wife?"

Duncan hesitated, but then offered a hint. "I know much more about her than you. Especially her prior life in Philadelphia. She's up to no good, I assure you."

"I respectfully disagree," Hart said. "She seems like a wonderful woman, bright and refreshing, just what the city needs."

"Perhaps," Duncan muttered, scanning those that walked the streets. "But I suspect otherwise, as do others."

Hart offered no reply. He studied the colonel, a man he

wouldn't want to count as an enemy. But he suspected at some point, he might not be able to avoid it.

"I was going to lay another trap for Blaine," Duncan said, pensive. "But it might be better to snare Mrs. St. Clair. Don't you agree?"

73

Patrick Blaine was building the cabinet for a grandfather's clock, the top an oval shape with carved molding wrapping it, when Ian came back in the shop. He paused to admire the craftsmanship.

"Philip, the watchmaker, asked me to build the cabinet," Patrick said. "He's working on the face and mechanism."

"It's beautiful," Ian said. "Perhaps your finest work. Who commissioned it?"

"Silas Barton, a banker," Patrick said. "He lives past Vine, on the outskirts of the city."

"I'm sure he'll be pleased with it," Ian said. He scanned the showroom to make sure no one was there. "Are you ready?"

"Is it time?" Patrick asked.

"A little early. But Abigail sometimes goes for a walk."

"I'll go to the rectory and wait for her to leave. Then I'll follow her to the cemetery."

"It's only a few blocks," Ian said. "It should be easy to see if someone is watching her."

"A soldier is unlikely. And Duncan must be somewhere close."

"Let's hope that everything has been a coincidence and Abigail is not under suspicion."

Patrick was quiet, studying his son. "I don't believe in coincidences," he said as he grabbed a broad-brimmed hat. "Let me get underway, and we'll see."

Patrick went out the back door of the shop, down the alley to Third. He walked to Walnut and down to Second, stopping to see Barnabas, who stood outside of the City Tavern.

"Any information?" Patrick asked as he approached.

Barnabas eyed a passing wagon and ensured no pedestrians were nearby. "Edward Walker is a wealthy Tory," he said. "He controls much of New York City, very quietly, of course—on behalf of the Crown. He specializes in personal loans to public figures, but only those who can't repay them."

"He owns the people instead of an asset," Patrick said, completing the explanation.

"Exactly," Barnabas replied. "Not a nice man."

Patrick was quiet, wondering how he was tied to Abigail. Through her father, perhaps?

"He's an older man," Barnabas continued, "late fifties and in very poor health."

"Married?"

"Yes, to a commoner named Alice Simpson."

"That's strange," Patrick muttered.

"It is," Barnabas agreed. "His first wife recently passed, and he married Alice shortly thereafter. She's much younger, in her twenties."

"After his money?"

"I'm not sure," Barnabas said. "Rumors claim she married him to secure passage from London, and that the family fortune is controlled by Walker's children from his first marriage."

Patrick was conscious of the time. "If you learn anything else, let me know."

He left the tavern and walked down Second. He passed the lane that led to the rectory, and watched the building from the corner, standing behind a wagon parked along the pavement, pretending he waited for someone.

Ten minutes later, Abigail left the rectory. She went down the alley to Third, but walked in the opposite direction, toward Market, glancing over her shoulder as she did so.

Patrick rushed to get closer. He had expected her to turn down Arch. But she was walking around the block, using the extra time to take a longer route, making sure she wasn't followed. He crossed to the other side of the street and saw her when he reached the corner, just over a block ahead. She paused to look in a shop window, waited a moment, and turned abruptly to look behind her. Then she started walking.

Patrick followed at a distance. He studied the people between them: a pair of British soldiers, patches of pedestrians farther ahead, a young boy, maybe twelve or thirteen, probably running errands for his mother. An older man, walking briskly given his age, was just behind her. As she continued down Market, the same people followed, while a sprinkling of others came and went, entering stores or turning down side streets.

When she reached Fifth, Abigail turned toward the cemetery. The crowd continued, most remaining on Market, where many shops were located. The two soldiers went straight, leaving the older man, the boy, and a young couple strolling behind her.

As Patrick turned onto Fifth, he discounted pedestrians that came from different directions, and focused on the few that had been on Market. British soldiers passed on horseback, a wagon carrying heads of lettuce rattled by, as well as a carriage, the lettering near the floorboard showing it was built by the Malones, Missy's family.

As Abigail approached the graveyard, she turned to study

those behind her. When satisfied none posed a threat, she stepped into the cemetery.

Ian was waiting somewhere behind the brick wall, pretending to mourn at an unknown grave. As Patrick came closer, the young couple passed the cemetery, the older man turned on Arch and headed west. That left the young boy.

Abigail was being watched by a teenage boy.

74

———

Surrounded on three sides by brick walls four feet high, accessed via an opened iron gate, the Presbyterian Burying Ground sat on the corner of Arch and Fifth. Abigail took one last look at those around her before entering the cemetery and noticed no one suspicious.

She found Ian in the last row of graves, standing behind a crooked tombstone. The rear of the cemetery faced open space with which to expand, defined by a rotting split rail fence, and an alley that fronted the rear of properties lining Sixth St. She looked past him, at the grass and trees, and an empty carriage that sat in the alley. After deciding it was safe, she approached.

"No one followed me," she said.

He didn't reply, but looked toward the entrance, making sure no one entered behind her. "We should only stay a minute," he said reluctantly.

"I don't have anything to share," she said. "Only what I told you about the fort in Jersey."

He took her hand and held it tightly. "I just wanted to see you."

She frowned, knowing she had started something she

might not have the strength to stop. She let him hold her hand but focused on the war. "Were you able to warn those in Jersey?"

"Yes, we were," he said, letting go of her hand. "But we may not have the forces to defend against a large assault."

"This attack will be much bigger than the last," she said. "Based on what I heard."

"Tell me about the Walkers."

She looked at the cemetery entrance. No one was coming. They were alone. But it still wasn't time to tell secrets—or the place. "Not now," she said. "Just know that you can trust me."

He sighed, agitated. "I know I can trust you. Because of what we were, and probably still are. But others are risking their lives."

"I know," she said. "But I can't tell you anything more. Not now."

"Your entire life has been lived in the Crown's shadow. Why switch sides?"

"Because the time was right, and so were the circumstances that drove my decision. For now, that's all I can really say."

"Are you still in love with me?"

She closed her eyes. The truth sometimes didn't need to be told. "We should go. This isn't a good place to meet."

He studied her closely, knowing she hadn't answered the question. "We can try the library again."

"That might work. It's larger than the book store, so we can more easily avoid suspicion."

"Tomorrow?"

"No," she said. "The day after. At ten a.m."

He nodded, looking hurt, as if she was avoiding him. "I'm sorry for what I said. I had no right. You're the minister's wife."

She glanced around nervously. "Let's go out the back. I don't like it here."

They went to the edge of the graveyard, across vacant

ground. When they reached the rail fence, he took her hand again, and helped her over it. When they got to the alley, they checked both directions. No one was near.

"You go out toward Market," she said. "I'll leave by Cherry St."

He turned, his attention diverted. "Look," he said, pointing to Fifth St. Several redcoats on horseback were visible over the wall that bordered the cemetery. "What are they doing?"

"I'm not sure," she said uneasily. "Could they be here for us?"

"I don't know, but we better not wait."

"Go the opposite way," she said as she started to leave. "And I'll do the same."

She watched him hurry away and walked toward Cherry. The soldiers milled about the entrance, but they hadn't dismounted. As she reached Cherry, her view was blocked by trees. She went west instead of east, to avoid the British, and walked to Sixth, to the Northeast Square, and came back toward the rectory down Race St.

She saw no more soldiers. At least none that seemed interested in her.

75

When Ian arrived at the shop, Patrick was showing a wardrobe to an older couple, explaining how it was built and the craftsmanship required. Ian briefly made eye contact as he entered and went back in the shop to wait.

The customers were impressed by Patrick's presentation and decided to make a purchase. Ian waited while Patrick discussed cost and delivery, and then drew up a sales receipt. The transaction seemed like it lasted forever. About twenty minutes later, he heard the door to the showroom close and Patrick entered the shop.

"Barnabas got some information on the Walkers," he said. "He's an older man, very sickly, but powerful. It seems he lends money to public figures who can't pay it back."

Ian thought about Solomon, so fearful of spending money —maybe for a reason. "And then he controls who takes his money."

"Apparently," Patrick said. "I suppose that's how he got so much influence."

"What about her?"

"She's much younger, Abigail's age. Arrived from London a

year or so ago. She married Walker, who had just lost his first wife, shortly thereafter."

"Interesting," Ian mused. "I'm sure there's more than one riddle wrapped in that tale."

"That there is," Patrick agreed. "Abigail knows the answers, I'm sure. How did your meeting go?"

"It was short, but no issues."

"Did she think she was being followed?" Patrick asked.

"No, she was actually quite sure she wasn't," Ian said. "But a handful of soldiers appeared at the cemetery entrance, so we left after only a few minutes."

"What happened with the redcoats?"

"They didn't bother us."

"Did they come into the cemetery?"

"Not while we were there," Ian said. "But we left when we saw them. Just to be safe, we went through the back, into an alley."

"Did they follow you?"

Ian shook his head. "Not that I saw. They didn't even get off their horses. I went out to Market; Abigail went on to Cherry."

Patrick watched him for a moment. "They must not have seen you," he muttered. "But I'm sure they were there for you."

Ian hesitated. "It didn't seem like it. Why, what did you see?"

"She is being followed," Patrick said. "Whoever arranged it is very clever."

"Are you sure?" Ian asked. "Because she's very careful."

"No soldiers followed her," Patrick said, his Irish brogue rising in tone.

"Not just soldiers," Ian insisted. "She said no one suspicious followed her."

"No one who seemed suspicious did. But she was followed just the same."

Ian was confused. "By who?"

"A young lad," Patrick replied. "Maybe twelve years old or a tad older. He was good at it, too. I'm thinking he's done it quite a few times."

"A boy?" Ian asked in disbelief.

"Yes, a boy," Patrick said. "She's dangerous. Stay away from her."

"I can't," Ian said. "Not now. I have to warn her."

Patrick was quiet for a moment. "When will you see her again?"

"The day after tomorrow."

"Tell her then," Patrick said. "But make sure it's the last time you see her."

Ian wasn't convinced. "I have to tell her sooner. She might take risks without realizing Hart and Duncan suspect her. Maybe it was never me they were after. It was her."

Patrick looked at his son sternly. "Ian, I care about her, too. She's a wonderful woman. But she's married to someone else. She's not worth losing your life over."

"She deserves a warning," Ian insisted. "She would do the same for me."

Patrick hesitated. "Yes, she would do the same for you," he said softly. "But how do you get a message to her?"

Ian thought for a moment, searching for some way to see her. "I know," he said suddenly. "The minister said that Abigail could get a chest, but he didn't know what size."

"And what is that supposed to mean?"

Ian grinned. "It means I should go and ask her."

76

I an knocked on the front door of the rectory. He had to warn Abigail that she was being watched, or maybe much worse. Whoever had a boy follow her around Philadelphia, and he suspected it was Duncan or maybe Hart, may already have enough evidence to have her hung. If they didn't, they were getting close. But he was plagued by an unanswered question. What had she done to arouse their suspicion?

The door opened a moment later, Anna standing at the entrance. "Hello, Mr. Blaine."

"Good morning, Anna," Ian said. "Is Mrs. St. Clair at home? I came to discuss the chest she wanted."

"I'll see if she's available," she said. "Please, wait in the parlor."

A few minutes later Abigail came down the stairs, Anna close behind her. "Mr. Blaine," she said as she entered the parlor. "This is a pleasant surprise."

"Mrs. St. Clair," he said, acting as formally as he could. "The minister asked me to begin construction on the chest you wanted."

"Really?" she asked. "That's unexpected. He tends to delay

decisions, sometimes forever. Especially those involving finances."

Ian smiled, watching as Anna stepped into the next room. He suspected she stood by the doorway, within earshot, or by the fireplace, which was shared with the kitchen. "He was quite clear. But before I start, he asked that I confirm the size with you."

"What did we discuss?" she asked, pointing to the next room to alert him Anna was nearby.

"The sketch I provided was the larger chest. But when I was last here, we measured for a smaller version."

"Yes, I recall," she said. She moved closer, glancing over her shoulder, watchful for Anna. "Did the minister give any indication as to which he preferred?"

"No, he didn't," Ian said. Then he whispered. "You are being followed. My father confirmed it."

She looked at him, eyes wide. "Please, sit down," she said, "and we'll discuss it."

"Thank you," Ian said as he sat on one of the stuffed chairs. "I brought sketches for you to refer to, should you need them."

She sat beside him and held up a finger, motioning for him to stop. "Anna," she called.

A moment later, the servant appeared. "Yes, Mrs. St. Clair?"

"Can you get us each a glass of cider, please?"

"Yes, of course, ma'am," Anna said. "I'll get it now."

Ian leaned forward. "It's a boy, twelve or thirteen. Do you know who he is?"

She arched her eyebrows and glanced back at the doorway. "Are you sure?"

"Yes, he followed you to the cemetery. The soldiers who came may have been there for us."

"And the day Duncan came to the carriage house?"

"Probably the same," he said. "But we'll likely never know."

She leaned closer. "What should I do?"

"Use it in your favor," he whispered. "Now you know who is watching you. Go anywhere you like. Lose him if you can, avoid the destination if you can't."

She was quiet for a moment, digesting the information. "I can do that," she said. "I'll keep visiting the poorhouse and hospitals. I'll make them think I'm a saint."

"Who do you think the boy answers to?"

"Duncan."

"How about Hart?"

She shrugged. "I suppose it could be. He's so guarded I wouldn't know if he's involved or how suspicious he might be."

"Do you know who the boy is?"

She shook her head and glanced back at the hallway.

"I need to see you," he said abruptly.

"Where?" she whispered. "At the library tomorrow?"

"No, too risky."

"We can't go back to the square. Or the cemetery. And the bookstore looks suspicious."

He thought for a moment. He knew there was danger, regardless of the location. But they could manage it, especially since they knew who followed her. "There's a carriage house next to mine, set back a bit farther but with a back door that exits to my property. Do you remember it?"

She thought for a moment and nodded. "I do," she replied. "Doesn't Benjamin Raus own it?"

"Yes, he does, but he's with Congress in York," he said. "We can meet there." He handed her the sketches so she could pretend she was reviewing them. "Tomorrow at nine a.m. If anyone challenges you, say you're coming to the shop to discuss the chest."

She hesitated. "It still seems dangerous. We almost got caught in your carriage house. Why would the building next to it be safer?"

"Because no one would ever suspect it. If you're being

followed, and can't get away, don't go. Duncan doesn't know you went to my carriage house before. He thinks you came to the shop. He'll never suspect we're meeting in a building owned by someone else."

She looked back at the doorway. "I don't think we should."

"We'll only meet there once," he promised. "It's best we don't repeat locations anyway."

She hesitated. "Maybe, but I can't commit."

He listened for Anna, but she still wasn't coming. "Give me a hint about Walker."

She held up the sketch, pretending to look at it. "He's dying, and she's—"

Anna walked through the doorway, handing each a mug of cider.

"Thank you, Anna," Abigail said.

"I'll be in the kitchen should you need anything else," Anna said.

Ian waited while Anna left, but he suspected she stood just past the doorway. He pointed to the foyer. "Have you decided which size?"

"Yes, Mr. Blaine, I have. I'll get the smaller chest. I think that might be best. The minister is so frugal, and I would hate for him to fret over the cost."

77

"Please, try to engage in conversation," Missy Malone said as the carriage stopped in front of the rectory.

"I will make the attempt," Hart said, smiling. "Even though I prefer not to."

The coachman hitched the horses to the post and opened the door, helping Missy step down to the pavement. Hart followed.

"It'll be nice to see Abigail again," Missy said as they walked to the door.

"Were you friends when she lived in the city?"

"We spent some time together. Not close, but friendly."

Hart knocked on the door, and Anna led them into the parlor. Abigail was sitting on the end of the couch, while Duncan and the minister stood, glasses of port in their hands.

"Miss Malone and Mr. Hart have arrived," Anna announced.

"Greetings," the minister said. "Come join us."

Missy sat next to Abigail on the couch, with Oliver beside her.

"We were discussing a theology book Mrs. St. Clair

purchased for the minister," Duncan said. "A comparison of the world's religions."

"But we'll gladly change the subject, should it not interest you," Solomon said, knowing his passions for theology and philosophy weren't shared by all.

"No, please don't," Missy said. "I'm sure it's a fascinating discussion."

"What are you reading, Mrs. St. Clair?" Hart asked, pointing to a book on the adjacent table.

Abigail handed him the volume. "*Shakespeare's Sonnets*," she said. "I purchased it at Bells book store."

Hart took the book and flipped through it. "I'm a great admirer of Shakespeare."

"Really, Mr. Hart," she exclaimed. "I am as well."

"I'm partial to the histories, but love the tragedies, as well."

"I'm quite surprised," Abigail said. "I thought your reading would relate to ships at sea and how to better manage them."

Hart smiled. "Some of my reading is devoted to my profession. But it's a small percentage. Shakespeare ranks first."

"Oliver, please," Missy said, lightly touching his arm. She turned to the others. "I asked him to engage in conversation. He tends to be so quiet, as I'm sure you're aware."

"He does speak when he has something important to say," Duncan said. "Especially when relevant to business."

"But I had no idea he planned to discuss Shakespeare all evening," Missy said. "Maybe the group would find the theological discussion more entertaining?"

The room filled with laughter as Hart handed the book back to Abigail.

"May I see that?" Duncan asked.

"Yes, of course," Abigail said. "I wouldn't have counted literature among your passions."

Duncan scanned the book briefly and returned it. "You bought the book at Bells?"

"Yes," Abigail replied. "I go there often."

"And the minister's book as well?" Duncan asked.

Abigail hesitated. "Yes, actually. Although I also frequent Honey and Mouse."

Duncan smiled, although his eyes didn't show it. "Do you go to bookstores often?"

Abigail looked at him curiously, as did the others in the room. "Yes, I do," she said. "Probably once a week, usually while enjoying a walk"

"But I thought your walks were devoted to the waterfront," Duncan countered.

Abigail suspected he had an agenda. "Often they are," she replied. "As you well know, since you accompanied me on one occasion."

"I just find it interesting, Mrs. St. Clair, that you visit so many places," Duncan continued. "I guess you see many of the same people."

"Is it my turn for questions next?" Missy Malone asked, realizing Abigail was uncomfortable. "I walk along the river sometimes, too. But it's usually to Oliver's office so I can drag him home for dinner."

Everyone laughed, including Duncan.

"Maybe I was prying," the colonel admitted. "Although it wasn't my intention."

Hart watched Duncan closely. The questions he asked Abigail, and his prior comment about laying a trap for her, made him wary of what Duncan had planned—although he suspected it was already in progress.

78

Barnabas went out the back door of the City Tavern around 10 p.m., leaving the establishment in the capable hands of Dolly Clarke and a few of her helpers. He walked down Walnut toward Third.

"Good evening, Mr. Stone," a British officer called as he passed on horseback.

"Captain," Stone nodded. "Have a pleasant evening."

He turned at Third and walked toward Chestnut. When he almost reached the corner, he went down a narrow alley, past a cluster of carriage houses, to the rear of Patrick Blaine's cabinet shop. He tapped on the door and, a moment later, Patrick eased it open, peeking out.

"Come upstairs," Patrick said, as he led him into the residence. "I've got a mug of ale waiting for you."

"Just what I need to quench my thirst," Barnabas joked. He followed Patrick up the stairs to the residence and found Ian sitting by the window. "How are you, lad?"

"Just trying to stay a step ahead of the redcoats," Ian replied.

"We all are," Barnabas said as he sat on the couch, taking

the mug that Patrick offered. "Another discussion with your source, I'm told."

Ian nodded. "My father proved she was being followed. I had to warn her."

"By a teenage boy, no less," Patrick muttered. "The English know no bounds."

"Did she have more information?" Barnabas asked.

Ian nodded. "But she couldn't tell me. Not with the housekeeper there."

Barnabas sipped his ale, wondering what secrets might soon be revealed. "Does she know who the boy might be?"

"No, she never noticed him," Ian said. "She constantly checks to see if she's being watched, but she assumed it would be a soldier or a Loyalist."

"Which does make sense," Patrick said, defending her. "No one would suspect a child."

"Duncan," Ian muttered with distaste. "He's a devious man. Unless Hart is behind it."

Barnabas was concerned. The enemy was closing in, and he couldn't let that happen. "Did she tell you about the Walkers?"

"Just a little," Ian said. "Edward Walker is dying. But she never finished what she was saying about Alice Walker. She was interrupted."

Barnabas was perplexed. "What would a mismatched couple in New York have to do with what's going on in Philadelphia?"

"Especially as a motive to support the rebellion," Patrick added.

"And why all the mystery?" Barnabas asked.

Ian shrugged. "I assume it's a long story she hasn't had time to tell."

"It makes me doubt her credibility," Barnabas muttered. "Even if she has provided valuable information."

"I don't understand how the Walkers relate to anything," Patrick said. "How can they be so critical?"

"I don't know," Ian admitted. "I suspect they wronged her family. That might explain why the minister came to Philadelphia."

"Ian," Patrick groaned, rolling his eyes. "You revealed her identity. Watch what you say."

"Abigail is your source?" Barnabas asked.

"Yes, she is," Ian confessed. "I'm sorry. I should have been more careful."

Barnabas shrugged. "I was better off not knowing. But now that I do, I could have guessed if I put some thought into it. You loved the woman once."

"Still does, I'm thinking," Patrick added softly.

Barnabas leaned back in his chair. "But I am surprised. Especially with her family so loyal to the Crown, moving to New York when the rebellion began."

Ian sighed. "I've made it all worse."

Patrick tried to console him. "You can't do anything about it now. Best get the whole story out."

Ian nodded and slowly began. "Abigail is my source. You know the different places we've met to communicate—Northeast Square, cemetery, carriage house, library. She obtains such valuable information because Duncan is billeted at the rectory."

"The arrogant fool boasts about his military genius," Patrick said, chuckling.

"The minister frequently hosts Hart," Ian continued. "Which leads me to believe he's heavily involved with Duncan."

"But I'm still skeptical," Patrick said, "because Abigail won't tell us why she does it. That makes me suspicious. Why betray country, given her loyalty to England, and her husband?"

Barnabas knew many motives existed. He had heard most

of them. She only had to name one. But for some reason, she wouldn't, and he had to understand why. "We need to know," he said and then drank more ale. "We've given her enough chances to persuade us."

"More than enough," Patrick mumbled.

Barnabas nodded, knowing this was a riddle that had to be solved quickly. "When will you see her again?"

"Tomorrow," Ian said. "We're meeting in Benjamin Raus's carriage house at nine a.m. She'll tell me everything then. Assuming she comes."

Barnabas weighed the risks, knowing there were many. "It seems dangerous," he said warily. "Especially when Duncan almost caught you in your own carriage house."

"But he thinks we were in the shop," Ian said. "No one will suspect we're on someone else's property. It's private, so we'll have more time. She'll tell the whole tale."

"What about the boy?" Patrick asked.

"If he's following her, or if anyone else is, she won't come," Ian said.

"Why don't we watch Raus's carriage house when you go?" Patrick suggested. "We'll see if she comes alone."

"That seems safer," Barnabas said. "I would help, too, but I have a commitment—someone I have to meet. I'm sure you understand."

Patrick gave Ian a wary look. "I don't like this," he said. "Especially if Barnabas can't help. Maybe you shouldn't meet her."

"We need to know what she's willing to share," Ian countered. "It could be far more valuable than we suspect. We may never have the chance again,"

Patrick and Barnabas were quiet, weighing his words. "He could be right," Barnabas conceded.

"I suppose," Patrick said, not convinced. "I'll watch the back of the building from our second-floor window, just to ensure no one approaches."

"I'll make sure it's safe." Ian assured them. "Or the meeting won't occur."

79

Abigail left the rectory shortly before 9 a.m. Solomon was in his study, writing a sermon, Anna Knight was in the kitchen, cabinet doors opening and closing. Abigail stood by the front door for a moment, listening to ensure they were occupied.

She left the rectory and crossed the street. Instead of walking down the cobblestone lane, she entered the cemetery beside the church. A sprawling chestnut tree sprouted from the edge, close to the short wall that defined the graveyard, near an iron gate on Second St. that marked the entrance. Abigail stood by the tree and looked up and down Second St., searching for any teenage boys, ensuring none were nearby.

After pausing for a moment, she found nothing but the usual street traffic—wagons and carriages, a few soldiers on horseback—and a pedestrian or two walking down the pavement. She stepped onto Second and turned south, passed the back of the church, and walked toward Market. She resisted turning around to see if she was being followed. It was too soon.

When she reached Market, she rounded the corner toward

Third, then abruptly crossed the street and paused, looking into the window of a hat store. She tried to use the reflection off the glass to see behind her, but when it proved ineffective, she turned, acting as if she was about to cross the street, and studied those approaching. When no one seemed to be watching, she went back to the corner and turned onto Second.

She maintained a brisk pace, pretending to hurry, her blonde hair bouncing on her shoulders. She crossed the street, looked in a bakery window, and went back to the other side of the road, eyeing those around her. She saw no one suspicious.

Walking quickly down Second, she went all the way to Walnut, past City Tavern, turned the corner and came up to Third, and walked north—in a circle. She stopped when she reached Chestnut and studied everyone on both sides of the street. She saw no faces from her last check and felt safe, convinced she wasn't followed. She continued down Third and turned into the narrow alley that led to Ian's carriage house. Just before she reached it, she veered to the left, walked a bit farther, and entered the building owned by Benjamin Raus.

"I was afraid you wouldn't come," Ian said as she entered, quickly closing the door behind her.

"I almost didn't. I needed to be sure it was safe."

The building was empty—the Raus family took both their carriage and wagon to York—but crates, small tables, two chairs and some clothes were scattered about, belongings that most likely didn't fit in their wagon. Ian took Abigail by the hand and led her to the rear of the building, where a wall defined the empty stable.

"No sign of the boy following you?" he asked.

She shook her head. "No, no one followed. Maybe your father made a mistake."

"I don't think so. He doesn't make many mistakes. He seemed certain."

"Maybe more than one person follows me," she said. "But I was careful."

She looked at his face, rugged and handsome, his eyes trained on hers. No words had to be spoken, their thoughts and emotions on display. He took her in his arms, pulled her close, and kissed her. She didn't resist, her body limp against his, her arms embracing him and pulling him tight. When the kiss broke, she pulled away.

"Stop, Ian," she said. "We can't relive yesterday."

"You're right," he said reluctantly. But he didn't stop. He lifted her head and moved his lips to hers.

She kissed him, then pulled away. "We shouldn't be doing this."

"No, we shouldn't," he said, kissing her again.

She broke the embrace. "This is wrong," she said. "Please, stop. We can't."

He sighed audibly and paused, as if waiting for his racing pulse to slow. "You're right," he said, gazing in her eyes. "We shouldn't."

"It was a mistake for me to come."

"I had to see you," he said. "I need to know. Tell me about the Walkers."

She closed her eyes, wondering whether to reveal a secret. After a moment passed, she looked at him intently. "I should go," she said. "I don't have any military information."

"No," he said, lightly grasping her arm. "Tell me first."

She paused, collecting her thoughts, not making eye contact. "I told you I would never forgive my father for what happened. But I realize he only did what he thought was best for me. At the time, it seemed like he was right."

Ian listened, the story about to unravel. "I suppose I would do the same for my daughter," he said softly. "Protect her from the unknown."

She nodded. "He did what he had to do. When we got to

New York, he became active in certain social circles, and met both Solomon St. Clair and the Walkers."

"He chose your husband for you?"

"In some ways," she admitted. "But not in others. It may not seem like it, but Solomon and I do have much in common. We married six months after we met. Almost a year ago."

"Where do the Walkers come in?"

"They were close friends of both Solomon and my father," she explained. "They actually arranged for Solomon to leave London and come to New York."

Ian listened intently but looked confused. "I still don't understand."

Abigail hesitated but realized now was the time to tell the tale, to share the secret she had so carefully kept, one that had torn her apart. "Edward Walker is almost sixty, very sickly, and currently on his deathbed. He's expected to die any day if he isn't dead already."

Ian was getting impatient. "Yes, I know," he said. "I believe it was in the newspapers. Barnabas at City Tavern told me."

"Alice Walker is my age, wed to Edward for almost eighteen months."

"And removed from any inheritance, I'm told."

"Not quite, but most of it. She'll receive a tidy sum when her husband passes."

"But I don't see any connection. Why would you surrender your Loyalist beliefs?"

"I was never a devoted Loyalist," she said. "I only sided with my family, as I did in New York. It's easy to change sides in Philadelphia."

"But it still isn't reason enough to betray your country, your family and your husband."

She looked at him sadly, hesitant to reply, her eyes starting to mist.

"Is something wrong?"

"Alice Walker is pregnant," Abigail said, her gaze fixed on his. "She's due any day and may have given birth already."

He looked at Abigail, a vague understanding started to show in his eyes.

She struggled to continue. "About six weeks ago, I learned she's the reason Solomon left New York. He's the father of her child."

80

Ian stared at Abigail with disbelief. He was about to reply when a shadow passed the window in the carriage house door.

Fear flickered across Abigail's face. "Who is that?"

He held a finger to his lips and peeked from behind the stable wall.

A British soldier stood outside the entrance, his rifle drawn, bayonet fixed. Another was behind him.

"We know you're in there!" someone called from the yard behind the building.

"It's Duncan!" Ian hissed.

Abigail hurried to a window. "Soldiers are everywhere! What are we going to do?"

Ian moved beside her. Duncan stood in the yard, near the lean-to, with four soldiers beside him. More redcoats gathered at the front door.

"How did they know we were here?" Abigail hissed.

Ian frowned and shook his head. "How could I be so stupid! My father warned me not to do this. But I wouldn't listen."

"Should we surrender?"

"I don't know," he said, trying to think. "I'm sure they're here for me. Maybe they don't even know you're here."

"What's the meaning of this!" Patrick Blaine bellowed as he stormed from the shop into the yard.

"I'm arresting your son," Duncan announced loudly, ensuring any onlookers could hear.

"For what?" Patrick demanded. "He's done nothing wrong."

"Come out the back door, Ian Blaine," Duncan called.

"Should we go out?" Abigail asked, eyes wide. She peeked through the back window.

"I have to. If I don't, they may start shooting."

Patrick hurried toward Duncan. "You have no cause to arrest him."

"I'll decide that," Duncan said smugly.

Ian glanced out the window, and then to the front of the building where the redcoats stood guard at the door. "There's no escape. We had best do as they say."

"You have ten seconds, Blaine," Duncan shouted. "If you don't come out, we start shooting."

"It's me they want, not you," Ian said.

"We go out together," she insisted.

"I'm coming out the back door," Ian called. "I'm not armed."

"Prepare to fire," Duncan called. "Come out slowly, Blaine. Hands up."

"Are you ready?" Ian asked Abigail.

"Yes," she said, her face pale, her eyes wide.

"I'll open the door and walk out," Ian said to her. "Stand in the doorway, let them see you, and then follow."

"Are you sure?" she asked. "Shouldn't I be with you?"

"No, it has to be this way," he said grimly. "I can't risk you getting hurt should anyone start shooting."

"I'm counting, Blaine," Duncan announced.

"I'm coming out," Ian called.

He opened the back door, stood in the threshold for a moment so they could see he wasn't armed, and stepped out.

"Hands up," Duncan ordered. "And walk forward. Slowly."

Ian did as he was told. After he had taken a few steps, Abigail appeared in the doorway and followed, a few steps behind.

Duncan stood at the ready, sword drawn as if he faced a ferocious enemy. Patrick was behind him, restrained by a British soldier. Three other soldiers flanked Duncan.

"Keep coming forward," Duncan commanded.

Ian advanced as directed.

"Halt!" a British soldier ordered. He moved toward Ian, rifle lowered, until the bayonet was inches from his torso.

"Don't hurt Mrs. St. Clair," Ian demanded.

Duncan laughed. "You're such a fool, Blaine."

Ian looked at him quizzically. "I'll do whatever you say," he said. "I swear. But leave her alone."

Duncan went up to Abigail and bowed slightly. "Mrs. St. Clair," he said with the utmost respect, ensuring all could hear. "His Majesty's government thanks you for your assistance in helping us snare this traitor to the Crown."

81

Abigail was startled. "Colonel, what are you talking about!"

"It's all right, Mrs. St. Clair," Duncan said, looking at Ian with disgust. "You have nothing to fear from this scoundrel any longer."

"But, I never—"

"I'll protect you," Duncan continued. "You have my personal assurance."

She looked at Ian and shook her head, but he gave her a horrified look, as if his heart had been ripped from his body. "Ian, I swear," she muttered, tears welling in her eyes.

"It's traumatic, I know," Duncan said, rushing beside her and wrapping an arm around her shoulder. "But you played your part well."

"Colonel, I have no idea what you're talking about," she insisted.

Duncan turned to his men. "Tie the traitor's hands. Bring him to the city jail."

"No, you can't do that," Patrick protested. "He committed no crime."

"He's right," Ian said. "I've done nothing wrong."

"Save it for your hearing, Mr. Blaine," Duncan uttered with disgust.

"Stop!" Patrick demanded, still restrained by a soldier. "You're not taking him anywhere."

"You can always join him, Mr. Blaine," Duncan said. "If you don't cease your obstruction."

"But you can't do this," Patrick wailed.

"Yes, I can," Duncan replied. "And I will."

"Should we take him now, sir?" one of the soldiers asked.

"Yes, please do," Duncan said. He turned to Abigail. "I'll escort you home, Mrs. St. Clair. You've had a trying morning. But your efforts are greatly appreciated by his Majesty, I can assure you."

Abigail turned, trying to see Ian, but Duncan blocked her view. She wanted to scream that it was all a lie. But she knew she couldn't. "What are you doing?" she cried.

"You're safe, and that's all that matters," Duncan said. "I have a carriage waiting on Third."

He led her from the property and onto the street. A crowd was gathered in front of the watchmaker's, straining to see down the alley and into Blaine's yard.

"It's the minister's wife," a woman said, aghast.

"You're right, it is," said her companion. "Mixed up in spy business."

"Let us through," Duncan demanded. "I have to get this brave woman home."

"What happened, Colonel?" an older man asked.

"At great personal peril, Mrs. St. Clair courageously led us to a rebel spy," Duncan announced to the crowd.

"She's a heroine," an elderly woman called.

"That she is," Duncan confirmed grandly. "We should all be honored to have her in the city of Philadelphia."

"What happens to the spy, Colonel?" asked a man standing in the back of the crowd.

Duncan looked at Abigail smugly. "He'll hang by the neck until dead. The punishment given to all traitors."

Cries and mumbled voices came from the crowd. The Loyalists were vocal in their support. Those loyal to the rebellion were quiet, knowing not to speak, watching in fear.

Tears welled in Abigail's eyes. "Colonel, please, I don't know what you think happened, but Ian is not a spy."

Duncan stopped as they reached the carriage and turned to face her. "Either he is, or you are," he said sternly. "Do you understand what's at stake, should you choose to disagree with me?"

She shivered at the cruelty shown on his face, the coldness of his tone. "But you're wrong," she said. "I came to see him about the chest I'm purchasing."

"Madam, you may be able to fool the minister," Duncan said. "And apparently you have. But you cannot fool me. I know all about your history with Ian Blaine."

"Colonel, please, I beg you."

He opened the carriage door. "Get in," he said, extending a hand to help her.

Abigail had no choice. She stepped into the carriage, ignoring the stares of soldier and citizen. She sat on the bench seat, as far away from Duncan as she could, and looked out the window, shaken and afraid.

Duncan climbed in behind her. "What shall we tell the minister?"

"I intend to tell him the truth."

He smirked. "That you came to buy a chest? Or that Blaine is both your former and current lover?"

"That's not true," she said. "I did know Ian before I left for New York. But we're not lovers. I came to buy a chest."

"Then why were you in the carriage house?" he asked.

"Wouldn't you be in the store if you intended to purchase something?"

"I was on my way to the store when I saw Ian in the carriage house."

Duncan started laughing. "My dear Mrs. St. Clair. I don't believe a single word you're saying. I suggest that you tell your husband exactly what I intend to tell him—that you heroically led us to the rebel spy, Ian Blaine."

"I refuse to say that," she insisted. "Because it isn't true."

"You will say that, Mrs. St. Clair," he said firmly. "I promise. I will tell your husband that you worked closely with me, setting the trap. That is also what the newspaper headlines will read tomorrow. Within a day, the whole town will know that you betrayed Ian Blaine."

"But I didn't," she said as tears dripped down her cheeks. "And I won't."

"Yes, you will," he said gravely. "Because the alternative is too horrible for you to even comprehend."

82

Ian was pushed to the wagon by British soldiers, his hands tied behind his back. "Where are you taking me?" he demanded.

"Walnut St. jail," the soldier said as they shoved him in the back of the wagon.

"You're making a huge mistake," Patrick called as he watched them take Ian away.

"Just doing what we're told," one of the soldiers said.

"He's an innocent man," Patrick declared. "As you'll soon see."

The crowd looked on, casting suspicious glances at Patrick and Ian, whispering among themselves. Ian looked at their faces, neighbors and friends, a few strangers among them. Some showed contempt while others shared a knowing glance. He met the gaze of the watchmaker, an older man with his shop next to the Blaine carriage house, and the man simply nodded, as if to show his support.

As the wagon pulled away, headed south on Third, Patrick called to his son. "I'll come see you," he said. "We'll get this all straightened out."

Ian nodded, struggling not to break down. He had been betrayed by a woman he not only trusted but had been in love with for as long as he could remember. Or had he been betrayed? Did Abigail really help the British set a trap, snaring him while he obsessed with a love that was lost? Or had she been innocent, only followed by the enemy and caught unaware, just as he was? But if that were true, she would go to jail with him. But she didn't. She left with Duncan, treated like a heroine.

The Walnut St. jail covered most of the block at Walnut and Sixth, stretching to Locust. Only a few years old, it was built of white stone, two stories high, a rectangular building with a cupola centered atop the roof. When constructed only a few years before, most residents thought it sheer folly. There was little or no crime in Philadelphia. Certainly not enough to warrant a jail as huge as this. But it was built anyway.

Ian sat stoically in the back, meeting the stares of onlookers watching from the pavement as the wagon rolled down Walnut St. Minutes later they arrived, accompanied by a half dozen soldiers on horseback, went to the main entrance, and halted. Ian was pulled from the back of the wagon and shoved into the building.

The jail held a handful of those suspected of treason, colonial soldiers captured in battles that led to the occupation of Philadelphia, mainly officers, and the few criminals who thought it an opportune time to commit crimes during the chaos that ensued when Congress and their staunchest allies fled. Just inside the entrance, off to the right, was a long wooden table with three British soldiers behind it. They stared at Ian curiously as the soldiers brought him in.

"This is Ian Blaine," one of the soldiers said. "Arrested by Colonel Duncan."

A soldier sitting at the table wrote down the information. "Place of residence?"

Ian at first didn't reply, but then one of the soldiers rudely smacked him. "Answer the man," the soldier snarled.

"Chestnut St.," Ian said. "At Blaine and Son, Cabinetmakers, between Third and Fourth."

"Age?"

"Twenty-seven."

The magistrate looked up at the soldiers. "What are the charges?"

"Treason," one of them replied.

The magistrate showed no expression. He merely documented the information, completing the records required. After a moment passed, he turned to two soldiers standing behind him. "Cell number eight."

The soldiers came from around the table and took custody of Ian. "Come with us," one of them said.

They led him around the corner, still on the first floor, past seven cells to the eighth, and opened a heavy wooden door with a small opening centered in the top. British soldiers stood guard at each end of the hall, others were passing by, moving from one corridor to the next. It seemed heavily guarded, a jail once meant for pickpockets and drunks converted to a military prison.

"Give me your hands," the soldier said.

Ian did as he requested. As his hands were untied, he memorized all he saw—where guards were stationed, the location of exits, how far he was from freedom should he have the chance to escape. Once untied, they shoved him in the cell and slammed the door.

It was cramped, walls made of stone, no windows, a cot and small oval table and chair. The only light came from the corridor—and the large windows that made the side of the building—streaming through the tiny opening in the door.

Ian sighed and sat on the cot, thoroughly dejected, wondering why Abigail would ever betray him.

83

"I control your future," Duncan sneered as the carriage reached the rectory. "You must never forget that."

"I betrayed no one," Abigail insisted. "Even if I could, I wouldn't."

"You betrayed your husband, and you betrayed your country. For now, that will be our secret. But you must do exactly as I tell you. If you don't, you'll suffer the consequences."

A soldier opened the door to the carriage and helped Abigail step out. Duncan was right behind her. He led her toward the front door.

Just as they reached the entrance, the door opened and Anna was standing there, watching them closely. "Is something wrong?"

"No, all is well," Duncan said triumphantly. "We just apprehended a traitor."

"Oh. my," Anna said as they walked into the parlor. "I'll get the minister."

"I won't lie," Abigail hissed when Anna left.

"You'll lie if I tell you to," Duncan said firmly. "Now sit down and prepare yourself. Because you had better play your part perfectly."

Abigail didn't reply. She was nauseated, worried about Ian and wondering what Duncan wanted in return for protecting her.

Anna led the minister into the parlor. He looked confused.

"Sit, Solomon," Duncan requested. "I will tell the tale."

Solomon sat beside Abigail. "Can you please tell me what has happened?"

"Quite frankly," Duncan said, "the best way I can explain the tragic events that occurred today, is with a simple sentence. Your wife is a heroine."

"A heroine?" Solomon asked, his gaze fixed on Abigail. "Please, enlighten me."

Abigail watched him. He truly was confused. She didn't want him hurt. He was a good man, his infidelity excepted. Maybe it was better if she listened to Duncan and did what he said.

"Yes, please tell us," Anna urged, standing at the edge of the room.

"While working closely with me, Abigail laid a trap for the traitor, Ian Blaine," Duncan said. "We captured him in his neighbor's carriage house only moments ago."

Solomon's eyes widened. "I had no idea," he exclaimed. "Although I wondered where you were always off to."

Abigail believed him; he would have no idea. He lived in a world of sermons, philosophical discussions, the debate of theories and ideas. At least to those who knew him. But he also led a second life, a world wrapped in lies, deceit, and secret rendezvous. She hadn't known it existed until only a few weeks before. Now he seemed like a stranger, someone she didn't know as well as she thought she did, and might not even know at all. She had not only lost all respect for him, but she no longer loved him.

"Mrs. St. Clair laid the trap?" Anna asked. "I'm shocked. How brave you must be."

Abigail shifted her gaze to her housekeeper. Rarely, if ever, did Anna participate in discussions—even if invited. But it was a monumental announcement.

"Yes, she did," Duncan replied. "Philadelphia is much safer, thanks to Abigail St. Clair."

"I wish I, too, could make a contribution to the Crown," Anna said with awe.

"Someday you shall," Duncan assured her.

Abigail studied Anna closely, conversing so easily with Duncan, not as servant and master, or employee and employer, but as an equal—as if they had many similar discussions. The answer to a lingering question arrived. Abigail had been careful in route to Ian's house. No one had seen her—not even the boy who Patrick found following her. Someone knew where she was going and when she would be there. Someone who over-heard a conversation—the hushed discussion Abigail had with Ian.

"It'll be in the newspapers by morning," Duncan said. "The whole city will know what a courageous woman Mrs. St. Clair is."

"Darling, why didn't you tell me?" Solomon asked, his eyes wide behind his spectacles. "Although I would have been terri-fied had I known the peril you faced."

Abigail decided to play the part. It was best for all involved. At least for now. "I couldn't put you in danger, dear husband," she said, wanting to vomit as she spoke the words. "You play such an important role to the citizens of this community. It wasn't worth the risk."

"Such a brave woman," Duncan muttered, looking on in admiration.

Abigail kept her gaze fixed on Anna, watching as she shared glances with Duncan. It was easy to see. Anna had betrayed her. Nothing could be done about it—at least not now. But Abigail would use it to her advantage, planting doubts and mistruths when needed most. One question had been answered—she knew who betrayed her. But two questions still remained.

Why was Duncan protecting her? And what did he want in return?

84

I an barely ate, even though the food seemed adequate, and he slept restlessly, pondering his fate. At first he was frantic, sure he was about to be hung. But when he considered what had happened, he wasn't sure Duncan had any evidence. Even if Abigail did betray him, all he told her was that he may have been seen observing the British army at Trudruffrin. Every other discussion they had concerned her giving him military secrets. Although he doubted she or Duncan would tell the truth, especially if they were in on it together.

Shortly after 8 a.m. a British soldier appeared at the door. "You've got visitors, Blaine."

Ian stood, anxious to see anyone. A moment later the door opened, and his father came in with Barnabas.

"Ian," Patrick said as he rushed in the room and hugged his son. "Are you all right?"

Ian held his father tightly, not wanting to let go. "So far."

"They're not torturing you, are they lad?" Patrick asked anxiously.

"No," Ian said. "At least not yet."

They sat, Ian and Patrick on the cot, Barnabas in the lone chair. Ian put his head in his hands, totally defeated.

"I told you not to trust her," Patrick said in a fatherly tone, not scolding. "She's not the same woman you loved. People change."

"I still can't believe it," Ian said as he looked up. "There has to be another explanation."

Barnabas held up the *Pennsylvania Ledger*. "Not according to this. The article claims she and Duncan have been plotting to trap you for weeks."

Ian frowned. "They got their information from Duncan. It's all false."

"It does seem like she led the redcoats right to you," Patrick said delicately, as if he wanted to spare his son the pain.

Ian sighed. "I know it looks that way, but I don't believe it."

Patrick frowned. "You mean you won't believe it. There's a difference."

"I saw Abigail coming down Third," Barnabas said. "I should have stopped her or tried to intervene when the British came."

Ian tensed, haunted by a dozen questions. Barnabas claimed he had a prior commitment and couldn't watch for the British. How did he see Abigail approach the carriage house? Maybe Abigail didn't betray him. Maybe Barnabas did. Missy Malone told Abigail someone close was watching—someone they wouldn't suspect.

"Are you listening" Patrick asked. "She had to betray you. There's no other explanation."

Ian hesitated, but then replied. "I think she was tricked. Just like I was."

"We should assume she helped Duncan," Patrick said. "If you find out differently, then all the better."

Ian didn't know what to think. He refused to believe Abigail betrayed him. And he doubted that Barnabas, a lifelong friend, did either.

"Although I still question why she did it," Barnabas continued, as if he too had doubts. "She shared information for weeks. Why betray you now?"

"Maybe Duncan suspected something between them," Patrick suggested. "And she betrayed Ian to save herself."

"It can't be changed now," Ian said, totally defeated. "Regardless of what's true."

Patrick sighed, pulling his son close. "We'll get through this. I promise."

"What comes next?" Ian asked.

"You'll have a hearing tomorrow morning at 9 a.m.," Barnabas said. He then frowned. "Although I have an appointment. I'll have to change it so I can attend."

Patrick looked at him with astonishment. "What can be more important than this?"

"You're right, of course," Barnabas said apologetically. "I'll find a way."

"I don't see why you wouldn't," Patrick declared.

"It's just that I already changed it once," Barnabas said.

"'It must be extremely important," Ian mumbled, trying to hide his mistrust.

Barnabas shrugged. "I didn't meet my contact yesterday. I got word just as he was due that he rescheduled for tomorrow. That's when I saw Abigail coming down Third."

Ian sighed with relief, smiling slightly. How could he ever suspect Barnabas? "I could never doubt your friendship."

"Nor should you," Barnabas said, looking at him strangely.

"Was your contact another spy?" Ian asked.

Barnabas started laughing. "Lord, no," he said. "He's a trader, although I do give him information. But I'm only trying to buy produce. If I don't get it, we won't be making any shepherd's pie."

Patrick and Ian managed a smile, even given the circumstances.

"Can't you send someone else?" Patrick asked. "After all, my boy's life is at stake."

"I'll think of something," Barnabas assured them. "No need to worry."

"Good," Patrick said, "then we'll both be there. But we'll defer to Barnabas. The redcoats trust him."

"The British know that Patrick and I are friends," Barnabas said. "But I still need to be careful. I have to preserve their image of me—one of the most trusted Loyalists in the city."

"Who questions me?" Ian asked. "It isn't Duncan, is it?"

"No," Barnabas replied. "It's a solicitor. Colonel Wentworth."

"What's the process?" Patrick asked. "Is it anything we can prepare for?"

"I don't think so," Barnabas said. "The British present three witnesses—Duncan, Abigail, and Oliver Hart. When they're finished their testimony, they may ask Ian questions."

"Is Colonel Wentworth the only judge?" Patrick asked.

"Two other officers will be present," Barnabas said. "I don't know their names yet, but I do know that they're both captains, so they'll defer to Wentworth."

"I'm doomed," Ian said, shaking his head in defeat.

"Maybe not," Barnabas said with a sly grin.

"Why is that?" Patrick asked, eyeing his friend curiously. "What do you know that we don't?"

"Colonel Wentworth loves my shepherd's pie," Barnabas said with a wink.

85

Abigail lay in bed, tossing and turning, sleep elusive. She wished she could get a message to Ian, to tell him she didn't betray him, that it was all a trap, but she couldn't. She wasn't able to leave the house, not even to get word to Patrick, and she couldn't visit Ian in jail—Duncan would somehow stop her. She was physically ill, knowing he sat in a prison cell, thinking she had betrayed him.

After lying there for at least an hour, she climbed from bed and went to the window, gazing out at the stars. It was quiet, no pedestrians or carriages on the little lane that ran beside the rectory. She saw candles flickering in windows of nearby houses, some residents not yet in bed. She had to somehow get her mind off of Ian, and her testimony the following morning, or she would lay awake all night.

She decided to get a glass of cider. She walked to her door and gently opened it, not wanting to wake Solomon should he be sleeping. But as she stepped into the hallway, she heard voices, a murmured conversation in the parlor below. She tiptoed to the end of the landing and leaned over the railing. She could just about make out the conversation.

"When I testify tomorrow, I'll claim that Anna overheard their conversation, and that's how we knew they were in the neighbor's carriage house," Duncan was saying. "Best keep you out of it."

"Anna must be prepared to state as such, should the authorities question her," Solomon said. "The Crown might be interested in her son's testimony, as well. Especially since he followed Abigail about the city."

"I'll ensure Anna is prepared," Duncan replied. "But it wouldn't be the first time she overheard them, even if it were true. She's been a valuable asset."

Abigail could barely breathe, as if her lungs had been robbed of air. Solomon was plotting with Duncan?

"Abigail didn't know I came in the back door," Solomon continued. "But when I realized Blaine was in the parlor, I had to hear what they were saying."

"It's good that you did," Duncan said. "No one had to follow her. We knew where she was going and when."

"I did talk to General Howe. Of course, as an old friend, he'll support whatever I need."

"I suspected as such," Duncan said. "The plan worked nicely. Even my promotion to general has been approved—as soon as Blaine hangs,"

"Howe will have all the documents ready to sign," Solomon confirmed, "and the Church has been alerted."

"I do think an annulment is the best approach," Duncan mused. "But divorce papers are prepared as well—they're just a bit more scandalous."

"You're assuming Abigail will sign the documents."

"She will, I assure you," Duncan replied. "She has little choice. Now that she's trapped in her web of deceit."

Abigail could not believe what she was hearing. Solomon, with Duncan's help, had somehow staged an annulment, or a divorce if needed, framing Ian as part of the process. Why hadn't he just asked her? She would have cooperated. Why ruin lives in the process?

"Blaine will get what he deserves," Solomon said. "I had no idea he and Abigail had once planned to marry. I never would have let her near him if I had."

"It all worked as intended," Duncan said. "She walked right into the trap."

"How do we make sure she does the right thing?"

"I'll take care of that," Duncan assured him. "I've already threatened her."

"But she testifies tomorrow."

"And I intend to present her options at the jail, just before she enters the courtroom," Duncan said. "I'll guarantee she makes the right decision."

Abigail listened carefully, convinced she could outsmart them. But she had to know everything they had planned. She strained, listening intently, memorizing every word they said.

"Are you sure she'll cooperate?" Solomon asked. "I can't afford to have any nasty gossip spoil my plans."

"She has no choice. I'll ensure she understands that. Her first option is to testify against Ian and sign the annulment. After Blaine is hung, she disappears."

"I don't care where she goes," Solomon said. "But it can't be Philadelphia, New York, or London."

"Agreed," Duncan said. "Her second option is to resist. Then she's exposed as a spy, Blaine's lover, and you're granted a divorce. We have plenty of evidence. We've been following her since you arrived."

"I don't want her hung. I did care for her once. I can't be that cruel and vindictive."

"General Howe would never execute a woman," Duncan assured him. "He'd send her to one of those prison ships docked outside of New York. She'll spend the rest of the war there and, if she doesn't die of disease, no one will even remember her."

86

The following morning, Ian was led into a makeshift courtroom by two British soldiers who then stood guard at the door. It wasn't what he expected. The room wasn't very large, a rectangular table at the front where three British officers sat. A single chair was placed before them, for the witness, while a second chair for the accused was off to one side. A half dozen chairs for others that might participate were located in the rear of the room. As Ian entered, he saw his father and Barnabas already seated, with no other observers present.

"Come in, Mr. Blaine," an officer said. "And be seated." He pointed to the chair off to the side, near the visitor's seats.

Ian sat where directed. He wouldn't be able to see the witness as they testified unless they turned to face him. Maybe that was better. He looked at Patrick and Barnabas, nodded his thanks for their presence, and hoped that Barnabas had been able to intervene on his behalf, or at least provide a credible reference to the colonel in charge of the proceedings.

"Mr. Blaine, I am Colonel Wentworth, and I'll be directing today's proceedings," said the officer seated in the center of the table. He was older, perhaps sixty, wearing a white wig. He was dressed in the red coat of the British army, very dignified, his face stern.

"Thank you, sir," Ian said, his voice quivering. He made eye contact with Wentworth, who gave no clues as to what his thoughts might be.

"My associates are Captain Milton and Captain Hyde," Wentworth said.

Ian nodded to each in turn. Milton was about forty years old and stout. He didn't wear a wig but had powdered hair, his round face showing no expression, almost as if he was asleep with his eyes open. Captain Hyde was about the same age, but lean, his brown hair pulled back in a short ponytail. They each eyed Ian curiously, if not sternly, and much like Wentworth, neither gave any indication of how they might rule.

"Our first witness is Colonel Alexander Duncan," Wentworth said. He motioned to one of the soldiers flanking the entrance.

Duncan strutted in a moment later. He ignored Ian, never looked at Patrick or Barnabas, and sat straight in the witness chair, his hands folded in his lap. He looked comfortable, as if he was gracing the room with his presence and nodded to the three British officers who faced him.

"Colonel Duncan," Wentworth said. "I'm Colonel Wentworth and, with my colleagues Captain Milton and Captain Hyde, we'll direct the proceedings. Please state your name and rank for the record."

"Colonel Alexander Duncan."

Wentworth hesitated, getting his notes in order. "Colonel Duncan, you have accused Ian Blaine of treason for spying on His Majesty's government. Please provide your evidence,"

"Of course, Colonel," Duncan began, sitting back in the chair. "I have identified three occasions where the accused has committed the specified act."

"Please, continue," Wentworth said, writing notes as were the other judges.

"First, on the evening of September eighteenth, Ian Blaine was seen observing the British encampment at Trudruffrin," Duncan stated. He leaned toward the judges, as if sharing a secret. "For nefarious purposes, I'm sure."

"How did you know it was Mr. Blaine?" Captain Milton asked.

"I was in the company of a Philadelphia citizen, Mr. Oliver Hart, who identified Blaine."

Milton arched his eyebrows. "But you could not identify him?"

"No, I couldn't," Duncan said, squirming in his seat. "I did not know Mr. Blaine at the time. But I have reason to believe it was the man now in the courtroom."

"I would suggest that this question is best suited for witness Hart," Milton interjected.

"Agreed," Wentworth said. "Colonel, did you take any action for this alleged activity?"

Duncan hesitated, as if he realized the proceedings might be different than expected. "I planned to arrest Blaine shortly after the occupation," he explained, speaking slowly and succinctly.

"But you did not?" Wentworth asked.

"Apparently he was in Jersey," Duncan said. "He didn't return until the following day. I was told by his father, and later by Barnabas Stone, owner of the City Tavern, that Ian Blaine had been back and forth to Jersey and had actually gone on the eighteenth and could not possibly have been at Trudruffrin as specified."

Wentworth looked at Barnabas and Patrick. "Gentlemen, if Mr. Blaine made several trips to Jersey, how are you certain he was there on the eighteenth?"

"Payment from one of our Jersey customers was due the

eighteenth," Patrick explained. "It was critical, for the sake of our business, to obtain the funds as soon as they were available. Our livelihood was at stake."

The judges each scribbled notes, not revealing their opinion on the testimony offered.

"Describe the second event of alleged treason, Colonel Duncan," Wentworth directed.

Duncan eyed the judges warily. "Mr. Blaine warned the colonials of the attack on Fort Mercer."

"How did he obtain such information?" Captain Hyde asked, speaking for the first time.

Duncan shifted, leaning closer to the judges. "It was discussed at a dinner at the rectory, where Mrs. St. Clair became aware of it, and then at the church while Mr. Blaine was performing some carpentry work," he said, not as confident, his tone not as strong. "Mrs. St. Clair mentioned the attack to the minister, unaware that Mr. Blaine overheard. I would add that Mrs. St. Clair has been very cooperative, critical to the apprehension of Mr. Blaine."

"Then it seems, based on the testimony provided, that the question is best suited for Mrs. St. Clair," Captain Hyde said, his observation consistent with Duncan's first claim.

"Agreed," Wentworth said, scribbling in his notes.

Ian dared let a small sigh escape. It seemed that the judges had effectively negated Duncan's first two assertions, or at least delegated the response to Abigail and Hart.

"What is your last accusation, Colonel Duncan," Wentworth continued.

Ian knew Duncan was angry. He had expected the judges to accept all accusations made. So far, he couldn't have been more wrong. Ian was relieved he couldn't see Duncan's face, given how the seating was arranged.

"Two days ago," Duncan said, his tone harsher, "Mrs. St. Clair led us to Blaine, hiding in his neighbor's carriage house.

She had pretended to offer him more information, and this was the site of their prearranged rendezvous. This can be confirmed by Anna Knight, the St. Clair's servant, who overheard their conversation."

Ian cast a guarded glance at Patrick and Barnabas. He hadn't been betrayed by Abigail. They had both been betrayed by Anna. But somehow, Duncan thought Abigail was the mastermind. Maybe she was.

"Mrs. St. Clair, at tremendous personal risk, has been providing information on Blaine's activities," Duncan said, his confidence returning. "We allowed the interaction to continue until yesterday, when Blaine was apprehended."

The judges whispered among themselves while Ian glanced at Patrick and Barnabas. It was difficult to discern by their expressions what their thoughts might be. After they finished talking, they sat back and faced those in attendance.

"That will be all, Colonel Duncan," Wentworth said. He turned to the soldier at the door. "Bring in Mrs. St. Clair, please."

Duncan rose from the chair and walked to the spectator's section, prepared to sit down.

"I'm sorry, Colonel," Wentworth said. "The witness testimony may not be observed. But you may wait outside if you choose."

Duncan's eyes lit with anger, although his face remained passive. He pointed to Patrick and Barnabas. "May I ask what they are doing here?"

"They're assisting in the accused's defense," Wentworth said. "Now, please, sir, kindly observe the rules of the court."

Duncan's lips were taut, his face firm and flush. He glared at the judges, started to speak but apparently thought it best that he didn't. He marched to the door, his heels echoing on the wood floor, and stormed out, just as Abigail came in.

"Mrs. St. Clair, please sit down," Wentworth said.

87

Abigail was still shaken when called to testify. Duncan had presented his ultimatum, with the available options, just before he was called in to the courtroom. Solomon sat down the hall, feigning disinterest, reading the Bible as if it served to save his soul. She pretended to be terrified and agreed to all of Duncan's demands, including the testimony she would offer. But he had underestimated her, as many had her entire life.

She entered the courtroom, dressed in a flowing green dress with white accents, and sat where indicated. She avoided looking at Ian—she had to appear impartial—and didn't acknowledge Barnabas or Patrick. She had planned every detail of what she intended to say, hoping to snare Duncan and Solomon in a trap from which they couldn't escape. Most of what she said would be true, although some falsehoods were needed to protect Ian.

"Mrs. St. Clair," Wentworth said. "I'm Colonel Wentworth, and I will direct the proceedings with my colleagues Captain Milton and Captain Hyde."

"I understand, sir," she said softly, her heart beating against her chest.

The three judges whispered among themselves, read over their notes, and then began.

"Mrs. St. Clair, when did you first meet Ian Blaine?" Wentworth asked.

Abigail hesitated. She wanted to give the correct answer, but she didn't want to reveal too much. "I was raised in Philadelphia," she said. "I've known Ian Blaine most of my life."

"How long were you absent from Philadelphia?" Milton asked.

"About two years."

"When did you first see Mr. Blaine upon your return?" Hyde asked.

Abigail breathed a sigh of relief. They didn't know she and Ian had been lovers. And they didn't know enough to ask. "At the party hosted by the congregation," she said. "It was a few days after the occupation."

"Did you have any private discussions with Mr. Blaine on that day?" Hyde asked.

"I did," she replied. "We briefly discussed the wine."

"Did he mention any trips to Jersey?" Hyde asked.

"He did not."

Wentworth continued. "How many times have you talked to Mr. Blaine since then?"

Abigail hesitated. She had to be careful. "A half dozen times. I conversed with him on several occasions while he built a pew at the church."

"Did you share information with him about the attack on Fort Mercer?" Milton asked.

Abigail pretended to consider the question. It was now that she must be her most convincing. "Not that I recall."

"Colonel Duncan was quite clear that you did," Wentworth said.

She studied the judges, her mouth dry, and replied softly. "I'm sorry, but I don't recollect having said anything in that regard."

The judges watched her a moment, none speaking. "What was your purpose for going to Benjamin Raus's carriage house?" Wentworth asked.

"I ordered a chest from Mr. Blaine," Abigail explained, "and he said he would load it on his wagon for delivery the following morning. After our discussion, I changed my mind, preferring a different design, and went to his carriage house to tell him. As I approached, I saw him enter the neighboring building. He was concerned that the owners, who are away, had left some belongings, and he wanted to ensure they hadn't been disturbed. I went in the building with him while he checked. We were about to exit when the soldiers arrived."

Wentworth glanced at the other judges warily. "You do realize there are serious repercussions for not being truthful?"

"I do, sir."

"We have a written statement from Colonel Duncan," Wentworth continued. "He stated that your maid, Anna Knight, overheard your discussion with Mr. Blaine and confirmed you were meeting him at his neighbor's carriage house."

"I know nothing of her statement," Abigail admitted. "But I suggest that she overheard only fragments of conversation and misunderstood what was said."

Hyde continued. "But you did confer with Colonel Duncan, planning to trap Blaine at the carriage house."

Abigail tried to appear calm. The next set of questions would be difficult. "I did not, sir."

Those in the room stirred, muttered among themselves, and shared astonished glances. Hyde leaned toward Wentworth, showing him a message scribbled in his notes.

"Are you saying the colonel was not truthful?" an incredulous Wentworth asked.

She took a deep breath. She might soon hang beside Ian. "I am, sir," she said softly.

Wentworth gasped. He turned to Hyde and Milton, who observed Abigail closely, eyes wide, their mouths agape. "Mrs. St. Clair," an astonished Wentworth continued. "Why would the good colonel, who has an impeccable reputation, ever lie?"

Abigail hesitated, started to speak, but stopped. She looked at each judge, hoping they would find sincerity in her gaze. "May I speak frankly?" she asked meekly.

"Yes, please do," Wentworth said. "The court finds your testimony quite concerning."

"I believe Colonel Duncan staged all that occurred," she said softly.

Wentworth stared in disbelief. "Why would he ever do that?"

Milton intervened. "Do you realize you're making a serious accusation?"

"Yes, sir, I do," Abigail replied, eyes lowered. "It's an accusation not made lightly."

Milton glanced at his two companions. "Please elaborate, Mrs. St. Clair," he said. "What was Colonel Duncan trying to accomplish? Choose your words wisely."

She took a deep breath, her next statement critical. "I think Colonel Duncan tried to bargain for my silence."

"For what purpose?" an astonished Milton asked loudly.

Abigail eyed the judges, disbelief written in every wrinkle of their faces. "I saw something that I wasn't supposed to see."

The judges again shared surprised glances and whispered comments. "Please, Mrs. St. Clair," Wentworth said. "Enlighten us. What did you see?"

"A transaction, perhaps, between Mr. Oliver Hart and Colonel Duncan," Abigail said. "Which I witnessed on more than one occasion."

"What are you suggesting?" Wentworth asked, losing his patience.

"I believe Oliver Hart makes payments to Colonel Duncan for goods his ships bring to the city."

88

Oliver Hart paced the floor outside the conference room, waiting to be called as a witness. He debated what he should say—what Duncan had instructed or the truth. But nothing could be more harmful than the truth.

Hart glanced at the minister reading the Bible. Solomon seemed content, as if unaware that the testimony given could result in a man's death. But maybe that's why he read the Bible. Maybe he prayed for Ian Blaine.

Colonel Duncan had stormed from the court room, a scowl on his face, cursing the way the proceedings were conducted. With a warning to Hart to tell what must be told, he had left the building, pressed to perform duties elsewhere.

As Hart paced the hallway, the door abruptly opened and Abigail stepped out, a soldier beside her. He met her gaze, her face impassive, not revealing what she may or may not have said. She passed without speaking and turned down the hallway, opposite from Solomon. Hart watched her, confused, when the soldier urged him into the court room. He entered, avoided eye contact with Ian, Patrick, or Barnabas, and wondered what had already been said. But he knew what mattered most was the testimony about to begin.

"We appreciate your presence, Mr. Hart," Wentworth said. "I'm Colonel Wentworth and I'll direct the proceedings with my colleagues Captain Milton and Captain Hyde."

"Thank you, sir," Hart said as he sat down. He assumed it was a preliminary hearing and that Ian Blaine was treated like any other subject that the Crown intended to try for a crime.

"Do you know the accused, Ian Blaine, Mr. Hart?" Wentworth asked.

"I do, sir," Hart replied. "More as a passing acquaintance than a close friend."

"Do you hold any animosity toward Mr. Blaine?" Milton asked.

"No, sir, I do not."

Wentworth pursued a different line of questioning. "Were you at the British camp in Trudruffrin on the evening of September eighteenth?"

"Yes, I was."

"What was your purpose?" Wentworth asked.

Hart wanted to accurately describe his motive, whether harmful to him or not. "When the British advance began, I asked General Howe, through an intermediary, if I could help get supplies to the city. He agreed to discuss the matter, and I was summoned to Trudruffrin."

"So, as a Loyalist, you offered to assist the British army?" Captain Hyde asked.

Hart hesitated. "I did agree to cooperate in getting supplies to the city. But it was actually the residents who I had hoped to help. I was afraid they would starve."

The judges looked at him curiously as Ian, Patrick, and Barnabas shared furtive glances. Hart's statement was different from what every resident believed to be true.

"Regardless of your motive," Wentworth continued, "you were at Trudruffrin."

"Yes, I was," Hart said. "General Howe assigned Colonel Duncan to meet with me."

Hyde shuffled his papers. "During that meeting, a rebel was spotted observing the camp."

"A man in civilian clothes," Hart replied. "I'm not sure if he was spying."

"Duncan also saw him, and he asked if you knew him. Is that correct?" Milton asked.

"Not quite," Hart replied. "When the man appeared, I squinted in the approaching darkness, trying to see who it was. I believe I mumbled, 'Is that Ian Blaine?' As the man fled, Duncan asked who Ian Blaine was, and where he could be found."

Hyde whispered in Wentworth's ear, and the colonel nodded. "Could you have been mistaken?" Hyde asked.

"Yes, I easily could have been," Hart admitted. "It was dusk, and the man was in a wooded area, not clearly visible. It was a fleeting image, at best."

Wentworth continued, the line of questioning different. "Do you know Abigail St. Clair?"

"I do," Hart replied. "I have been a guest at the St. Clair household on several occasions."

"Did you know Mrs. St. Clair when she formerly lived in Philadelphia?" Hyde asked.

"No, sir, I did not. But I did know her father and her older sister Emma."

Wentworth leaned close to Milton and exchanged a few comments.

"Mr. Hart," Milton said, his tone stern, his face firm. "During Mrs. St. Clair's testimony, she made serious allegations that concern you and Colonel Duncan. Are you aware of that?"

Hart sat quietly and considered his response. His next few

replies could cost him his life. But sometimes honor super-
seded, good overcame evil. "No, I did not. Can you elaborate?"

Wentworth interceded. "Mrs. St. Clair alleged a financial
arrangement between you and Colonel Duncan. Does such an
agreement exist?"

Hart squirmed. "Yes, sir, it does."

Wentworth arched his eyebrows. "Can you describe this
financial arrangement?"

Hart nodded. The most difficult questions were coming.
"When I met Colonel Duncan at Trudruffrin, he demanded
compensation for assisting my efforts delivering supplies to the
city's residents."

Hyde sat back, his arms folded across his chest. "What
compensation?"

Hart hesitated. He wanted to describe their arrangement
precisely. "He would receive a twenty-five percent commission
on any profits I earned shipping cargo into Philadelphia. But
only for the residents—not the military."

Ian shared glances with Patrick and Barnabas, astonished
looks on all their faces.

"That's a serious accusation," Wentworth said gravely.

"I'm aware of that, sir," Hart replied. "But I assure you, it's
the truth. Colonel Duncan told me on several occasions that
much of his family fortune had been lost when cargo he
financed was confiscated by the colonials. He was determined
to recoup those losses—regardless of how he did it."

"How did Mrs. St. Clair become aware of this arrangement?" Wentworth asked.

"She saw a transaction I conducted with the colonel," Hart
said. "I think she could easily decipher what she observed and
reach the correct conclusion."

"Did she share her suspicions with you?" Hyde asked.

"She didn't have to," Hart replied. "I could tell by her

expression that she knew she saw something she wasn't supposed to see."

"She testified to the same," Wentworth remarked. "And mentioned more than one occasion in which she was the observer."

"I wasn't aware of other occasions," Hart said. "But I do not dispute that they existed."

Wentworth spoke with the other judges, wrote some notes, and looked at Hart. "One last question, Mr. Hart. Do you have any reason to believe that Ian Blaine has been spying on British forces in Philadelphia?"

Hart hesitated, eyeing each judge in turn. "None whatsoever, Colonel Wentworth. I do not know Mr. Blaine well, but I do know him to be an upstanding citizen, a man of good character with irrefutable references. Quite frankly, if I heard such accusations, I would not believe them."

89

The judges dismissed Oliver Hart and conferred for a few minutes, referring to notes they had taken during the proceedings. Finally, Colonel Wentworth spoke. "Ian Blaine, please stand."

Ian stood, glanced at his father with the most loving look he could muster, and prepared to meet his fate. He tried not to tremble, even though it was difficult, and faced the judges.

"Ian Blaine," Colonel Wentworth announced. "You are hereby released from custody with no further questions or charges."

"Justice is served!" Patrick cried as he came forward and hugged his son.

Barnabas was right behind him. "Good for you, lad!"

"Thank you so much," Ian said as he vigorously shook Barnabas's hand. "For whatever it was you did to sway this court."

Barnabas chuckled. "Very little, actually. The witnesses were more than enough."

"Let's get you home," Patrick whispered. "Before they change their minds."

They left the room and went into the hallway. Only Oliver Hart remained, standing in the corridor, waiting for the verdict.

Ian looked at him, and for a moment their eyes locked.

Hart nodded respectfully. "Well done, Mr. Blaine," he said. He looked to make sure no one was nearby. "I look forward to working with you."

Ian smiled and stuck out his hand, shaking Hart's firmly, one Patriot to another.

"Come on, Ian," Barnabas said. "We've got some celebrating to do."

They left the jail, went down Walnut to Second, and entered the City Tavern, arriving just before noon. There were only a few patrons, dinner was served at two, so they took their normal table, able to speak freely.

"Dolly, three mugs of beer, please," Barnabas called as he sat down and joined them.

"Coming right up," she said, moving behind the bar. "Is there anything else, you'll be needing, Patrick Blaine?"

Patrick laughed, as did the others. "Your company is always welcomed."

"Then I'll see that you get it," she said as she delivered their beers. "I'll stop after closing. It seems we have some celebrating to do."

"We do," Patrick said, smiling. "Sharing it with you makes it all the more special."

"Aww, Patrick Blaine," she crooned, leaning over to kiss the top of his head. "There's hope for you yet, isn't there?"

They all laughed. A patron called for a refill and Dolly went on her way, waiting on the few tables that were occupied.

"We've much to be thankful for," Barnabas said, raising his glass in toast.

"We do," Ian agreed as they clinked their glasses.

Patrick took a sip of beer. "Your lady didn't betray you."

"No, she didn't," Ian said. "I'm sorry I doubted her."

"Who wouldn't?" Barnabas asked. "It surely seemed she had laid a trap."

Ian sighed, reliving moments best forgotten. "It was my own stupidity. I should have known to be careful around Anna Knight. We never should have met at the carriage house."

"Don't forget that in days to come," Patrick said. "It was a painful lesson, but I hope you learned it."

"Best treat it as a misunderstanding when you next cross paths with Mrs. Knight," Barnabas suggested. "Act is if you've no ill will."

Ian realized he had much more than Anna to worry about. "I still need to be wary of Duncan. Especially now that he's exposed."

Barnabas nodded. "Although he's got his own problems. The Crown doesn't take lightly to thievery. Especially among its senior officers."

"We couldn't have been more wrong about Hart," Patrick said. "I feel badly for thinking so poorly of the man."

"The truth will come out," Barnabas assured them. "It always does."

Ian wondered what it was like to be a Patriot living the life of a traitor. But Barnabas did it, too—while making valuable contributions to the cause.

Patrick sipped his beer. "What a brilliant performance by Abigail. She outsmarted Hart and Duncan."

Ian smiled. "I knew I could trust her—even if I did waver when the trap was laid."

"You were right," Patrick said. "But don't look for something that no longer exists. Leave the past where it belongs."

"You definitely need to avoid her now," Barnabas warned.

Ian nodded, his thoughts elsewhere. He was focused on a secret he couldn't yet share.

90

Abigail walked down Third at 9 a.m. the following morning, wearing a lavender dress, her favorite white shawl wrapped around her. It was a brisk day, the streets almost bare, leaves dancing along the pavements in a gentle autumn breeze. British soldiers rode by on horseback, others walked past shops and houses. Wagons and carriages rattled by, their wooden wheels clicking on cobblestone—all just another day in the occupied city of Philadelphia. But for the first time since she had arrived, she strolled down the street without looking over her shoulder, nary a concern about being followed.

She hoped to find Ian in the carriage house, even though no arrangements had been made. But she knew he had been released from jail, innocent of all charges. The newspaper headlines screamed the verdict, and citizens discussed it as they walked down the streets. She suspected that he realized, if he wanted to see her, that's where she would be—an unplanned rendezvous where they had shared their first kiss in over two years.

As she approached the corner of Chestnut, she turned

down the slender alley. It was deserted, as she expected. She went directly to the carriage house and stepped inside.

Ian was waiting at the rear of the building. He smiled as she approached. "I was hoping you would come."

"And I was hoping you would be here," she said with a grin.

She stopped in front of him, her gaze locked on his. For a brief instant they only looked in each other's eyes, seeing more than words could say.

He came closer and took her in his arms. When she didn't resist, he hugged her tightly and kissed her, long and lovingly. It seemed like two years of separation had never existed.

"We have to be careful," he said, aware of the risks. "Duncan will really be out to get us now."

She laughed. "I don't think so."

He looked at her quizzically. "Why not? The man must despise me. And you, too."

She couldn't contain her excitement. She was quiet for a moment, letting his apprehension linger, the drama increasing. "Duncan was sent to London this morning. A fresh start, I suppose."

"He'll be dealt with severely," Ian said. "Deservedly so."

She shrugged. "Maybe not, given the circumstances," she said. "Apparently, he desperately needed to recover the funds he lost—his father sits in debtor's prison as a result. And his wife is very sickly, his children not yet grown, and costs involved are severe."

Ian tried to find compassion. "I suppose even a scoundrel has a redeeming quality or two. His obsession with a promotion and all his thievery makes more sense now."

"I suppose he had his reasons. But he's gone. No one is watching us."

Ian looked confused. "What about Solomon? Surely he lurks somewhere."

She gazed in his eyes, showing the love that held her heart. "Solomon left with Duncan."

Ian's eyes widened. "He's gone?"

She nodded. "It was Solomon plotting with Duncan to get you. Missy tried to warn me, but only said it was someone I would never suspect. It wasn't Anna Knight."

He slowly shook his head, summing the information received. "Solomon and Duncan have been working together?"

"Yes, although each had their own motives. Hart was never involved. It just seemed like he was. If he was watching you at all, it was only to prove your innocence."

Ian was starting to understand. "What happened with Solomon?"

She hesitated, the story painful to tell. "He's returning to London, but with Alice Walker and her baby, a boy born a few days ago."

Ian stared at her, trying to process what she just said. "And Mr. Walker?"

"He died last week. Alice received some inheritance, not much, but enough to return to London."

"As Solomon's wife?'

Abigail nodded, her gaze still trained on his.

"It makes sense," he said with a shrug. "She avoids a scandal and all the gossip that comes with it. Solomon does, too."

"I signed the annulment paperwork yesterday, right after I left the courtroom. Solomon was never what he seemed, and certainly not what one would expect of a minister."

"He did well in the pulpit, though," Ian said, "I'm forced to admit."

"He does have his talents," she agreed. "But he either had to leave or be forever disgraced. It's his chance to start over, too. As well as mine."

He opened his mouth as if to speak, and after several unsuccessful attempts he managed to continue. "I can't believe this is happening."

"It's all true," she said, hugging him tightly. After a moment, she pulled away. "I also moved out of the rectory after I signed the papers. A new minister will be sent shortly."

"Where did you go?" he asked, struggling to keep up.

"My family's home on Pine St. It was leased by a cousin. But now there's a room for me. It had been occupied by a British colonel, but he took Duncan's room at the rectory."

"This is incredible," Ian said, slowly shaking his head. "It changes everything."

"It does," she said, smiling coyly. "But we have to be extremely cautious."

He looked at her, confused. "I don't understand. Why would it matter?"

"Two British officers are lodged in my father's house with my cousin and me. I'm sure they'll reveal quite a bit of information. But we have to be careful in how we handle it. Duncan outsmarted us, but he was a crook and in the end it didn't matter. And who would ever believe a minister could be so dastardly. But from now on—"

"Abigail," Ian interrupted. "This all seems too good to be true. Can everything be like it was? Before you went to New York?"

"No," she said with a mischievous twinkle in her eye. "It'll be better."

ABOUT THE AUTHOR

 John Anthony Miller writes all things historical—thrillers, mysteries, and romance. He sets his novels in exotic locations spanning all eras of space and time, with complex characters forced to face inner conflicts, fighting demons both real and imagined. Each of his novels are unique: a Medieval epic, a Cold-War thriller, five historical mysteries, four WWII thrillers, and *The Minister's Wife*, a tale of the American Revolution. He lives in southern New Jersey.

To learn more about John Anthony Miller and discover more Next Chapter authors, visit our website at www.nextchapter.pub.

The Minister's Wife
ISBN: 978-4-82414-437-9

Published by
Next Chapter
2-5-6 SANNO
SANNO BRIDGE
143-0023 Ota-Ku, Tokyo
+818035793528

8th June 2022

9 784824 144379